SHORT SEASON

⊖ and other stories ⊖

by Jerry Klinkowitz

Collier Books
Macmillan Publishing Company
New York

For Marshall Adesman

This is a work of fiction. Names, characters, places, and incidents are either the product of the author's imagination or are used fictitiously. Any resemblance to events or persons, living or dead, is entirely coincidental.

Collier Books
Macmillan Publishing Company
866 Third Avenue, New York, NY 10022
Collier Macmillan Canada, Inc.

Library of Congress Cataloging-in-Publication Data
Klinkowitz, Jerome.
    Short season and other stories / Jerry Klinkowitz.—1st Collier
Books ed.
        p.   cm.
    ISBN 0-02-044141-X
    1. Baseball stories, American.   I. Title.   II. Title: Short
season.
[PS3561.L515S5   1989]
813'.54—dc19   88-31591   CIP

"Eddie and the *Niña*" appeared in the *North American Review*. "Ball Two" won the 1985 PEN Syndicated Fiction Project and appeared in the *San Francisco Chronicle* and the *Village Advocate*. "Five Bad Hands and the Wild Mouse Folds" won the 1984 PEN Syndicated Fiction Project and appeared in the *Chicago Tribune*. "Ambience" appeared in *Art & Artists*.

Cover painting by Bob Dorsey

First Collier Books Edition 1989

10 9 8 7 6 5 4 3 2 1

PRINTED IN THE UNITED STATES OF AMERICA

☹ Contents ☹

Contents

⊗ Pregame ⊗

Sweet Loretta Martin, thought she was a woman, but she was another man, and the ball sizzles off his bat and tears across the left-field wall. Eddie likes hitting to the Beatles, and if the station plays another he could go five for five—get fired up in batting practice and it stays with you all night. For infield warm-ups they may put on some newer music, but while Eddie's hitting it better be sixties rock. *Goin' to Kansas City, Kansas City here I come,* all right! He speaks little English but knows these tunes like his prayers. The pitcher throws a fastball and Eddie lifts it out to center field, catching gold from the evening sun, and it's gone.

Gates open at half past six with the end of BP and some fans are drifting in, so Jeff the GM turns off the radio even before the batting cage is pulled away. Paying customers mean a man collects royalties, so let the guys take their final swings in silence. Fifteen bucks to ASCAP is more than six box seats, and for most of this week the boxes have been thin. Four-hundred-some regulars will show up tonight, but they'll save fifty cents by sitting in the grandstand. Last year they'd spend it on a beer, but now a can costs ninety cents—blame the distributor and the new deposit law. Hot dogs are eighty-five, "same as the New York's famous Central Park," he jokes with people, peanuts half a dollar. A fun night with the Mason City Royals costs you less than four bucks, Jeff says in the ads, ten for the entire family. But filling the boxes is still a struggle. And where's Eau Claire? It's quarter to seven and the Kings have missed their own BP and infield. Did their bus break down again?

"Goin' to Mason City, Mason City here ah come," Mitch is hollering out in his hillbilly-pimping voice as the team bus chugs across the Fourth Street bridge into town. He's had a song for each occasion since they left Eau Claire two hours late this noon, even "Old Man River" as they crossed the Mississippi at Prairie du Chien. By now it's on everyone's nerves. Mason City means no visitors' locker room, changing on the bus, a motel with roaches, and not a single cheap restaurant open after the game, not even a Mac's. Plus they'll be stiff all night without warm-ups.

Plus they'll probably lose. Mason City is in first place by four games, they're in last, and that's the way it will be as long as they're a co-op. Kansas City bankrolls the Royals, but the Eau Claire Kings are a cooperative team used by the Red Sox, Phillies, Mets, and Twins to dump their odd players who can't move up. Last year the Kings' infield had three shortstops and a converted catcher, and this season they can't find a pitcher who'll last five innings. May 1 and they're 2–10, worst in the league. With no central budget, meal money comes by the month instead of week. Mitch regularly loses all of his the first day and has already borrowed two hundred dollars from the trainer. The bummest poker hands are dealt to guys on co-ops.

Time for line-ups to the umps and still no Eau Claire. Eddie hits clean-up, has been punching out an awesome .328, which is third in the league, and he plays every night. But even starting for a first-place team can't erase some problems. Like his salary—it's the same $630 per month as the benchwarmers. Right now he's playing good enough to make a Triple A club where the paychecks start at fifteen grand a season, but the Royals are so rich with infielders that it's debatable he'll see Chattanooga next year. A trade? Nobody trades Class A players except as throw-ins, too much can change in three or four seasons, so you're stuck with the club that signed you till protection year. Or get released. Half of last year's Royals are back on the farm, after a whole season of low pay and cheap meals. A summer of motels from Madison to Cedar Rapids. Three days of every other week you spend on the bus, sometimes half the night. The manager keeps telling him he could play with Tacoma next year, top of the minors, but Eddie's sure that's just talk to keep him up.

Less than one in twenty Class A players ever sets foot in a big-league park, unless it's as a fan. And who can be a fan after that? Too many years of this and Eddie fears he'll lose his taste for baseball. Is this fun?

There's fun in the grandstand. A bunch of the four hundred are already here, catching the last swings of batting practice and settling down to the night's gossip and junk food. If Eau Claire doesn't show they'll still have their hour of entertainment before game time. Jeff is quickly walking up and down the aisles, seeing if everything's clean but really just to joke with the fans. Old Lew the retired grocer is standing next to his season seat, shuffling the three programs and nine bingo cards he's bought for the players' wives, a heartbreakingly beautiful group of nineteen- to twenty-two-year-olds he sits with every night. Ever try to find an apartment and feed a ballplayer on $630 a month? Their common secret is three boxes of macaroni and cheese a day, leaving $600 intact for rent, car payments, clothes, and occasional treats. They complain, but for three hours each night Lew makes them feel like favorite daughters.

In front of the Royals' dugout Freddie Guagliardo is tossing some soft pitches to Keith Henley. Keith won't start for another couple days and Guagliardo is strictly short relief, but it's early in the season and they have to keep loose. The two are a study in contrasts. Keith is a clear-faced Floridian, straight from the college draft. With his cap pulled over the crown of his long, straight hair, he looks the image of a young Tug McGraw. Freddie's from Chicago, a scrappy kid who spells *college* with one *l*. He's dark-complected, Sicilian, with short curly hair. You can spot his car in the parking lot, a block-long Lincoln waxed to perfection, sporting personalized Illinois license plates that read DA FONZ— he wears his ancestry proudly but with humor.

Old Lew, who worked in Chicago's wholesale produce market as a younger man, once tried joking with Freddie about the mob. "I see Smooth Sammy Mazonni got acquitted yesterday," Lew mentioned to him, expecting a laugh. But Freddie was all seriousness.

"Hey man, that's good, that's really good to hear," he nodded. Turns out Mazonni is an uncle, his mother's older brother. When Jeff got wind of this he tried to play it out, asking Freddie "What do you call him? Uncle Sammy? Or Uncle Smooth?" Once more Freddie didn't laugh, and when Jeff bugged him about his Mafioso Lincoln the short reliever gave him a stern lecture about how he'd worked three winters in an auto-trim shop saving up. "I paid cash for that car, all my own," Freddie insisted, "and all earned by myself!"

So no mobster jokes for Freddie Guagliardo. But when he walks in to pitch the Royals out of a late-inning jam, he lets the stadium

announcer play *The Godfather* love theme. That's only movies
and that's okay, just like his TV nickname. A little girl who wears a
Yankee cap and T-shirt lettered "Catfood Hunter" has shown him
her mimic routine and he likes it: squaring her shoulders toward
an imaginary plate, she shakes off two signs, nods at a third,
reaches back, delivers, and looks up and over as the phantom ball
sails past her head for a home run. "Aaaaaaaaaaaaayyyyy!" she exclaims, and Freddie cracks up every time. This is, of course, what
often happens, as he has a wide-breaking curve that fools the hitters till he gets behind, at which point they're looking fastball and
pop it out of the park. This is Freddie's fourth year of A-ball.

Eau Claire's within half an hour of forfeiting this game, and
neither Keith nor Freddie minds very much at all. Lew is standing
at the screen, sipping his first of two Budweisers, when Keith
comes over to retrieve a ball. "What you guys going to do if the
Kings don't show?" Lew asks, and Keith tells him that he's looking at it in his hand. But Carl Peterson, the field manager, is getting antsy. He hates to make up games. Sitting out tonight will
break his training routine, and he's got discipline problems
enough with this year's team. "These kids are crazy," he's been
complaining to Mack Ptaszynski, his pitching coach, an old
Washington Senators reliever nearly half again his age and less
inclined to take these youngsters' high jinks so personally. But
they're both concerned about their own no-show, reserve infielder Buddy Knox. Buddy has rolled in late before, once stunk
up with beer and unable to find his locker. That time Carl and
Mack pulled him into their office, where he took it as a joke. "No
problem, Skip," he kept laughing, "me and Elliot Ness just raided
another brewery."

Peterson is thinking back to that when he sees some traffic
coming off the highway into their parking lot. It's Eau Claire's
bus, horn ablare—what is this, a Hollywood arrival? He calls
Mack over to the locker-room door so they can flip them the bird
together, when he sees what the driver has been honking at.
Buddy's old rusted-out Camaro has run into the ditch to pass
them on the right, and now he's spinning a perfect doughnut,
tires screaming and gravel shooting out all the way to the clubhouse as he pulls up preciously close to Guagliardo's immaculate
Lincoln. Carl is beyond words, he can't even swear. Mack has a
grin on his face but the Skipper is beet-red. "Knox is on suspen-
sion," he growls through his teeth. "Send him home. Call Kansas

City. Don't let that little sucker near me or I swear to God I'll kill him!"

And now for the evening's anticlimax, nine innings of Class A professional baseball. Freddie will come on in the eighth and strike out two batters, then retire another three on strikes in the ninth, happy as a possum eating candy till he showers, civvies up, and finds the stone chips riddling his car. This will lead to a whole other story, which minor-league baseball is full of. There's even a story about why Eau Claire was late. At four this morning, with only a few hours sleep after their date with Cedar Rapids and the usual poker game afterward, their outfield plus the trainer had loaded up their rods, reels, and gear into a rented Ford for some daybreak fishing. At five they were back, dragging behind a DX tow truck, the left side of their Pinto fully caved in. They'd stopped for a light near the bank downtown but started off again when the time-and-temperature sign they'd been studying flashed from 58 degrees to 4:10. A farmer's pickup with the green broadsided them. The guys didn't settle with the police until noon, hours after their bus was due to leave for Mason City.

Carl hears the story as he exchanges line-ups at the plate, and trots back to the dugout to share this misery with Mack, who finds it a lot funnier than he does. With the national anthem the game begins.

☹ Short Season ☹

Carl Peterson's out doing all the things that make managing a job and a half. Walking the outfield, seeing that those gopher holes in left have been filled in and the sprinkler plate behind second covered with some Astro Turf. Dave Alpert took a spill on it last night, and Carl's had to remind the grounds keeper and the GM how Mickey Mantle's career was almost ended by an injury like that during a World Series game at the Polo Grounds. But he sees Jack's got it covered up with an extra three inches on each side, so that's one less worry.

It's May 3, and after two weeks' shakedown the field's in good enough shape for undistracted play. The base lines have been straightened and filled, the nails on those advertising signs along the fence pounded in where the springtime sun had bucked them out, and the drainage problem behind home plate solved. Three weeks ago the place was hardly fit for play—no wonder, since Jack told him that just ten days before the opener it had been under a foot of ice and snow, making any work impossible. But twenty days have produced a miracle in the weather, with afternoons touching the sixties now, and Carl pauses to think about the strange cycle minor-league baseball has become for him.

Technically the Mason City Royals are a full-season Class A club, because they start in mid-April instead of June like the rookie leagues, but for him A-ball is still the short season because it comes and goes so fast. April turns to August sooner than you realize, but not to look at these players who develop even faster than the summer months fly by. Take Eddie Sanmarda—in just the dozen games played so far he's learned to hold his ground in the batter's box and charge the ball at short, making him a foot taller in Carl's view. Billy Harmon's coming out of his shell, and Robin Haas is good enough for two more innings each start—by mid-month Carl expects to see some complete games from him. Even veterans like Lynn Parson and Freddie Guagliardo no longer seem so out of place among these younger kids, as day by day their field play and clubhouse manners have shaped them into a coherent team. It all happens so fast, Carl's been thinking again and again. It probably means he's getting old, just too many seasons long and short alike, so that months seem like days and days like hours. The hour he's spent out here so far has flown by like ten minutes.

He must be older, for the team sometimes treats him like a father figure. Especially kids drafted out of high school like Billy, and older players still growing through a second adolescence like Freddie, or "Guags" as the rookies already call him. The first week in town Guags, who's played three seasons of A-ball already, most of it here, got in a hassle with his landlord about a parking space. As many as five guys will share a two-bedroom, and, if more than two have wheels, parking becomes a problem. There's extra storage, but it's always down at the end or out in back, and Freddie wants his manager to explain how his car's special. A mammoth Lincoln with vanity plates, immaculate inside out and showroom shiny, it simply can't sit out in back for the vandals. So instead of fastballs and training rules Carl's found himself opening the season by dealing with parking spots.

Then there's roommates. Finding a place to live is the player's own responsibility, but kids from the college draft act like they're still on scholarship. Carl can't knock it that their coaches took such personal care of them, but he's a professional baseball man, not a professor of intercollegiate athletics, nor is he paid like one. Nor is there a booster club, alumni association, or any of the perks these kids enjoyed when their Saturday afternoon contests dominated campus life and ABC-TV as well. "Football players!" Carl scoffs, kicking away a clod of dirt unraked behind third base —God save him from any college gridiron stars who've signed a baseball contract with the Royals this year. Those kids would find a big-league clubhouse shabby. He spits in the dust and kicks his way over to the dugout, where Jack, the grounds keeper, is scraping away at some peeled-back paint.

The infield's been troubling both of them. It's the original ground from 1946 when the park was built, and nearly half a cen-

tury's weathering has turned it back into something not that far
from virgin Iowa prairie. Meaning it rolls, a gentle undulation
from behind the pitcher's mound toward second, then a sharp set
of washboard ripples along the grass toward first. The area between short and third has simply sunk, and other than collecting
water during rainouts it presents no real problems for play. But
the last of those ripples where the second baseman stands creates
a nasty lip—the Durocher effect, Carl calls it—and poor Billy
Harmon's risked a broken nose twice already as hard grounders
have defied true hops to strike him in the face.

After the last time, when it looked for a moment like Billy might
have to come out, Jim Smith got him laughing by offering the
bruised and bleeding infielder his catcher's mask. But Carl hopes
good grounds keeping can correct the problem, and so he's been
leaning on Jack every time the poor man's not reaching for a rake.

"I rolled it twice, then dug it up and rolled it again," Jack complains. "I watered it for ten hours and parked the tractor on it
overnight, and that damn lip's still there." He scratches his head
and fiddles with his cap. "I swear to God," he implores Carl,
"somebody's buried under there!"

They laugh, but Carl keeps on him about the hazard, and Jack
promises to keep wetting it and rolling it down.

Into the dugout, and Carl's reminded once more how they're too
small. Again it's a case of 1946 and how much things have
changed since when this park was built. Back then Mason City
played in the Three-I League, and even though its classification
was a bit higher than A-ball now the rosters were much smaller,
just a total of sixteen players plus the manager. So that's what the
dugouts were built to hold. And none of them taller than five foot
eleven, Carl believes, as he frets at the low roof which keeps him
and over half his team in a perpetual stoop. Today he's got twenty-
three players alone, plus five nonroster kids killing time till rookie
season starts in the New York–Penn and they're shipped down to
Elmyra. And these days teams carry a pitching coach and trainer,
so no way can his outfit squeeze into this tiny bunker not much
bigger than a duck blind.

So come game time all but the regular starters are sent down to
the bull pen—unhappily, these early days in May when the
nights get nippy. Not that they'll like it any better when the
weather warms, for there's a nasty May fly hatch coming in a few

weeks which will bury them in clouds of insects falling from the light standard up above their unsheltered bench. Then June bugs all over everything and, when they're gone, mosquitoes. As compensation, these boys who haven't got the stuff to pitch as starters will have free access to the groupies who haven't made the pass list. Fifty cents gets them into the bleachers if they're nineteen or under, and their favorite spot is right behind the bullpen bench. Here they'll spend a few nights making friends and getting on that pass list. Which is downright silly, Carl thinks, because once a pitcher signs them in they're gone forever to the boxes and he's left out here in the cold.

His starting rotation sits closer to the action, but still outside the dugout. Another open bench runs from the dugout edge on down the line, and here the half-dozen players who can't fit spend the evening in their warm-up jackets. Carl gets less complaints from this end because the players are right next to the amenities of Gatorade and dip, plus they've got the best seats in the house for action at third. It also gives them a great position for riding the manager when he's coaching on the field and can't strike back, but what makes these seats easiest to sell is their closeness to the fans.

The bench sits squarely at the end of the grandstand ramp. Box seats start above the dugout, then continue on around behind the plate, but there's an open space along the wall which makes a great little pen for the kids to congregate in, and among them can be found something interesting for everyone on the team.

There will be little kids eight or nine years old—some just seeking autographs, but others who can talk baseball with amazing knowledgeability. Carl remembers a happy movie he once saw about a child this age taking over the New York Yankees and managing them to yet another pennant—or was it some hapless wrecks like the Senators or A's that the kid guided to beat the mighty Yanks? Either way, there are kids out here who know as much about the league as he does, and one night he's actually taken some mental notes as a ten-year-old told him how to recognize when the Giants' top base stealer would telegraph his move.

One or two of the college players like talking with these baseball wizards, especially when the kids can tell them their number in the draft and where they played. But there's a subtle match-up that Carl has noted between the kids signed out of high school and the eight-year-olds down here just to cop bubble gum and broken bats. Billy in particular has hit it off with a youngster just as blond as he is, and Carl suspects the second baseman misses a little brother at home. There's also some affinity between the Latin players and these younger Mason City fans. Each is a curiosity to the other—these small-town Iowa children seeing their first dark-skinned person up close and hearing a foreign language all at once, and kids like Sanmarda, Escobar, and Naboa hearing their first English unaffected by locker-room slang.

What Carl doesn't like about the bench is the angle it provides for teenage romance. The spot's become a way station for future groupies, the manager believes, and regrets it that guys like Andy Thompson and Johnny Mueller let these twelve-year-olds send them love notes and chatter with them mindlessly till the game begins. So far the girls have kept to groups of three and four, but once a bold one starts coming down alone Carl will step in. Still too early for that, he notes, for in the short season that stuff doesn't start happening till school's out in June. But these little ladies are surely warming up their charms in the early days of May.

From the dugout Carl turns into the clubhouse tunnel, grabbing last night's line-up card but being careful to leave the two strips of adhesive tape holding it for tonight. The tunnel's built for five footers just like the dugouts, and Carl remembers little Luis Aparicio played his first pro game here in the forties when the White Sox had the franchise. Who else broke in here? Carl asks himself, figuring mostly American Leaguers since the affiliation moved from Chicago to the Red Sox, then Cleveland, and now K.C. Carlton Fisk, that's one. Bet this tunnel cramped him crazy. Carl struggles through it till he comes into the locker room and throws the light switch near the door.

Water's been leaking from where Jack's hosed down the stands. Thankfully he's spread plastic sheeting over the top shelves, or the players' gear would be soaked. Andy Thompson's stack of college paperbacks for when he's tossed out of games, Billy's Bible, and any number of hair dryers and portable radios. Six different stations these guys play while suiting up—Carl hears it as utter cacophony. But after a win Johnny Mueller's always first one in, and it's his tradition to turn up his huge tape player for a victory dance. When they lose, nobody plays nothing.

For Carl the locker room is foreign territory. It's the players' turf and he tries to leave it to them, just as his office past the trainer's room is posted with a Knock First sign. There are several stages between, and each has its separate protocol. The smell of laundry soap lingers in the hallway past the washers and big oversized dryer, and the table opposite it where guys jimmy up their tricks. Freddie's taught the hitters how to save on broken bats—heat the barrel over a low alcohol fire in a can top, then rub it down with resin, filling in the cracks from which a shatter can develop. Sometimes corking a bat, though the K.C. office has discouraged this because it's too easily discovered in the bigs and distorts their player development stats. Then into the trainer's room with its hydro bath, rubdown table, and shelves of tapes and bandages looking for all the world like a doctor's examining room. Carl doesn't like the ambience at all, but the players—especially pitchers—love it, as they flock around Chet like gossips in a corner bar.

Then his office, a tiny windowless cubicle just ten feet long and seven across, where Mack will usually stretch out on the battered couch while Carl sits more properly at his desk and files. It's half past two, which means he has over an hour free for reports to Kansas City. The paperwork has grown each year, as farm directors have begun requesting charts and graphs on every aspect of each player's game. And then they tell him how to manage.

That's been Carl's irritation working A-ball, especially when some wizard down in K.C. starts telling him to pull one guy out of the rotation and leave another in for six full innings each start no matter what. He's stood there in the dugout taking all sorts of fan abuse as someone the farm director wants to read about gets shelled in the early innings. "What's the matter with you, Peterson?" the crowd will yell. "Warm somebody up out there! What the hell you doing?" Little do they know it's not winning ball games, but generating stats for the home-office types.

He looks at the stacks of papers on his desk and wonders if they'd like him to write a novel. Why not, he's got good enough stories already to fill a book. Eddie hitching in from the airport without a word of English. Billy in tears when some teammates wrapped his Bible in a *Hustler* gatefold. Old Mack recalling good times and bad with the Washington Senators as he spreads out on the couch before games.

Posted on a wall is a jumbo postcard Carl's daughter has sent him from Paris on her junior year abroad, showing scattered rooftops sloping down the Left Bank toward the Seine. He gazes out across them before turning back to his desk. Old Ernie Hemingway, he thinks to himself, that's who I really am, as he wonders what brilliant story to concoct tonight for his boss in Kansas City.

☻ Rain Date ☻

Of all the Mason City Royals, Freddie Guagliardo loves rainouts the most.

Not to spend the night drinking. That's for beer hounds like Buddy Knox and his friend Tex from the bleachers, who's been caught sneaking six-packs out to the bull pen, where Buddy hides with the middle relief.

Or for fishing like the country boys with their Georgia drawls and endless stories about hunting dogs and boat rigs. Freddie's a Chicago kid whose idea of blood sport comes from getting caught in the wrong neighborhood after a high-school game away. Sent into the alley behind his aunt's to kill some rats, he used his cousin's air rifle to take out three rear windows in the old lady's place across the way. That was fun and, unlike Buddy with his cans of brew hidden here and there, he never got caught.

Freddie loves rainouts because they break the routine. Class A minor-league baseball is a steady grind—no more than two days off from April through August with nightlong bus rides every three to six days. So even the dead certainty of a doubleheader in the dog days of summer makes this late spring rain a welcome sight, when their first six weeks as pros has many of these kids reeling and aching already.

Freddie likes the way Lynn Parson sings in the dugout, the damp concrete echo making it sound like classic Motown. "Feel so bad," Lynn is booming out, "feel like a ball game on a rainy day!" But the fact that Lynn hollers "bad" with three or four syllables, savoring the word and making it count for half his song, lets Freddie know that Lynn thinks this rainout is just fine.

"You and Little Milton," Freddie laughs over to him, and sings back a line he's heard the shaggers use. "Sometimes," Freddie croons slowly, "sometimes bad is BAD!" Lynn cracks up and tosses a can of dip at Freddie's spikes, so now he's dancing as well.

The manager scowls at this as he worries over the now-useless line-up card. "We got any rain dates with these guys in Madison?" he asks the trainer, who's reaching for the schedule as Freddie interrupts.

"Hey Skip!" he shouts. "This here's my rain date right now. Watch me take my laps!"

With that, Freddie climbs over the top and sprints across the field. The rain has made it a mess, and as soon as he hits the base path mud flies up past his ears. But using home plate as his starting block, he lowers his head and covers the ninety feet to first base in what looks like under four seconds.

The trainer is amazed. "You ever see Guags get out of the box that fast in practice?" he asks the manager, to whom Freddie is waving and grinning as he stands on first in a sea of mud. But before the Skipper can answer Guagliardo is off again. Ten feet from second he dives into a Pete Rose bellyflop, hitting the bag head-first as water and muck shoot up on either side.

He stands, displaying his Royals uniform now coal-black in front, and takes off for third. Here he executes a hook slide, fouling the left side of his pants and jersey as Buddy and Lynn cheer and the rest of the team hurry up the clubhouse tunnel to see what's going on.

"Come on, you chickens!" he yells to Buddy and Lynn. "It's drill time: suicide squeeze!" With his friends just ten steps behind he barrels for home, sliding feet first under an imaginary tag. Now he's mud from head to foot, but he's cleared a nifty furrow for Buddy and Lynn, who splash through what's mostly water in a parody of the dusty practice sessions suffered through this spring. As they slide in Freddie tackles them, flopping around the batter's box till all three look like creatures from the murky deep.

The other guys are lined along the dugout, cheering and clapping like mad. But the manager is all seriousness. He strides through the standing ovation and marches resolutely to the plate. His words are few.

"Parson! Knox!" he barks out. "Twenty dollars! Twenty dollars!" He checks off the fines, turning from Lynn to Buddy. For the suddenly silent Freddie he makes a significant pause.

"Guagliardo—one hundred!" He turns on his heel and stalks back to the quiet dugout.

For a moment Freddie is speechless, eyes darting about in confusion. It's not the money—he can clear a hundred hustling cards with the losers from Eau Claire's sorry co-op team. But the Skip has shown him up and, what's worse, spoiled the fun.

But it's not over yet. His eyes have settled on a cherished boyhood sight—keys in an ignition—and as he leaps onto the grounds keeper's tractor Freddie has some words for the boys.

"One hundred's the max, fellas," he shouts to the dugout as the tractor fires up. "Look what a hundred bucks can buy!"

Freddie has started the snout-nosed light utility tractor in gear, and with a nasty backfire it lurches forward, almost bucking him from the seat. With muddy arms and legs flailing, he finds the clutch and shifts into second, his favorite gear for when the chips are down. This baby has torque, he notes to himself, as he spins around to send a spray of sod and gravel into the scattering dugout crowd. He keeps the rpm's up and plays with the ignition, rattling off more backfires, which resound through the ball park.

He's heading for the plate when the team's general manager and two half-dressed umpires come running through the empty stands. They're just in time to catch a bath of mud as Freddie downshifts to make the big turn at first. He's heading toward second on two wheels and everyone knows the best is yet to come.

⊗ Cheap Seats ⊗

There's lots of reasons for Jeff to close the second set of bleachers out along each line. For one thing, having them open spreads the crowd too thin, making the park look empty and that's depressing, especially when the sports-page photos are shot against a background of sparsely populated seats. Better to squeeze'em all together in the sections over first and third. Plus he can pay the clean-up crew ten dollars less when half the bleachers have been kept roped off. It's good for public image and makes sound business sense.

The meaner side of it is sociological. Those far seats are nearly three hundred feet from the backstop screen where Al, the stadium cop, spends most of his time bumming peanuts and pop. He's titanically overweight, and the ball-park punks are sure the foul corners are safely beyond his range. Tired of all the firecrackers and underage drinking down there, Jeff feels better with the distant bleachers closed.

He's got little regard, anyway, for the kind of folks who'd want to view the game from three hundred feet away. All that's close out there is the bull pen, with the bench set right along the knee-high wall between the field and the stands. Here the grizzled winos try to talk baseball with eighteen-year-olds fresh from the Dominican or small-town Legion teams, and the groupies spend the evening charming their way onto the pass list.

The players change each year, keeping the Mason City Royals a perennial age eighteen to twenty-two. But for the three seasons Jeff's been here the same familiar alkies have held onto life and the price of admission, and the groupies have remained the same loitering bunch. One of them, a stringy blond he thinks of as

"Scarey Mary," showed up at the VFW hall that Saturday in March when he and the board members were interviewing kids for summer jobs.

"I was at Double A last year," she told Jeff proudly as he ran through some routine questions on experience.

"You mean to say you played professional baseball?" he was just about to ask in disbelief when she straightened out his obvious confusion.

"You know, some of the guys were moved up to Chattanooga and I went along," Scarey Mary explained, and Jeff could hardly hold his laughter. So here we have a groupie who couldn't hack it up in Double A, he chuckled to himself—she's being sent back down to A-ball with the rest of our batters who can't hit curves.

What bothers Jeff the most about these cheap seats in the shadows is the subculture growing out here. At least Scarey Mary and her friends are of age—he could close the bleachers altogether and they'd still be free to fill the booths and barstools at Tony's and the Fourth Street Station, where the team hangs out after games. But the left-field corner, a world away from where Jeff and his cop and ushers can control things in the stands, is a breeding ground for sexual delinquents. He remembers cute little eleven-year-olds from his first year in Mason City, running from the box seats with popcorn money from their parents, now strutting like hookers past the better seats on their way out to the second set of bleachers, loaded with eye make-up and poured into downsized jeans.

Thirteen years old, Jeff notes to himself, and ropes off the gate with the hand-lettered Section Closed sign he must remake for every set of home-stand games.

⊖ BP ⊖

Batting practice happens every day unless the grounds are wet or taken over for special promotions like a pregame softball contest between the local D.J.s. Carl's hand-lettered poster lists the daily ritual—4:00, report; 4:30, in uniform on field; 5:00, BP; 5:45, visitors' BP; 6:30, infield; 6:50, visitors' infield—and only the shaggers and a few old retired guys with nothing else to do but hang around the ball park know how the Mason City Royals' workday has begun over three hours before the game's first pitch.

At the single-A level of minor-league ball there's a lot of emphasis on instruction, and so the players get twice the swings they'd take in the bigs.

Not that BP's a home-run-hitting contest. The practice balls are nothing like the once-used game balls the big boys use, and such heavy duty day after day has many of the PBs softened to the consistency of cheese. So a healthy slam may sometimes just squish the ball out behind second base, where pitcher Al Elgin dutifully picks them up and fills the bucket for old Mack, who's throwing from behind the BP screen on the mound.

Pitchers shag the outfield while the Royals' utility men sharpen their skills around the bags. A screen protects the first baseman, whose eye is often off the ball as he takes the infielders' throws from previous pitches, but the guys at second and short get plenty of action, while third's the hot corner indeed. Mack lobs them in at three a minute, and if there's a high infield pop-up chances are a liner can come screaming past your ear while you're still staring up among the clouds. That's another reason for a quick-paced BP, since nerves go soft during the long waiting game baseball can become in the thirteen hundred innings from April through August.

The fastest play on the field, however, is the verbal stuff around the hitting cage. There's no catcher, but six or seven guys stand waiting their turn at either side, and a few more are down the line a few feet to snare the mandatory bunts that start each hitter's sequence. There's usually lots of kidding as each batter squares away to lay one down . . . but even when it's line-drive and dinger time there's plenty of talk, all nicely punctuated by the crack of ball on wood.

Lynn Parson is a favorite in the cage, since his California smoothness is a natural target and when he has to concentrate on Mack's throws the other guys have a rare advantage. He's the team's only black American—the rest are from Mexico or the Dominican Republic—and the white guys play this factor for all it's worth, pussyfooting with the sociological side of race while never thinking about a physiological slur.

"Hey Lynn," Johnny Mueller shouts as the smooth left fielder lifts one out beyond the wall and Carl calls "ball over" to the shaggers who chase them down, "you hit that way in high school?"

"Didn't play in high school," Lynn replies without taking his eye off Mack's next pitch, which goes sailing almost as far, thudding off the plywood fence, which sports a dozen and a half advertisers' signs.

"Parson didn't go to high school," Andy Thompson shouts from the other side of the cage.

"He didn't?" Johnny calls across the sound of a solid liner that almost nips a distracted Buddy Knox at third. "How'd he manage that?"

" 'Cause he was in jail," Andy laughs, "weren't you, Lynn?"

Lynn laughs too but keeps his eye on Mack. The old coach has been listening and bears down with a fastball. A solid whack lifts it out beyond the scoreboard, well into the giant maple tree the players know is 420 feet from home. "Ball over," Carl yells, and even Mack turns around to admire Lynn's shot. "How'd he do that with a practice ball?" Andy Thompson asks himself, and Lynn takes a second to glance back, satisfied he's made his point that all the jockeying in the world is no distraction.

"Good thing he can hit," Andy says as a comebacker to the guys waiting behind him. "With no real high school he's a bit deficient when it comes to basic skills in the world."

"Yeah," Johnny agrees from the base line, where he's darted out to grab a few balls, "all Lynn knows is what he learned making license plates. His first one was ABC 123. Had a hell of a time spelling 'California.'"

A second later Johnny's desperately spinning away as Lynn pulls an inside pitch and sends a rocket down the line. This shuts him up, and for the next few minutes the only sounds are the crack of Lynn's bat and Carl's sharp "ball over" to the shaggers.

Out in left four pitchers are covering what's usually just one fielder's spot, so no one has to move more than a step or two to snag Lynn's liners when they fail to clear the wall. Their fielding style looks odd out here as they keep their bodies rigid, just waving up their gloves to pocket Lynn's liners like sharp tosses back to the mound. An equally easy motion sends the balls to Al, who's bagging them behind second. Smooth and supple, all fluid motion—that's the style for pitching these days, and no one would mistake these guys for position players. Unlike the Royals' line-up, which has resumed chattering around the batting cage, these starters, long men, and short relievers hardly say a word, so customary is their isolation once they're on the mound. Pitchers only talk sitting down, spinning endless girl-friend or hunting stories when they mingle together in the dugout or huddle along the bull-pen bench. But out here shagging BP there's not a lot to say, and they make a point of not listening to the horselaughs and imprecations filtering out across the field.

Angel Naboa's up, and after his five obligatory bunts he peppers sharply hit infield shots to short and third, winding Buddy Knox and Herman Escobar, who struggle with the pace. Andy tries some banter in Spanish, but Angel ignores him and Eddie Sanmarda answers back in English. But when Andy himself steps in to hit he's greeted with a long barrage of heckling in several languages, even some Japanese cusswords the guys have learned since that exhibition with the Seibu Lions this spring.

"That's a bad bunt, man, who taught you?" Lynn Parson yells as he pops it back toward the mound. "Feo, Feo," Angel Naboa adds.

"Ugly like the man himself," Lynn laughs, and plays around with the word. "He ain't just bad-looking, he's uuuuuuuuugggg-LY!" Andy tries to rip one as Lynn ties off his word, but only squibs a little spinner out toward short, stopping several steps in front of Herman Escobar, who laughs along. When the guys can get to someone in the cage they'll show no mercy, and pretty soon the "ugly" jokes are making it around the field.

"He so ugly when he born," Herman shouts in, "his mama try to put him back!"

"Ugly?" Lynn asks from down the line. "He was such an ugly baby his folks had to tie porkchops around his neck to get the dog to play with him!"

"Yeah, and look at him now," Billy Harmon adds from behind the cage. "When he dates a girl he's gotta promise to wear a bag over his head."

"That's in case the bag on *her* ugly head breaks and she sees him," Lynn responds, and collapses around his bat.

"Ball over!" Carl yells from centerfield as somehow Andy's hit one out. But now the PA announcer's here to play some music, and the Royals take their final swings to the sound of more level-headed rock-'n'-roll.

☻ Eddie and the *Niña* ☻

Jolene is a Class-A shagger. For two hours before each game she sits on the concrete retaining wall beyond the left-field fence and chases batting-practice balls that make it out. Six or seven do every late afternoon, sometimes a dozen or more, and today has been especially good—fifteen practically new Midcontinent League balls fill her pockets and batting helmet by six o'clock. Most of them are scuffed just three times: the first that took them out of last night's game, second by the wallop out of the park to-day, and third for the grass, gravel, or concrete where they hit just now.

The Mason City Royals' GM will pay her a quarter for each ball when she reports her total at the month's end. But tonight she carries a higher mark of distinction, for her hero, Eddie San-marda, has sent a screaming liner to the top of the left-field wall, just a foot away from the foul pole, and with a momentum-gain-ing bounce it's taken a beeline for Jolene's ankle and stung her good. For a while she mugs it up and walks with an exaggerated limp, but fifteen minutes before game time it's swelled up and hurts real bad.

A fan takes her to the dugout. "Mr. Peterson," he says to the manager who's worrying over his line-up card, "one of your shag-gers caught a line drive on her ankle, maybe the trainer could give her some ice." Carl lifts her over and, dream of dreams, she's in the Royals' dugout. Chet the trainer pulls down her sock, feels that there's no break, and applies an ice pack. He listens to her story then calls Ed over to see his work. Eddie speaks little En-glish but he knows his sockamayocking rampage has hurt this little *niña,* so he grabs a clean game ball and presents it to her as his first trophy of atonement. Then he chases back to concessions for a hot dog and big orange drink, his spikes clattering on the steel walkway. Bill White, the stadium announcer, has introduced the managers and umps, the first three hitters, and is waiting on Eddie as he stumbles back through the boxes, so Ed runs out to his position from the stands. Bill is two-thirds down the line-up and the whole infield is out there before anyone notices Ed standing at second, gloveless, dripping mustard and orange pop on the bag.

That night Mason City wins 6-2, a good game with no errors and three home runs. Ed hits the first but pulls up lame rounding first base. Carl has to help him around third to home and in minutes his leg is packed in ice. Jolene's still there in all her glory so she bums two quarters from the trainer and fetches Ed a Coke.

If Ed Sanmarda makes the major leagues he'll be the first starting shortstop who can feed an entire team for less than five dollars, another minor-league skill gone to waste in the bigs. By mid-June in his first year with Mason City he has fed his teammates, all twenty-two of them, on eight successive Sundays. Meal money is passed out Monday mornings and it never lasts a week.

Spanish-American cooking? Yes, in a way. But nothing Eddie or his family ate in Panama. His down-and-out enchiladas are purely a concoction of American convenience food, a mélange of cheap ingredients chosen after his first half-hour in an Iowa food store.

Three packages of supersoft tortillas at 69¢ each, full count twenty-four, which answers for every man on the team. A can of mild taco sauce for these soft-mouthed gringos, only 19¢. A round of Colby cheese, the biggest investment at $2.44. That leaves 30¢ of his five (hidden in his hatband Monday) for some closed-out jalapeño peppers he's found at the Swiss Colony Gourmet Shop, unquestionably the best food buy in Mason City and perhaps the whole United States. These are for himself, Joey, and Manuel; the Yankee boys tried them once and howled for water, like throwing gasoline on their fires until Eddie told them just to suck on sugar for a while. "Panama Pizzas," Donny Moore called them, refusing to roll the tortillas like Eddie showed. One of these babies, a foot long and three inches high when tightly rolled and broiled, keeps their bellies filled from Sunday night to Monday morning, when the meal money comes and it's back to Mac's and Burger King.

Given his relatively few words of English Eddie finds it amazing he can have so many Anglo friends. When the Royals' scout told him he'd start in Mason City his parents were concerned—How would he get along, with whom could he even speak? The scout, a veteran of the Mexican leagues and the majors, assured them there would be other Latin players—Herman Escobar from Cuba by way of Miami, Angel Naboa from northern Mexico, Monterrey, plus there was Andy Thompson from Ybor City in Tampa, half-Spanish, who was majoring in Romance languages at South Florida—but that even without these Spanish-speaking kids Eddie would find it easy to get along.

Baseball has its own language of movement, the scout explained and Eddie soon found out. On the field the game's natural rhythm of threes—three strikes, three outs, three bases, nine innings, nine players—gave his actions a familiar mold. Playing deep for the first two outs, in on the grass when he expected a bunt, pegging the ball to first and running off the field with his teammates—all this made Ed and the guys partners in a dance that flowed between the base lines. In the dugout they became a captive audience to the other team's spectacle with its own echo of the same old song.

Warm-ups before the game, the cadence afterward of bagging bats and balls, loading the bus, fifteen minutes back to the motel, and then a couple hours' cards or TV before bed. The five months from April through August across eight midwestern towns flowed easy, like a river, its currents obvious from the first time around.

Assigned to share a room with Billy Harmon, whose Spanish was as weak as his own English, Eddie found no trouble—their body language carried directly from the field, and as roommates they had more to say to each other than Angel and Herman, or any of the English-speaking pairs. "¿Quieres algunos chips y Pepsi?" Eddie would call from the kitchenette and Billy would nod and answer, saying "Sure, bring some cheese if we got some." One night around a darkened motel pool they talked for hours, their voices floating through the dusk like music from another world. Eddie spoke of his parents back home, Billy about the ball he'd played in high school, and though neither knew for sure what the other was saying each felt good about their talk. When Ed and Herman played the infield they laughed aud chattered, rattling the batters with their private jokes. But with Eddie at short and Billy at second they played with the quiet of brothers.

Eddie had been signed in August off a sandlot team organized by the United Methodist mission in Panama City. He was nineteen years old and had never played much ball before that summer, favoring jai alai up to then. But the Methodists had been pulling kids off the courts, and Reverend Styles, their coach, was so struck by Eddie's natural talent that he wrote every major-league club about his find.

Scouts from Kansas City, Chicago, and Toronto answered his letters, and during the All-Star break a man from the Royals flew down. This was the day Eddie hit two home runs and played the infield like a dervish—to show him off, Reverend Styles shifted him around every two innings from third to short to second and to first. The scout took his report back to Kansas City on the next plane and three weeks later called with an offer. As a crack infielder who could hit, Ed would be their number-one pick from the nondraftable Latin Americans. Report to Sarasota in March for rookie camp and then, depending on the older utility infielders, he'd have a spot with Double A Chattanooga or A-ball's Mason City. In his part of Panama City, $630 a month American was a fortune, so Ed gladly signed. The Methodists were right: jai alai would waste him and he was too small for soccer.

In Sarasota he was rudely disappointed. The American players showed off tricks he'd never dreamed of and the coaches ignored his lusterless play. But in the second week when the veteran players came in for workouts the Royals' starting shortstop broke an ankle on a practice slide and everyone moved up a notch—the reserve infielder to short, Neddy Ralston from Triple A Tacoma to the Kansas City bench, Mason City's shortstop to Chattanooga—and Eddie had the A-ball job by default.

Carl now gave more attention and liked what he saw. He spent more time with Eddie, showing him how to watch the ball's rotation: bottom over top a fastball, top over bottom a curve, sideways with a white dot in the middle a slider, which was thrown three-quarter arm as well. Mack threw ball after ball with Carl catching and calling each of them for Eddie, who was soon sending every one to the wall. Woody Brown, the Chattanooga manager, now watched, too, so Carl cut the practice sessions before he lost his man.

On April 2 camp was broken and the parent team headed up to K.C. for the opener. The farm kids were given the chance to ride along on the charter and Eddie said yes to see his first pro game. He spent three days in Kansas City sick on Yankee food—the players ordered thick rare steaks so he did too and nearly vomited; a steak in Panama means well-cooked, cut-up beef in rice and bananas. He found a taco stand near the bus station, and, even though the putrid little things were made with hamburger, he bought his own jalapeño sauce at a nearby Quik-Trip and made them edible.

He rode a bus from Kansas City up to Chicago, twelve hours, just to spend a day walking among the tall buildings on Michigan Avenue. In the Art Institute he prayed before the El Greco he'd seen in his mother's Catholic missal. At the Y they spoke Spanish, more Spanish than English, and the Honduran clerk told him it was better to pay the ninety bucks and fly to Mason City, bus connections were that bad. On the airline bus he sat with a Mexicana stewardess who took him to the Ozark ticket counter and then all the way to gate F-11, through this airport bigger and busier than any he'd ever seen. Forty minutes in the air a passenger pointed out the Mississippi, way over its banks at flood stage, and Eddie couldn't believe it wasn't a long, wide lake.

At the Mason City airport, so small and desolate, he was lost. Seeing no buses and afraid of cabs, he started walking down the highway toward town. A sheriff's deputy picked him up, saw his baseball gear, and drove him to the Quality Inn, where the ball players stayed. Thankfully Carl was in the lobby to book his room. Tomorrow he'd have his apartment with Billy, the blond and baby-faced second baseman who'd been his friend in camp.

April 13 was the home opener, then a second game with Wisconsin Rapids before heading up to Eau Claire. Right off Ed was hitting and hitting well, surprising himself in this cold weather when sometimes fewer than fifty fans came out for the night games. Other players were complaining that their hands stung and their joints ached, wanting the managers to shift the weekend games to afternoons, but Ed was in his glory. The night lights made the ball's seams stand out like scars on his uncle's cheeks, and Carl had taught him to watch so well that he routinely sent the fastballs screaming through the hole and lifted a few hanging curves out beyond the wall.

By May 1 he had twenty hits and fifteen R.B.I.s, an amazing clutch percentage. By June 1 he was up to fifty-five and forty, and in one amazing week—June 6–12, against Madison, Quad Cities, and Cedar Rapids—drove in another fifteen runs, virtually the only Mason City player producing scores. Carl would surely have faced losing him to Chattanooga by now, but Kansas City's All-Star shortstop was coming back and the organization had an extra infielder plugging up the tubes.

Lynn Parson, the hip black outfielder from Berkeley, California, started telling Eddie about "making his hundred." Poor in English and worse in slang, Eddie groped for the meaning, so Joey came over to explain. One hundred R.B.I.s is an achievement even in 162 major-league games; in A-ball's short season of 140 it is a rare accomplishment indeed. "You gotta make your hundred," Lynn crooned and Eddie got the idea. "Ninety-nine," the black player sang, "and a half won't do."

School's been out since June 9 and Jolene's been here for batting practice each afternoon. By coming in for the games she risks her job, because the GM wants the shaggers to stay out and chase fouls or home runs. But her ankle still hurts, she tells him, and she can't strain it running in the dark when the teenage beer-drinkers out on the bank give her competition. The GM's New York savvy has been flashing "lawsuit" ever since that line drive nipped her, so he doesn't complain. "Are you shagging BP tomorrow night?" he asks and Jolene answers with an impish grin, heading down to play some catch with Ed.

Hitting .340 with all those R.B.I.s exempts Eddie from the team's ribbing, so he's started being more forward with the kid. Johnny Mueller the superstar sits on the outside bench taking love notes from the little girls who scamper back and forth down the grandstand runway. Billy's perched on the wall, laughing at Johnny and wishing for some adulation of his own. But Jolene is Queen of the Silver Dollar, reigning monarch of the Mason City Park Commission Stadium, where she stands along the base-line tossing balls back and forth with Ed.

"Eddie," she yells so everyone can hear, "here's my slider," and with her glove she waves that brush-cross motion the pitcher makes in warm-ups to indicate a fast-breaking ball. "No, no, *niña,* no no!" Eddie shouts back—kids shouldn't try to throw breaking stuff till their arms are developed; she could hurt herself for life. But Jolene's slider floats in soft as a butterfly, hardly any spin, and Eddie hopes they come at him like this during the game. "Your slider," he tries in English as he flips the ball back, "she is a beeg balloon!" The bench laughs. "Okay, nut face," Jolene snarls, and sends a smoking fastball at his groin.

For three nights' running Jolene comes in for catch, and after Friday's game she's perched on the dugout roof as the team troops in after a 1-0 win over Cedar Rapids. Eddie's been hitless, a seventeen-game streak broken, but the sight of his little *niña* cheers him. "Wanna cone?" Jolene asks, and Eddie, puzzled, looks to Andy Thompson who says "*Helado,* man, *helado.* 'Cept it ain't *helado.*"

There's a Dairy Dreem just three blocks from the ball park, and Eddie, who rarely carries money, reaches into the deep lining of his fine broad hat for Sunday's five.

"And what does your daddy want?" the lady asks as she hands the girl her Chocolate Whip special, and Jolene doubles over in a barely held laugh, snickering up at Eddie with that twisted impy smile that's been haunting all his dreams.

⊖ Ball Two ⊖

Costy Pedraza's first pitch has been low and outside, almost past the catcher, forcing him to lunge head-first toward the base line and start this first inning with a snootful of dirt. He swings back on his heels and pumps his mitt upward, urging Costy to keep the slider from breaking too soon, then snaps the ball back to him on the mound.

Billy Harmon, who's playing second this game, wanders over to the bag between pitches and motions to Eddie at short. Eddie's English isn't much, but still better than Costy's, and so he's the guy who translates minor-league plays and instructions from the manager. Eddie's from Panama, though, and since Costy is only eight weeks off the plane from the Dominican their Spanish can get mixed up, meaning utterly different things.

One wet afternoon when Eddie suggested taking their raincoats to the park Costy thought he was talking about rubber diapers. Another time Eddie saw Costy talking with a pretty young woman near the dugout and walked over to compliment her hairdo. But Eddie's *pelo* was not at all what the word meant to Costy, who almost decked him right there. So Eddie's wound up thinking that this new kid is a little bit bananas, and vice versa.

But the little bit of English Billy and Eddie share—evolved as roommates through spring training and the first weeks of A-ball —keeps the middle infield free of ambiguities and fistfights. Billy has caught the pitcher's signal to them, a shrug of the left shoulder, which means he'll wait until the catcher calls for a fastball, so any grounder will surely go to Eddie's side of the bag. "Your ball, man," Billy says with his glove shielding his lips. "You bet," Eddie answers, his favorite American phrase, which handles just about anything.

As Costy paws the mound and the infield gets back into position, the benchwarmers pick their topic for the day. The madly erratic clubhouse shower that scalded one of them and nearly froze another has them thinking about water, and after a bit of grumbling Buddy Knox, the reserve infielder whose beer gut is growing with each day's lack of play, starts the second-string outfield on their pet obsession: discovering the headwaters of the Mississippi.

The Mighty Mississip' is a big item in their lives this year. Two of the clubs they play in Iowa are river towns, and for road games in Wisconsin and Illinois they cross it every trip. Lynn Parson, whose California hipness finds everything about the Midwest cutesy quaint, has been telling the bench how he and Rafael Quinones traced it to its source during three days of rainouts at Eau Claire last summer.

Out in the bull pen the long-reliever, two middle men, and the reserve catcher are—like the pitching coach who's joined them— just slouching and staring as if their game hasn't begun. The players sit quietly and Mack isn't thinking about anything at all. Costy paws while all the action's in the dugout.

"It started that first day we'd planned on the Eau Galle," Lynn recalls. "Yeah, you said the reservoir was full of walleyes," Buddy adds, and for a moment there's some thought about Wisconsin game fish. Their rivals in Madison, after all, are called the Muskies, and the fans have a fish cheer and everything. But now Lynn reminds them that the Eau Galle looked mean that day. "Storms?" the new bat boy asks. "Nope, bunch of boys in campers acting like the place was locals only," Lynn scoffs. "So Rafael and I took our little All-Americas tour to the river and just headed on up. When we found Lake Wabedo Raffy phoned to be sure the game's called off and we fished all night."

"Fish stories!" Billy spits across the dugout as he says it and notes that Pedraza is shaking off a lot of signs. Some game, if this is only his second pitch. Mack spots the delay from the bull pen and leans out from the bench to see if the manager wants his help. But Carl is motionless on the dugout step, just resting on his knee and staring like the others toward the field.

Lynn fills the gap as Costy fidgets and Carl stares. "Hey, these good folks at Wabedo felt bad we didn't get a walleye strike, so next day they sent us further north." "Still raining?" Buddy asks and Lynn says sure, they decided to chance it and see how the Mississippi looked north of Reginald. "I hear you can step right across it, there," Carl turns around to say, surprising everyone that he's been listening, but Lynn protests to all of them: "No way, kids, all the way through Sainer it's still a good twenty-feet wide and faster than a demon." Carl turns back, remembering those long-distance calls from a half-day's drive away. "We rained out again, Skip?" What could he have told Kansas City if they'd called—a left-fielder and star shortstop were two days A.W.O.L., looking for a place they could straddle the Mississippi River?

The catcher goes back to one finger—fastball—and this time Costy nods okay. What's this, he can't read numbers? The catcher's flashed it to him twice before, but now he gets the message—this shrewd Dominican is confusing the batter, making him think all sorts of exotic pitches and locations, when in fact it's going to be the straight one down Main, okay!

Costy fingers the ball and leans back in his stretch. Billy glances over to check that Eddie's in position, but Eddie's not with it at all—he's mooning over toward the dugout where Carl's perched on the top step, trying to ignore the jockies behind him. Billy wants to yell a "Hey, man!" but Costy's spooked enough from that first bad pitch. What on earth is Eddie up to? There's his little *niña*—the cute young shagger who's been flirting with him ever since his fence-hopper in batting practice nipped her ankle. She's in the first-row box over the dugout, where kids don't belong anyway and certainly not when they're shagging. "Hey man, *trouble*," Billy wants to yell, but he doesn't have the words and what a can of worms, what a crazy Latin mess to get into. Maybe one of the older Spanish players—Quinones if he comes back down from Chattanooga—can straighten Eddie out. Mason City, Iowa, sure isn't Panama, or anyplace else but Iowa for that matter.

"Quinones, my man Raf-a-el!" Lynn is musing. "Wanted me to play winter ball in Colombia, said we'd get to Venezuela, meet his wife and kids." "Yeah, but what about the river?" Buddy prompts, now obsessed himself. "How far up did you guys get, did you ever see it get, like, real small?" He wants an answer—every third day this story gets started and then Lynn is called in to pinch hit or reserve, or following some other action just gets bored with it and changes subjects.

Lynn doesn't answer, as he's joined Carl in puzzling over Ped-

raza's actions on the mound. Costy's dropped his arm and has
stepped off the rubber, staring toward Jim Smith the catcher as if
he's in a daze. Smitty has called to Carl and is shrugging his
shoulders, asking if he should check with Costy on the mound.
"Sanmarda!" Carl calls to his shortstop, "Sanmarda, *vete*"—one
of the few Spanish words he knows, as he gestures Eddie over
toward the pitcher. "Settle him down, hey?" "You bet!" Eddie
thinks to himself as he trots in toward Costy.

"Mi amigo, mi compadre," Costy is thinking happily as Eddie
joins him on the mound, with Billy and the other infielders looking on suspiciously from their positions. But then Eddie greets
him with the words Costy would use to summon a waiter or correct a servant, and his grin changes to a pucker, ready to spit.
"What's the problem?" Costy says to break the tension, meaning
it friendly enough but Eddie takes it to mean his own problem.

"I got no problems, man, it's you that's not pitching."

"I am too pitching, why don't you play shortstop like these
Yankees pay you to?"

"I can't catch what they don't hit what you don't throw, baby!"
Eddie says, again meaning it friendly, doing his best to put the
funny words his teammates use into Spanish slang. But he's answered with a thick spray of tobacco juice across his uniform top.

¿"Niño? ¿Niño?" Costy is screaming. Eddie's looking down at
his shirt, wondering what he's said, and is knocked clean off his
feet by Costy's swift shove.

Costy is now bellowing insults and kicking at poor Eddie, who's
struggling in the dust to find his feet. He's halfway up, finding
unsure balance on the mound's steep slope, when Pedraza knees
him in the chin and sends him head-over-heels toward the plate.

By this time Carl is out there, pinning Costy's arms from behind, while Jim blocks off Eddie, who's standing again but some-
what tipsy from the two quick blows. Both benches have emptied,
but no one else is fighting—just the American players turning
toward their Latin colleagues to ask what on earth is going on.
"Shortstop called him a kid," the Angels' batter is telling the ump.
"Down in the Dominican you'd say that to your own child, but for
any other kid, not related, you know, it means a brat, a dirty kid
in the streets, you know." "No, I didn't know that," the umpire
says, not really listening, as he wonders how to discipline this
mess.

He walks toward Carl, who's released Costy on the mound. Not having the least idea what to say, he simply takes a schoolmar-mish, traffic-cop attitude and prepares to stare the manager down. "Don't look at me," Carl protests, "I don't understand these Latinos any better than you do." The ump is still silent. "Now don't go tossing anybody," Carl warns, anticipating an argument, "my boys didn't touch the other team, this is all my business, not yours." "Are they staying in?" the ump asks. Carl looks around to see that Eddie is still a bit woozy and bleeding from the mouth. "Shortstop's coming out," he decides, "pitcher stays in." The ump looks skeptical. "Hey, we played a doubleheader last night, I don't *have* anybody else!" Carl pleads, and the ump lets him off. But as he turns back to the plate he gives Carl a stern warning: "When I crew your game, *do not* play those bozos together, got me?"

As he passes the mound, Carl has three words for his pitcher. "Pedraza—hundred dollars!" He points as if to underscore, then stalks back to the bench. Costy looks about helplessly and settles on first baseman Andy Thompson, Spanish-speaking from home and college. Andy answers his mute question in clear, grammar-book language: "He's fined you one hundred dollars, Costy. Now behave!"

The players finally clear, but not until Lynn and the Angels' third-baseman have finished up their chat. "Hear your showers are out, man," the infielder has said, and Lynn is giving him the whole rundown on how old Mack came running out naked through the clubhouse, scalded and steaming like a lobster. "Old Mack?" the Angel twists his head, "That's awesome! Bet he'll get it fixed, those old guys don't put up with none of this shabby A-ball stuff."

Lynn starts in on the great shower-leak story as the two teams brush past each other toward their dugouts. "We looked for it all last year, figured there had to be an absolute source, something real small-like, you know," he's telling the Angel as Buddy and the bench jockeys pass by.

"So where'd you find it?" the third baseman asks, as Buddy and the others stop to hear Lynn's answer.

"In the hot-water tap for the sink, you never would believe it!" Lynn explains as he slaps his rival with his glove and trots back to the bench.

Buddy is transfixed by wonder and disbelief. "Hey Skip," he calls as he approaches Carl, "Parson finally told us where's the source!"

"The source?" Carl asks, not following and not caring.

"Of the Mississippi, of the river!" Buddy exclaims. "It's in some kitchen sink, some leaky faucet!"

Carl just stares, writing off this senseless line to the general lunacy that has prevailed since Costy's first pitch. He's thrown a few tosses to get loose again, and Escobar's in at short. The ump pulls down his mask and calls for play, squatting behind the plate. Smitty signals a fastball and it comes in high, a mile out of the strike zone.

☹ Baseball Bingo ☹

Bill White is the best PA announcer in the Midcontinent League. It's the one category in which the Mason City Royals score first each time, as the minor-league parks are rated on everything from pregame music to parking lots, locker rooms, and warning tracks. Their visitors' lockers are the pits, and without an outfield track Mason City's chances are whammied from the start. But Bill's their pride and glory, as he should be because he's a pro.

He's the sports announcer and fill-in D.J. for the local country station, a low-power AM affair that must get off WCFL's clear channel at sunset. But such a self-defined day job makes it easy for Bill to moonlight at the ball park, where even with his twenty dollars pay per game he's doing it for the fun.

His desk up in the press box is organized like a sound effects lab. He's got cassettes all over, labeled for their music and features, including several national anthem tapes, explosions for home-team four-baggers, the Beatles' "Help" for when the visitor's relief trots in, and the love theme from *The Godfather*, which he plays each time Freddie Guagliardo strides purposefully to the mound. He's tried "The Lonely Bulls" once for Costy Pedraza and the hot little Dominican complained, but Bill has got back at him by playing an assortment of tangos from the forties he'd never recognize, which gives the older fans a laugh.

The tapes are fun but they're the simplest part of his job. Fan promotions run all night, from lucky numbers to baseball trivia. Bill tries to do each one with special flair, and the trivia answers are usually good material. For uncommonly witless answers he has a noisemaker he sounds for the evening's "raspberry award" for prime stupidity—an answer like last night's "Frank and

Brooks Robinson" for the question "Which brother combination holds the record for home runs in the major leagues?" One night a puzzler about consecutive steals has the especially active group of fans down in box 28 sending up dozens of unlikely answers, the wackier of which Bill reads to the crowd—"Imogene Coca" is his favorite.

The best part of Bill's job is the perch he has up here. He can see everything—out to the bull pens, down into the dugouts and, of course, across the field. He's not exactly hanging out over the plate, but when the ump looks up to signal a line-up change or ask for stadium lights it really seems the guy is praying to the Lord above, and when Bill's voice booms out through the park's six speakers it's like God Himself talking to the fans. His words do sound omnipotent, opening the first-base beer bar if the crowd gets heavy, saying if a rain delay's to be lifted, and proclaiming what's a hit and what's an error. Umps can be challenged and jawed at, but when that mighty voice calls "E6, error on the short-stop" there's nothing anyone feels they can do but accept it.

But Bill's really not much of a deity up here. Or if he is, it's like one of those Greek or Roman varieties, always hungering for a piece of mortal action and getting messily involved in the lives of human playthings down below. There's one more feature of the park laid out before him—the main aisle, which skirts the boxes and parades down there in full view of the press box—which on some nights runs like a river of pretty girls. Bill's convinced they do it just to tease him, walking back and forth in their tight jeans and skimpy tops while he's tied down to his microphone, tape deck, and scoresheet up here.

Most heartbreaking are the players' wives and girl friends and even the better class of groupies who've won themselves a place on the pass list. They're down below him in boxes 29 and 30, and as they mingle and joke and wave to the field Bill often feels like a kid looking down into a dollhouse or into the town square of his Lionel train set. Maybe that's where real life is, Bill fantasizes—the social doings that go on around the artifice his announcing sets in motion. He counts innings, introduces batters, and scores the plays, all the while that human culture down there in the boxes develops around his game. At times he's tampered, slipping an especially pretty girl friend's name among the winners so that he can try flirting when she comes up to collect her prize. But it's never worked so far. His role up here is just too abstract, and the girls can't seem to see him as one of their kind. So it's become his fate not to be one of them at all.

His major link between the game on the field and life in the stands is baseball bingo. In the old days conventional bingo was called between innings, and it's still done sometimes for special promotions. But the normal order of business is to integrate it with the game. It works quite simply according to a chart of possibilities—if the shortstop grounds out, that's a B-16, whereas if he gets a single that means N-37, and so forth through all the plays and numbers. Only thing that doesn't count is a strike-out, both so that there's no chance a batter can fix it for a winning number and because it would be downright ghoulish for a hometown fan to cheer for such competitive misfortune simply because he needed the square filled on his card. Still, there've been some silly situations where a fan needing just an O-72 will yell at the pitcher "Hit him!" and another who lacks I-25 and B-9 hollering "Get a walk—then steal second on a passed ball!" But most times baseball bingo's excitement works in tandem with the field action, and Bill enjoys it when the rhythms of the two games coincide.

O-69—right fielder doubles. I-20—second baseman steals. And one of his favorites, B-11, which means the left fielder hits a home run. When Lynn Parson's in the groove Bill's come to think of him by that letter and number, and one night he nearly brought the house down when, instead of announcing Lynn's uniform digit with his name and position as he came to bat, he simply called out "B-11, Lynn Parson." Happily, Lynn obliged by driving one out and Bill did feel like God.

Ever since that night the fans have urged him to bring good luck by calling numbers in advance, but Bill's saving his fun with baseball bingo for something else. A favorite with the GM because of the professionalism he brings to the job, Bill can get away with just about anything. So Jeff has no objections when on a quiet night—a Monday when ABC-TV cuts into their already depleted sports entertainment market—the announcer asks if he can run the bingo game a slightly different way.

Among his pregame patter is the news that tonight baseball bingo will be played differently for one time only. Not off the game-play instructions, and not by lottery number between innings like years before. Instead, Bill will call the numbers between batters, based on his perceptions of what's transpiring down in the

box seats. Old Lew, the retired grocer who sits down there each
night, has given him in a rundown on all their doings, and Bill
can hardly contain himself when he introduces the special game
of his own devising: baseball wives' bingo.

"Baseball wives' bingo is played just like regular bingo," he
reads from the parody of his regular announcement for each
night's game, "except that the numbers conform to the actions of
our Mason City Royals' wives sitting down there behind the
screen. Each reported piece of gossip corresponds to a number,
and five across or down your card makes for a winner. Baseball
wives' bingo will begin in the bottom of the third inning, so buy
your cards now."

Whether Bill will really go through with this has the wives' box
buzzing, and as the bottom of the third rolls around all eyes are
on the booth where Bill waits for the first play to conclude before
calling a number.

Angel Naboa grounds out in a play that would ordinarily be an
N-40, but instead Bill calls out something new—"B-4, the center
fielder's wife overcharges the MasterCard account." Next batter
strikes out, which usually means no number, but for this new
game Bill has one ready—"O-70, the shortstop's girl friend calls
her mother in Hawaii and runs up a thirty-dollar phone bill." The
fans are howling and there's quite a bit of action in the boxes, as
the bevy of young women who surround Lew are one by one turning to confront him. Bill decides to end the inning with a big one
he's made up, and as the batter tops a sinking slider and rolls it
down toward first he reads a favorite he and Jeff cooked up this
after noon—"G-38, the pitcher's wife forgets two payments and
the Camaro's repossessed."

For the next three innings of home-team at-bats Bill reads off
his list of bingo situations. It adds up to a pretty good description
of life among this strata of baseball society, with security and
phone deposits lost when a player's moved up to Double A or down
to the rookie league, minor crises with the grocery list when the
paycheck from Kansas City is a few days late, and even the odd
sexual innuendos that filter through these players' lives. Of all
Bill's topics there's only one that's a bit mean: "Brooke Thomas"—
she's a notorious traveler, barely ranked above a common
groupie—"dates the starting line-up."

Baseball wives' bingo continues and by the seventh inning Bill
has paid off the first winner, a regular who's completed his five

across with the free space plus "O-67—short reliever's girl friend forgets to move her toiletries out when his folks come to visit." When a second winner scores in the eighth Bill begins a balancing act. He wants the game to continue through the ninth so that he can announce the last number with the final out. He's kept a close eye on box 30 downstairs, and the object of his call is still down there—like the players' wives, she's always loyal to the last out. But if a third fan wins, that ends the game. So Bill tries sneaking in some repeat numbers, skipping a few turns, and inventing some no-number situations that parallel their husbands' strikeouts, such as "third baseman's wife drops a tray of beer and Pepsi."

Finally it's down to one more out in the top of the ninth. With the Royals leading they won't bat, and as Freddie bears down on the hitter Bill readies his final call. "Don't forget, folks, we have one more number in tonight's bingo game, so listen after the final out." Several fans with cards one number short hang on his announcement, and Bill's pleased to see the young woman he's been studying all night is still following along. Grabbing his binoculars, which are used to spot the bull pen, he refocuses on her card below—I-22 is the slot she needs to win.

This makes it perfect. Bill's been mooning over her like a sick love song since she joined Dave Alpert's wife in the box last month. Small like Jayne, she's got a punkish cuteness that drives Bill wild. By a process of elimination he's discovered the music she likes and has played it to the exclusion of everything else, determined to keep her happy at the ball park. With her seat number she's won an amazing number of prizes, but has always sent Jayne or Lew to collect.

This afternoon he's asked Lew her name and sure enough she's Jayne's younger sister from New Jersey. There've been all sorts of ball park proposals, from airplanes trailing the question to scoreboard messages, so Bill feels he's in line with tradition when he makes his final call in baseball wives' bingo. And now it's time.

Freddie Guagliardo drops a curve past the Rangers' last hope, and as the crowd cheers Bill reads the winning number. "I-22," and Jayne's sister jumps up to applaud her good luck as Bill continues: "Carol Gallagher goes out to dinner with the Royals' PA announcer." She looks up, still smiling, and Bill knows it's finally worked.

☹ Beer Night in Bettendorf ☹

Bishop's Cafeteria at the Bettendorf Iowa Mall, and it's lunch before the team checks into the Travelodge Motel. Secretaries and saleswomen on their break are filing past the roast beef, potato salad, cottage cheese, pies, and coffee to the cashier, where the Mason City Royals' infield and a few other rowdies have taken a big table.

Johnny has passed out the cards, and as the first young woman walks past they flash their scores: 8-9-9-7-8. Oh, these Bettendorf girls. Within a minute there are five 9's and Johnny lurches after her in his Groucho Marx walk. It's an unwritten law among them that nobody but nobody rates a 10; 10's are for the one you'll marry, or maybe have already. But five 9's win an invitation to lunch with the boys. The lucky lady blushes, asks if her girl friend can join them. "We gotta vote on that," Johnny advises, and so the cards are shown one more time. The girl friend gets an honorary pass and so she's asked in.

Johnny is ready to ask for a date when the first young woman starts talking about her husband. "He's a rat-poison salesman," she confesses. "Oh, a mean one," Johnny says with a back-off motion, but the girlfriend giggles out, "Yeah, funny little eyes and whiskers." So maybe they mean business. But Carl and Mack are herding the team out and there's no time for heavy propositions, just a plea to come out to the game if the rain lifts. "And baby," Angel calls out in Spanish, "you can stop by the shower room and see what comes up." Eddie blushes, then laughs, while across the restaurant two Mexican busboys nearly drop their trays.

That afternoon the skies clear magically, a draft of cool Canadian air blows down river, sweetening even the Travelodge Motel, and Carl decides to field the team for some early practice. There's only one set of uniforms along, so the guys depart from conventional minor-league field dress and wear T-shirts and cutoffs. "Sandusky Football," "Tampa Bay I Do Love You," "Kansas City Royals," fond thought. "Tecate Cerveza," which Angel's father helps brew in Monterrey. "World's Greatest Lover." Eddie, dreaming of his cute little shagger in Mason City, misses too many pick-offs and is sent out to center field to chase flies and loosen up his sore leg. Carl teaches the kids a pick-off play he saw the Phillies' infield work on in 1962.

"Angel, you run toward the bag from short, then when the pitcher turns wheel off back to short. The runner will think it's a bluff or that the ball's in the hole and he'll make his move. But when Angel turns off, Billy, you slip in behind the runner from second and take the throw. Now listen, you have to be conservative with this play, second time it's easy to read—Angel, you explain it to Eddie—so only do it when you're sure there'll be a bunt or a hit and run with the runner going, but then it'll work every time. Okay, take your positions and we'll pull some plays out of the hat."

Six, play six, so Matt rears back on the mound, places his foot halfway between the plate and first, and fires over to trap the runner. "Balk, balk!" the crowd at first shouts—three first baseman and six runners are lined up for turns and none of them likes Matt's move. "Any ump would call that, every time," Andy Thompson argues, and everyone supports him. "What ump?" Matt protests. "This is A-ball, the ump's at second with a runner, he can't see my foot on this side of the hill." Carl strides over and tells Matt to cool it, both his talk and the move. "It's a bad habit," Carl says, the purist, but adds for practicality, "the other ump can see it from the plate."

Out along the left-field line the pitching coach is talking about habits, too. "You catch the bull pen like you catch the game," he yells at Jim Smith, who's let a few sliders sneak away beneath his glove. "Any habits you pick up here you carry down there." Smith feels he's been spotted out, as everyone on the field has heard this dressing down. "Dump it," he says, quietly.

That night it's a bad game all around. The rat-poison salesman's wife and her girl friend haven't shown. Costy Pedraza loads the bases twice in the first two innings and bang-bang they're down five runs. Nobody's hitting good, their fielding's shabby, and it seems like the hit parade and flashy play last night in Mason City has sucked out all the juices, burned out their fire. Coaches and players squabble.

What's worse, the fans are riding Eddie. Their announcer, trying for a little pizzaz, has sung out his name in mock-Spanish, "Eduaaardo Sanmaaarda," drawing out the a's like a Mexican folk song, and the drunks—it's fifty-cent beer night—have picked it up. "Hey, Eduaaaardo," they chant each time he comes to bat or takes a grounder. This will happen every night down here for the rest of the year, Eddie knows, and it could follow him through the league and maybe his career. Eddie is short, spare, with tight curly hair. He looks the kid and is a natural target.

Too rattled to continue at short or second, Eddie is shifted to the outfield in the fourth, where a fan beans him with a can of Miller's. Eddie is prepared to throw it back and Andy Thompson has tossed a punch at the first-base coach, who's been egging them on when Carl runs out onto the field. "All right, stop this stuff right now or I'm pulling my players off," he snaps at the ump. A conference: both umpires, the Quad Cities manager, head usher, and stadium cop. Word is sent up to the press box and the announcer makes his appeal. No interference. Spectators throwing objects onto the playing field will be ejected. And then the words that bring down the house: "The beer bar is closed."

Six hundred spectators rise as one, hurling scorecards, popcorn boxes, and aluminum empties down on the field. Players from both teams back off under the rain of debris. Carl, who's been holding the game ball, whips it back into the stands—at no one in particular, just an angry reflex, but it hits the press-box window dead-center and sends a shower of glass over the writers and announcer. Both dugouts empty again, and the teams start brawling purely out of habit. This quiets the stands, for now there's action on the field. Quarters are close, so there's no room for wind-up blows, just pushing, shoving, and bear-hug holds. Some players are laughing, rollicking in the joy of contact, and when the two police cruisers roar onto the field through the field gate all fifty young men turn around to give the cops a standing ovation.

The police, however, are humorless. Their squad cars are natural targets for the beer cans, and empties sail off their helmets left and right. Five of them charge a cluster of fans still holding their drinks—how could they have been the hurlers?—and flail away with night sticks. This is an ugly scene, but instead of provoking more violence it quickly clears both stands and field.

Eddie and Angel are safely outside the park—through the gate left open by the police, they've climbed up to the flood levee that surrounds the ball park, a weedy mound of hard gravel and rusty cans which, just beyond the stadium lights, is a haven a tranquillity. A young Mexican boy has been out here shagging balls and is now calmly toking on a joint.

"Compadres," he beckons when he sees these fugitive players are Latins like himself, and continues in Spanish, "come share my good smoke." The three sit along the concrete wall facing the brightly lit park and take long, slow draws. "Bueno," Angel exhales. "Si, si, si," Eddie agrees, like his grandfather used to say when smoking the same weed.

For a long time no one says a thing. The Mexican boy drifts away unnoticed, humming a tune of soft benevolence. The joint is gone, the stadium empty, the lights are going out one by one.

" 'Ey," Angel croons to his teammate, "Eduaaaardo . . . "

⊗ Five Bad Hands and the ⊗ Wild Mouse Folds

The Mason City Royals are bussing it across the state, and an hour out of Bettendorf catcher Jim Smith announces that he's finished up his league chart. "Bettendorf!" yells Johnny Mueller before Jim can even begin, "Smells like catfish in the showers!" "Dubuque!" Joey choruses in, "Cat yuck in the rugs!" One by one they check off the Midcontinent League cities, small burgs of forty thousand folks or so where sometimes there isn't even a Holiday Inn, not that their GM could afford it. The Royals go into each city four times a year, and Jeff has booked them seasonal rates in motels that would otherwise stand empty. And for good reason. "Madison: big June bugs mashed up in the sheets! Quad Cities: smells like dead stuff in the walls!" Eddie perks up, senses his turn. "Caedar Rapeeds!" he trills in his high Panamanian accent, "¡La cucaracha!" Jim shouts for order, claiming they've got it all wrong. He runs down his own list of sundry pests and vermin, noting approval and shrugging off complains ("The zitty waitress is in Peoria, moron"). But everyone agrees he's saved the best for last. "Eau Claire!" he sings out, and the whole bus answers in a single voice, "The wild mouse!"

Their four-game sweep in Bettendorf primes them for the Northern Division, and the luxury of an off-day's travel gets them into Eau Claire early enough for some serious poker.

> You gotta lend me five
> Just to keep me alive.

Donny the left fielder is making up a new ditty a for each hand, fitting the beat of slapping cards, jingling chips, and popping can tops. For a minor-league baseball club the Royals make a good

rhythm section when they're playing for blood; it sounds like a
bass line behind a nasty whining Mick Jagger song.

> I'd pay you back quick
> But my brother got sick,

and Andy is dealing out another hand. "Garbage," he calls, not
his hand but the name of this particular poker round, each dealer
calling his pick. Two queens, two deuces. Should he play on a
double pair when everybody's drawing three, tossing three, drawing two more?

> How about a ten
> till I see you again?

But he's a long way from borrowing. Nobody's had much good
stuff that night, so the pots and losses have been small. The game
was better on the bus up from Bettendorf, part of the crazy energy
from the ball-park riot two nights before. "Game called on account of madness" the paper read, the Royals won on a forfeit
called by the ump, and next night the stands were full hoping for
a repeat. Lots of action, but all legal—a dozen home runs between the two teams, tied a league record, score like a football
game, 14–13, one of the writers said he'd head it "Dodgers miss
point after." Plus all sorts of good baseball. Carl's sucker pick-off
worked three times; he was wrong, the runners never learn. Four
wins in Bettendorf on top of the game from Wisky Rapids puts
them way, way out front, and now when they finish in Eau Claire
they'll be looking at a lazy four game/four day series in Dubuque
odds say they'll sweep. Oh, oh, Eau Claire. Donny knows a girl up
here who'll cook for him all week, so that's six dollars meal money
for the poker pot each night. Right now she's across the courtyard watching TV with the players' wives.

Mitch is calling, the crazy bastard. He's the only Eau Claire
player they'll let in the game, and only because he's shot his credit
with his teammates. Calling the last five hands and the best he's
had is a pair of aces. The poor goof. Matt, who took counseling
courses when he pitched college ball, says the guy is lonely and
that he's only playing cards as a substitute for making friends,
which he can't seem to do. So he plays poker like a hyperactive
eight-year-old. Maybe he doesn't understand the game.

> Just lend me twenty
> and I'll show you guys plenty.

For sure, he doesn't understand that Donny is singing about him.

The guys turn in at two, and within an hour the motel is quiet. But sometime later Angel hears his roommate get up and head for the john, and in a moment it sounds like a war going on in there. He pushes the door open just in time to see Jim's bat poised over the commode.

The bat slams down with a vengeance, shattering the fixtures and sending shards of porcelain and ceramic tile to the corners of the room. "Take THAT," Jim growls, and swings to position himself for the next blow. But his target is nowhere to be seen. "Close the door, close the lousy DOOR," he yells at Angel, who is calling in Spanish for Ed to come on down and see the fun. It's 4:00 A.M., lights out was two hours ago, but everyone is waking up as word spreads through the Northland Motel—Jim Smith is clubbing out the wild mouse!

Jim is standing on the toilet, his thirty-six-ounce Louisville Slugger bearing his own stamped signature broken off in his hands. "Angel, Angel, you got a bat up here?" he calls, and Angel laughs back, "No, man, I don't sleep with my bat." "Get me something, come on, get me something," Jim screams again, but now Johnny and Buddy are at the door with the mosquito spray Buddy had brought for the murky Bettendorf dugout. "This stuff is industrial strength," he tells the room, "just turn off that fan, close the door, and we'll gas the thing through the ventilator." "It's in the can?" Johnny asks, and Jim shouts back, "Yeah man, it's in the shower and I almost had it but these bats go to pieces, you know."

Buddy's up on the dresser, shaking and spraying his insect repellent through the bathroom vent. Angel starts to cough and sneeze. "Hey, man, you're killing me, turn on the air conditioner." "Forget it, you want to pull it all out?" Buddy protests.

"Listen," Johnny says, "you need a ton of that stuff to even stone it, this is the wild mouse." Every night in Eau Claire this season the mouse has hassled them—chewing gloves, glutting itself on chip dip from the poker table, and one-by-one keeping them all awake. Of course they'd like to flatten it, with baseball bats, bug spray, or the TV.

"That's it," Johnny announces. "It's gonna want out of that bathroom real bad," he reasons, "so turn out all the lights and get me up here on the dresser with something big." "Smitty's behind," Buddy suggests, but Johnny already has the twenty-three inch vintage black-and-white TV in his arms. "Bombs over Tokyo" he yells as Angel slips open the door, the mouse scoots out, and the television is dropped from an altitude of seven feet. It hasn't been unplugged.

A sickening roar and phosphorous shower fill the room, condensers sputtering and the main power tubes flashing red and yellow and spitting out sparks. Everyone's yelling and cheering like mad. "Don't touch it, don't touch it," Johnny yells to Angel, "you'll electrocute yourself." He jumps down from the dresser and over to the wall, where he unplugs the guttering set.

"Oh boy, oh boy," Jim is repeating. Nobody's hurt but the room's a mess, from the smoldering TV to the sooted-up walls. They kick away the TV's shell and there's the charred corpse of a tiny mouse.

"Try mouth to mouth, I think it's still breathing," Johnny says, but nobody's laughing. The team has this entire wing so nobody's heard the bedlam, but tomorrow morning, oh tomorrow morning. "Is Carl's light on?" Jim asks and Angel looks across the court to the coaches' room and it's dark. "I think they're still out," Angel says, but no one knows how to cover this.

"Let's say we were robbed," Buddy offers lamely. No one responds. A few sparks from the TV and Buddy jumps. "Easy, man," Johnny cautions, "it holds two thousand volts, don't touch it."

"I'm calling Jeff," Jim says, and reaches for the phone. Eight for an outside line, 515 for Mason City, then their GM's home number. "You killed a lousy mouse?" Jeff screeches in his tinny Bronx accent, "a lousy MOUSE?" "Yeah, well you see there's some damage up here, not a lot, but if Carl thinks he has to represent it to you and Mr. Howard. . . . " Jeff agrees to put a call into Carl at the desk, he'll get it any minute now that the after-hours bars are closed, and try to take the guys off the hook. The six players in the room will pay all damages from next month's salary. The TV is the worst, maybe the bathroom, but they'll cover it. "And listen, man," Jim pleads, "from now on can you book us in some other place up here?"

"At their pleasure," Jeff assures them. "At their pleasure, I'm sure."

⊖ Workouts ⊖

The dead time of a road date means full workouts, fullest they've had since spring training. It's called for ten that morning, which means the bus leaves the motel at nine fifteen, quarter of an hour out to the ball park crossing most of Eau Claire, Wisconsin, and thirty minutes to suit up. Buddy finished three twelve-packs during the poker game, where everyone was supposed to stay with Pepsi, and he's trying to sneak off from running the outfield. He dreamed about the wild mouse all night and he's already lost his breakfast in the ashcan out back of Happy Chef. Chet gives him an Alka-Seltzer, which brings it up again.

They run the outfield twice, not sprints but just enough to shake the sleep and work off breakfast. Then Mack forms a center circle and calls out calisthenics, mainly stuff for arms and legs plus a few torso bends. The pitchers get down to stretch: fingertips grasping toes, rocking back, oh that feels good around the belt, they paw and preen like kittens in the sun.

Warm-ups. The pitchers are lollygagging, so Carl shouts over to take more throws, he wants them loose enough to move toward first. A few play catch, most rifle the ball against the concrete wall that loops from the dugouts back around the plate. A kid has come out with a glove, she's a girl who looks a bit like Jolene, and Ed would like to give her some throws but worries for the jeers. She sits in the stands, disappointed.

Now some pick-off plays, but this time to train the base runners and try some rundowns. "Stay in the base line, stay in the base line" Carl yells, and Johnny, flush from six great hands the night before, tears off toward right field with Angel and the ball in hot pursuit. "You think that's so funny, you can run ten laps," Carl calls after them, but he's laughing, too.

Afternoon out of town means batting practice for the pitchers, and even though it's two o'clock on a sunny Wisconsin afternoon you'd swear it was a girls' slumber party. Preening, primping, showing each other their best pitches and giggling at the exotic stuff like screwballs, knucklers, cross-breaking curves and palm balls, forkballs, things these kids will never really use till they're fifteen-year vets. All the pitchers are together, incongruously, with the real men—the hitters—far away.

No one shags because few balls even make it near the fence. In fact there's only one pitcher playing outfield to wander beneath the occasional deep pops. The Midcontinent League uses AL rules, which includes the designated hitter, so they'll never bat until they move to a higher league that plays National or perhaps wind up with a senior circuit club. But it's still part of minor-league basics, so they like their turns batting.

They're laughing and ribbing until Matt loses control of a hard curve and dumps Robin. This is never, never done in pitcher's BP, and three turns later Robin's first throw to Matt is a wicked fastball at his head. Not really meaning to, it takes his helmet square above the ear, splitting it cleanly to the crown and sending Matt into a dizzy descending spin. But he shakes off help, climbs up, and grabs his bat to stalk out toward the mound. There Robin stands, not moving an inch, staring him down. "You're a real creep, Robin, you know that?" Matt is growling, while everybody else is keeping far away. Robin is searching for words, wanting to dress him back good, when suddenly his eyes tear up and he chokes out, "Matt, I'm sorry, Matt, Matt. . . . " Matt turns and hurls his bat twenty rows up in the metal stands, where it bounces down, clattering and echoing for an eternity.

By now Mack is out of the clubhouse. He's muttering dark things to himself but, seeing that the fight is over, just calls out, "Okay, girls, we're running the outfield." Matt and Robin are nowhere to be seen.

⊖ Bus Trip ⊖

Earl Hansen's been the Mason City Royals' driver for a dozen years. This spring he tried retiring but was called back when his young replacement just didn't pan out. In June, when he signed back on, young Angel Naboa gave him a vivid picture of what his absence had been like.

"Earl," Angel greeted him his first day back, holding him in a deeply affectionate handshake while he proclaimed how glad he was to have the old guy driving for them, "it's so good you are working again. This new kid, he was no good at all!"

"No kidding, huh, Angel?" Earl laughed, but the young infielder continued with firm solemnity.

"Earl, this new guy, he did not know how to drive! Last year, you drove us to Peoria in four hours. This year, the new guy takes six, sometimes seven, hours. Earl, it is so good you are back!"

Now it's July and time for one more swing up north. First stop's been Eau Claire, a town Earl likes because the park's beer bar is just a few steps down the aisle from his seat behind the dugout. He'll go through half a dozen Millers on a normal night, and when friends are buying it's more like nine or ten. He cuts himself off in the late innings and downs a coffee or two before hauling the guys back to the motel, but more than once the manager's had complaints about the bus being left in the wrong place, blocking the drive or wedging in any number of cars. By breakfast, however, Earl's always back 100 percent, and it's relatively easy for Carl to pull him off his second glass of orange juice and have him clear things out of the way.

Today, however, he's halfway in the bag before the team is even packed. Eau Claire to Wisconsin Rapids is a short late-morning trip, but Carl's disturbed to see Earl wobbling a bit as he opens the pneumatic door and laughing hoarsely with Al Elgin and the trainer as they stow some gear. Carl's not that happy the GM's brought Earl back—his speeding may be just a case of tickets, but the drinking is a stupid risk for his own skin and for the future of the Kansas City Royals, who have two high draft picks sporting hundred-thousand-dollar bonuses riding here together with lots of solid talent. He hopes O'Reilly and the others in the farm director's office never put two and two together and find out the old stumble bum they sometimes see on visits to Mason City has been trusted with getting their investments from town to town in one piece.

While Earl's still jawing with the players, Carl settles into his seat up front. He sits directly opposite the driver and often wishes he has his own steering wheel. More than once he's jammed his foot down hysterically on an imaginary brake pedal. It's just an hour and a half to Wisky Rapids, but when Earl's this shakey in the morning it means he's hit the hard stuff, usually brandy in his coffee to get things going after a rougher night than usual.

When his veteran pitching coach climbs on board, Carl motions him over for a moment's candid talk. Old Mack has so much more experience that simply confiding in him makes the younger manager feel secure, but this time Mack has some specific advice.

"You bet he's loose on his pins this morning," Mack agrees, and says he's worried about making it to the next town too. "And it won't be any better once we get there, either," he adds, because Earl will open up the beer bar while they take their workout.

"Geez, look at this drive," Carl complains, reaching across the driver's seat for Earl's road map. All his life Wisconsin's struck him as a funny state—dairy cows at graze and muskies lunging out of turgid water—and even looking at the map makes Carl picture its outline on a rustic knotty-pine board, the way he'd seen at countless sports show exhibits in his youth. Given Earl's condition this morning the route looks treacherous, a mass of secondary roads winding around lakes and rivers and through tiny resort towns that will be clogged with boat rigs and campers this time of year. Short as it is, he doesn't relish the trip.

"Listen, if you can just keep Earl's attention, the trip will go fine." That's old Mack's advice and as usual it's right on target.

"All he cares about these days is his fancy new radar detector," Carl complains and shakes his head hopelessly, but Mack gives him a big reassuring smile.

"Then that will make it real easy for me to keep him on the ball," the old coach laughs, and sets his plan with Carl. Whenever Earl starts wandering—and that will be pretty obvious as Carl sees himself heading for the ditch or centerline—he should lift his cap, just like when he's signaling the bull pen. Mack will be spread out across the last row as usual, where he promises to have something guaranteed to keep Earl on his toes.

At eleven everyone's on board and Carl reaches over to summon Earl with a few rapid honks. The garrulous old boy's been standing by the newspaper vending machines, yammering away with someone or other he knows up here from their four trips in each year. Earl looks up, gives Carl a wave, and to his utter infuriation keeps on talking for another couple minutes. Carl's not about to honk again, but he's precious near to hopping over and pulling out the bus himself when Earl piles on and they're off, a half-hour late as usual.

Earl's not two blocks out of town on Highway 12 when he starts making up lost time. The bus shudders as he accelerates, and Carl doesn't have to look to know the speedometer's well past fifty-five and heading toward seventy. Seventy miles per hour Carl can take, but when Earl inches up toward eighty while he fiddles with his log book the manager decides this is enough. He takes his cap off, wiggles it a few times, and holds it away from his head until he gets some sign from Mack.

It's not long in coming, though the effect of it is quite a surprise. Earl jumps as his radar detector gives a little bleat, then another, and finally six or seven in a row. At once they're down to fifty-nine miles per hour, Earl's safe speed, and the driver's back 100 percent as he scans the roadway for the Wisconsin State Patrol. They're coming to Augusta anyway, having picked up Highway 27, and Earl decides to share some expertise with his sometimes disapproving field boss.

"I got this baby set on long range," Earl tells him with a grin, "but coming to a town I shouldn't."

"Why not," Carl asks disinterestedly, "does it poison little school kids or something?"

"No," Earl laughs, "instead of getting some Smokey who's set up over the hill, I'm picking up a speed trap somewhere in town.

Could be six blocks over there where County HH comes in, there's a shopping mall out that way gets all the traffic." He reaches over to change his unit's range and the bleating stops. "See?" he says proudly. "Nothing on our street." But by now they're in a 40 zone with crossroads congestion up ahead, so Earl stays under the limit for the time being.

Driving through town he's alert to everything, pointing out the local sights to no one in particular. Carl wonders who supports the store after store of moccasins and curios. Folks from Milwaukee, Racine, and Kenosha, he figures. Women wore them in the stands at County Stadium years ago when he came in on road trips with the Phils. Just perfect for a town whose team boasted Phil Neikro and Bob Uecker. Chintz city.

He's wakened from his daydream by a sudden roar. He looks up to see the small town disappearing as Wisconsin 27 opens up ahead. A sign says "Fairchild 13" and Earl's boasting "I bet we can make it in ten!" when Carl reaches for his hat. It's in his lap, so he puts it on, takes it off again, and waves it around till he's sure Mack has seen.

"Damn!" Earl yells as his radar trap starts sounding. He checks the range and tries two frequencies but can't shake the signal. "Okay, this means they're up ahead. There goes our time, dammit!" He slows to fifty-nine and holds it there a mile and then another, but so far nothing's seen.

"One of those sedans up there," he motions to Carl, "up ahead where that county trunk comes in. They use a lot of unmarked up here." But as they pass the crossroads Carl can see these are just old junkers, car-pooled from surrounding towns and parked here for the day while their drivers join in a van or station wagon for the forty-mile ride over to the cranberry processing plant in Marshfield. Still, there's nothing up ahead, so Earl's convinced one of these old sedans had to be it. Satisfied, he floors it, and the aging bus grumbles deeply in response. Soon they're sailing along at seventy with the driver whistling gaily.

As long as he holds a tune, Carl promises himself, he'll leave the hat alone. Once or twice Earl falters and the manager reaches for his brim, but the melody comes back and Carl rests his hands. Earl's happy to make Fairchild just a few minutes past his hysteric schedule, and Carl breathes freer when they turn onto U.S. 10, which gives them a straight shot through the prettier ski country of Bruce Mound and Powers Bluff. Along here Earl can drive as fast as he wants and there's hardly a need for radar, visibility is so clear and unobstructed. Carl watches for Wisconsin Highway 13, however, since U.S. 10 makes a T with it at one of those classic dead man's intersections and he wouldn't be surprised at all to see Earl overshoot it.

Things like that happen all the time in Europe, soccer teams and football clubs wiped out in a single crash. Images of buses plunging down Alpine ravines and massive pileups in those crazy French traffic circles he'd negotiated on leave in the service fill Carl's imagination, till he snaps awake to hear Earl leaning on the horn. They're stuck behind a milk truck on the single stretch between Fairchild and Neillsville with a no passing zone, and Earl—stalled at forty miles per hour—is going nuts.

"For Chrissake, Earl," Carl tries to settle him, "it's nearly noon!"

"I know that, and we should have been past Granton already! You want some practice drills today yet, don't you?" The old driver is blustery and irate, precious minutes ticking off the wildly impossible log time he's left himself to get to Wisky Rapids.

"I mean by noon that truck's all full of milk!" Carl corrects him. "Look at his max weight back there—that's what he's pulling and it's all fluid. You ever had a load shift on you? That's what he's got to reckon with on these turns. So give him a break!"

But Earl is dauntless, popping the clutch to give him more jump when a quarter-mile stretch of highway opens up. Carl's helpless—making the radar box beep, however Mack's doing it, won't mean a thing now that he's stuck fifteen miles under the limit, and with the mood Earl's in there's nothing that will stop him once he gets this monster Greyhound out in the passing lane. So he leans back in his seat and closes his eyes—Carl simply doesn't want to see it, good as the odds are that Earl will pull them through unscathed.

Seeing nothing, Carl has little to distract him from the sound and feel of the big old bus straining to overtake its nemesis up ahead. They must be on a slight downgrade, the manager senses, as the vibrations smooth out and he feels them pick up speed. He's no longer being pushed against the window—this means Earl has got them out in the lane. He counts the seconds until the bus's motion rocks him against the other armrest, and at ten he's desperate to open his eyes and see what's taking so long. But a heavy shudder tells him that they've hit another incline and Earl's unwilling to gear down. The engine struggles as its valves labor to put out in this high gear, and Carl listens to a running commentary from the driver's seat which paints the picture clear as day.

"Forty-five, forty-eight," Earl is calling off, "that lousy bastard's speeding up on me! Where the hell's the state patrol when you need 'em? That idiot's breaking the law!" Carl's tempted to beg Earl to pull back in behind, but that's no use. The man's caught up in his own world, like one of those Kamikaze pilots Carl would see in the war flicks of his youth. That's where Earl belongs—in the cockpit of a Mitsubishi Zero, scarf billowing behind as he glares down at an undefended aircraft carrier below. At least those Kamikaze planes didn't carry passengers.

Suddenly Carl's thrown sideways and then tossed ahead as Earl jams on the air brakes. He has to look now or lose his breakfast. What he sees is curving road, and what he hears is frantic honking from the milk truck just behind them. Thank God, Carl prays to himself, and leans back to find his shirt is drenched with sweat.

Two minutes later they're making the hard right onto Highway 13, which takes them straight into Wisconsin Rapids. For this homestretch Earl cranks her up to eighty, but Carl's too demoralized to complain. Besides, it's easy road and he's tired of bothering Mack. He takes his cap and stows it on the rack up top with his gear bag, catching the old coach's crafty smile as he turns to take his seat. For the first time Carl wonders seriously how Mack's tripped the radar box, but assumes it's got something to do with the bus's exposed wiring. It's something Mack likes to fiddle with, and Carl's too exhausted to give it much more thought at all.

But as they swing into the wide driveway of the Roadway Inn Carl hears the detector give a final bleat and sees Earl give it a disgusted whack with his map case. "This lousy gadget cost me more time than it saved," he complains with great offense, and Carl's glad to see a lesson learned in messing with the law.

Earl's first out, but Carl keeps his seat as the players file past and head out along the cargo door to grab their bags. Soon it's just him and Mack as the bus sways back and forth when the heavier gear's unloaded.

Carl's about to head down the stairs himself when he hears the radar detector start beeping like crazy. He looks out both windows and then ahead before he hears Mack laughing from behind.

The manager turns to see his pitching coach standing halfway down the aisle, hunched like a Western gunslinger as he quick-draws the radar gun used to time his pitchers' speed.

The gun lights up, the radar box screams, and Carl collapses in laughter as old Mack blows the imaginary barrel clean and stands above his victim.

⊗ Costy Pedraza's Greatest Pitch ⊗

The team's been up north for a solid ten days, giving Jeff an easy week at the desk—paying bills, filing travel reimbursements with Kansas City, and straightening out the hospital charges for all the player X-rays and examinations which have piled up since May.

Carl and Mack aren't due in until three, when they'll spend an hour doing their own minor-league reports, and so it's quite a surprise when the manager comes bursting into the office at quarter after nine—prime sleeping time for coaches and players alike—all red-faced and impatient.

"Don't you guys answer your phone?" Carl demands between breaths. "I've been getting that assinine Mason City Royals recording ever since six o'clock!"

Jeff looks over and sees he's left the answering machine on since closing up last night—this road trip sure has made things easy. He flips it off and turns to ask the harried manager what's happening, but Carl is already giving him the news that makes the team's ten days away a happy, placid memory.

"Pedraza's in jail! We gotta get him out! We need eleven hundred dollars!"

Jeff doesn't know what to ask first: what's Costy in the slammer for, or where on earth does Carl expect him to find that kind of cash? He's just cleaned out the checkbook with that stack of bills, and there hasn't been a gate receipt for a week and a half. But Pedraza's been a colorful enough character to outweigh Jeff's worries about cash flow, and so he tries to slow things down with a little humor.

"What'd Costy do, get caught knocking over a taco stand with

Sanmarda?" Jeff says this with a toothy smile, hoping to charm Carl into some decent behavior, but the grin is just gasoline on fire.

"Taco stand? Taco stand?" Carl is waving his arms around and looking like a John Madden commercial for Miller Lite. He'd like to throttle Jeff, who's now backing away behind his desk.

"Yeah, you know—burrito bandito?" Jeff laughs weakly but he can't deflect Carl's rage, which he knows has come to a boil because the man's now talking in a level tone just above a murmur.

"Pedraza's been arrested on a complaint of indecent exposure. He's been in jail all night and he doesn't speak a word of English, and we have to get him out of there and back in the clubhouse before O'Reilly flies in this afternoon."

Tom O'Reilly is the Royals' farm director, and with baseball operations out of his hair so long Jeff's forgotten that he's visiting Mason City this week to look things over. A player in jail is the last thing anyone wants him to see. But for Jeff, the whole thing's still pretty funny.

"What did Costy do, moon somebody from the bus last night?" Jeff asks, trying for a laugh again. "What time did you guys get in, were you in your pj's already?"

"Early—just past midnight," Carl replies. "The cops picked him up at the apartment laundromat."

"That's where he dropped his pants? What was he doing, washing every stitch he owns?" For all Carl's worry, Jeff still finds it hard to take this seriously.

But then the story unfolds. Carl explains how on the way back to his apartment Costy stopped off to start a load of dirty road-trip wash in the building's laundromat, only to find two police lieutenants waiting at the door. Neither spoke Spanish, but Costy didn't resist when they cuffed him—their badges and such jailhouse paraphernalia as handcuffs spoke a universal language that told him he was in Dutch with the law.

But which particular law he didn't know, and even when Herman Escobar and Andy Thompson came down to clear things up the befuddled pitcher couldn't understand what he'd done wrong.

"They say you exposed yourself to two women from the balcony last week," Herman explained, and Costy said so what.

"So what?" Andy Thompson cut in, in less idiomatic Spanish but showing his irritation nonetheless. "You can't go doing that, it's against the law and they swore out a complaint against you!"

"They complain about me? They not happy with what I show?" Costy beamed proudly, they told Carl, patting the crotch of his jail fatigues. "They crazy, those two ladies. Then I no like what they been showing *me!*"

Some of Costy's words were in a rural Dominican vernacular, which for Andy's sake Herman had to rephrase in academic Spanish. But the two of them soon lost patience with their teammate, who kept acting like he was back in his tiny island village, where a young woman's stripping down to a bikini bottom and laying on a blanket outside your door is not an act of ambiguity. Costy claimed he was only offering back, but Herman and Andy warned him that he's been here long enough since sunbathing weather to know that the half-dozen or so young singles out catching rays on the lawn are not advertising free sex.

"They no like, they no see again!" Costy was protesting as the two ballplayers left to look for Carl and some bail money, hopeful at least that when translated for the judge this might sound like good enough repentance.

Springing bail for Costy Pedraza is easy enough once Jim calls the bank and requests a letter of credit to cover their checkbook for a few days, but keeping the news quiet sure isn't. Not that the paper will run a story—the *Courier* cares enough about keeping Kansas City's minor-league team affiliated here that they'll even drop the report from the daily police record published right alongside the horoscope. But the inevitable ball-park gossip starts spreading the same day, and because there's so much room for humor no way can Jeff manage to keep it down.

The comic possibilities of a midnight laundromat arrest give the especially talkative fans in box 28 behind the screen some good material for their endless fictionalizing. The trainer's let it slip out that Costy's been arrested, and after a short rehearsal they call him back to try out some jokes they've devised.

"In the laundry room—right, Chet?" they ask him. "That's where the cops pulled their bust?" When the trainer confirms this the three fans pepper him with lines.

"A classic Dominican blunder," the older fan explains to Chet and the others. "I see it happen every year with these kids until somebody shows 'em how to do it right."

"What's that?" the younger box-mate asks on cue.

"Well, how to wash your clothes. Now we all know that when you wash your pants, you leave your undershorts on. And when you wash your shorts, you . . ."

"You put your pants back on!" the third fan interrupts, pointing out this logic to the unamused trainer, who regrets having brought the matter up.

"That's absolutely right," the older fan agrees. "But these young fellas don't always know that, and first thing you know the cops arrest 'em."

"Yeah," the younger fan admits, "that's what happens. But it was just bad luck the cops were there."

"Why's that?" the first fan asks.

"Because," the other explains, "they were responding to a call about ring around the collar. There they were, hauling this young housewife off to the hoosegow, when Costy forgets who's there and drops his pants." They all laugh and even Chet sees humor in it. Before game time the story's spread halfway round the stands.

Next night the trainer himself comes back with a tale, which to his satisfaction hooks the guys in box 28 but good. Seems the black players are particularly mad at Costy, he tells them as they're settling into their seats an hour before the game.

"Why's that?" they ask, rising to the bait like hungry sun fish in a pond.

"Because of that damned police line-up." Turns out, Chet explains, that Lynn and the two dark Hispanics had to stand with Costy for identification, just to be sure the women who complained had seen for real and could pick him out.

"You're kidding me," the younger fan objects, but the others want Chet's story bad enough that they're willing to play along.

"So the boys were all lined up, huh," the older fan asks, "with their pants down and peckers sticking out?"

"Yeah, you had to be there," Chet recalls, and switches to a silly falsetto, "'No, *that's* not him, he wasn't that *curly*. No, not *him* either, he's too . . .'"

"The younger fan cuts in with a line about how the ladies fainted when faced with the mighty Frito, but Chet's now made his point and is laughing his way back to the dugout, where players are waiting for tape.

For three nights Costy doesn't pitch but, with just a one-run lead against the heavy hitters from the Quad Cities, Carl asks his pitching coach if he thinks Costy's calm enough to go in there for an inning or two.

"Calm," old Mack replies, "that banana bandit has been yuck-ing it up ever since Jeff sprung him. He thinks it all some kind of joke."

"Some joke when the local jury sees him," Carl scoffs, but de-cides to use Pedraza anyway. What he doesn't count on is the reac-tion from the stands.

The stadium announcer barely gets his name out when the place erupts. There's no way anyone can tell who starts it, and the guys in box 28 are looking back to take it in themselves. But as Costy takes his warm-up throws the fans are tossing around all sorts of lewd advice.

"Hey, Mack," one loudmouth shouts to the pitching coach, "better keep a towel handy if Pedraza loses his pants!"

"Don't let him get behind on the hitter," another yells, and for the moment is happy with this unintended pun. But he tops it off with a better line: "Or he'll show the batter his high hard one!"

Three young women are just coming up the ramp when Costy pauses after his eighth and final warm-up pitch, and he hears quite well the names they're calling out.

"Hey," one of them cries, "is that Lynn Parson out there?"

"No way," her friend replies so half the field can hear. "That's Angel Noboa."

"How can I tell," the third complains, "when he's wearing his pants?" The cries dissolve into laughter as Costy turns back to the plate, ready to settle down till he sees what the batter's doing.

Naïve about it all because his team has bussed in that after-noon and he hasn't heard the stories, the first hitter has reached up to adjust his batting helmet, propping his bat between his legs. It's pointing right at Costy, and as he works his helmet around it jerks up higher each time.

The stadium roars as Costy throws his glove down in disgust, and Carl at once regrets his decision to put Pedraza in. "Now don't do nothing foolish!" he wants to call out to the mound, but can't get Eddie's attention at short to translate.

It's too late anyway. Costy has turned around to face the outfield and as the crowd shrieks he rips apart his belt and struggles with the waistband of his pants and shorts. "Oh no," Carl Peterson an-guishes to himself, and starts running to the mound.

Seeing he's too late, Carl turns to look if Big Al, the stadium cop, is anywhere in sight. Al's not at his customary post behind the screen, but coming down the aisle he spots Jeff ushering in a slick, cigar-smoking man in a neat banlon shirt and sports jacket who looks deathly like Mr. Tom O'Reilly from the K.C. office.

"My Lord in heaven," Carl prays aloud, as Costy bends to moon the hitter and the entire place erupts.

⊖ Ambience ⊖

Andy Thompson and Robin Haas are having an argument, which isn't at all unusual, since position players and pitchers rarely share the time of day. So if they're talking, it's surely on opposite sides of an issue.

The point they're batting back and forth is ball-park ambience. Just what is it that gives a baseball game it's special quality of experience, the two guys want to know. They're each philosophers of a sort, though from different schools. Andy is a talker, surrounding everything with words. Language is his net, and if he can just get the right phrase for something he's sure that he's made it his own. Robin will talk, but only after he's absorbed something, "feeling every atom of it" as he explains. It's quite a sight to catch him doing this, especially on the road, where for the first trip into each town he'll come out early and sit alone in the empty stands until he's got the special ball-park feel.

There's a different feeling for each of them, he knows—the dampness of the Quad Cities park in Bettendorf, the high-altitude crispness in Eau Claire and Wisconsin Rapids, and the fishy smell that pervades the stadium in Dubuque. The dustiness down in Cedar Rapids, the cold stone feeling of Peoria, all of which Robin has assimilated in his careful studies this spring. But what he and Andy are discussing looms larger, taking in fields from the Midcontinent League and on up through the high minors to the bigs—Just what makes being in a ball park a special experience?

It's the sounds, Andy insists. So much of a baseball game is given to empty pauses that there's lots of space to fill up with sounds. Vendors selling, fans calling out encouragement and voicing disdain, plus all the semimusical razzmatazz you get from the stadium organ when you have one. Even here in lowly A-ball the PA announcer has a shelf of tapes for each occasion, and of course there's the rock music for BP and all the promotions between innings. Even the bingo numbers these small-town fans insist on having become orchestrated with the game, and Andy can no longer imagine a home stand without them.

Then there's the sound of the ball. Everyone knows that unlike other sports, where shifts in position can be strategic and deserve constant attention, this game focuses everything on the baseball itself, from its position in the strike zone to the course it takes across the field—first offensively as a potential hit, then as the defense's weapon as its handling determines whether the batter is safe or out.

What impresses Andy is that for each movement in the game, the ball will make an appropriate sound, punctuating the action as distinctively as any comma, period, question mark, or exclamation point in English grammar. In fact, Andy's telling Robin, the ball's sounds make it more like a Romance language, something inflected like French or Spanish, where there are diacriticals galore to mark each special sense.

"Look at it this way," he appeals to Robin, "when you're out there pitching you get a sound from each throw—a pop in Smitty's mitt, then a softer smack on yours when you get the ball back. No sound, no pitch. And you can tell what you're throwing from the sound—hard pop for a fastball, duller thud for a curve, and that rattle-thump for a slider when you break it off in the dirt." Andy's carried away with his theory, the crowning proof of which is how you can chart a game blindfolded, just going from these sounds alone.

Then there are the sounds of hitting, a percussive crescendo rising from the dribbled grounder through the sharply hit liner all the way to the solidly cracked home run. And always the responsive sound of the ball in a fielder's glove—umpires will call close plays at first based on hearing that slap of horsehide against glove leather while they watch for the runner's foot to hit the bag. The one unanswered sound is baseball's most heroic, the uncatchable home run, where crowd noise celebrates the silence by effacing it.

"It's all in the sounds, man," Andy concludes, and notes that through this long philosophical lecture Robin hasn't said a word, just hunching over in thoughtful silence to take it all in.

He stays that way for a moment, and Andy's forced to listen to the silence that surrounds his words. Or what he thinks is silence. It's three o'clock on a sunny, slightly breezy afternoon, and they're out here at the park an hour early because Andy's dropped his van at Midas and Robin's given him a ride from there to the park. They're already in uniform simply out of custom, which makes them look a little strange sitting halfway up the right-field bleachers, overlooking the visitors' bull-pen bench. But it's a comfortable place to stretch out and catch some sun, and also to carry on the endless summer conversations they're famous for.

Except that half of Robin's points are made without the benefit of words. Andy knows enough that his pitcher friend wants him to listen, so he settles back to hear what's up. And sure enough things begin speaking to him. Though there's no one else in the ball park now, Andy can sense that the place is alive, rustling in understood anticipation of all that will happen tonight.

There's a slight but steady whoosh every time the wind comes up, as candy wrappers and peanut shells from last night's crowd blow down the aisles and beneath the bleacher seats. And then, as the breeze sweeps out to center field, the ping-ping-ping of the rope and pully against the empty flagpole. Andy remembers that sound from summertime playgrounds, especially in the half-hour before a late July sunset when there in the empty schoolyard it seemed the loneliest sound on earth. Here at the ball park, however, the sense is different, more like a Sunday church bell calling the faithful to come on in. And come in they will at half past six and the stadium will be full of noise again, awash in a tide of cigar smells and beery effluvience.

"See, you can feel we're in a ball park," Robin now tells him, and Andy realizes it's been done with sounds and senses far more subtle than the crack of bat on ball. "Close your eyes, man," he prompts Andy, "and tell me what you see."

"Hey, you're right," Andy murmurs with quiet relish. "Cloud coming over, just a small one, little breaks in the middle," as he feels his cheeks and arms cool then warm again. "Blackbirds feeding in the outfield," his hearing tells him, even though his eyes overlooked them completely, "and some nicer birds, like robins, sing sweeter, pulling worms around the sprinkler." Andy keeps his eyes shut for several minutes, naming all the little nuances of ball-park life which slip into his consciousness. "You got quite a system, man," he tells Robin. "I love it!"

"Only way to go," Robin laughs along with him, but Andy has a serious question—How'd he ever pick up this technique of getting inside experience?

"Paris, right there in the twentieth *quartier* of the fifth *arrondissement.*" Robin sounds the two French words with a flair of fine pronunciation, and the hard *ka* of the first and the deep *mon* of the second make Andy feel he's right there now. But what does Paris have to do with baseball?

It's getting inside the experience, Robin tries to explain. That was the first time he'd ever noticed there could be an inside and an outside to things, when during the twelve-week summer session he'd spent abroad gave him ten days in Paris while his better-heeled friends spent the break gallavanting around the Riviera.

"I was living in this little old hotel right there on the Place du Panthéon," he recalls for Andy, "and for the first time over there I was really seeing how there was another world outside myself."

"Like how?" Andy wants to know.

"Like when I was at the language school in Angers, I had my books and classes and a whole semester routine like college."

"Yeah," Andy acknowledges, but wants him to continue, which Robin is more than happy to do, since retelling it puts him back there again.

"But up in Paris I was in a real place, something which had more reason being there than I did—you know, a hard reality to it, a whole world going on, and it was up to me to either sit outside and miss it all or climb on in."

And climb in is what he did. But first he had to find a point of entry.

He started by learning the routines, then moving along with the ambience around him. Breakfast, for example, filled the hotel's lobby and reception area every morning from eight until half past nine, as the tables and chairs hardly noticeable against the walls were pulled out to form an impromptu dining room. But there were many sounds and smells surrounding breakfast, he learned—the concierge's instructions in the kitchen as early at seven, which he'd hear echo up through the rear courtyard; the rumble of the expresso machine and the first smell of that strong, dark coffee drifting up the spiral stairway all the way to Robin's room on the sixth floor; the flush of toilets on each landing as the guests arose, and finally the sounds of tables and chairs being pushed out, place mats slapped down, and the first diners being asked their choice of *"café—thé—chocolat?"* Afterward she'd make the same rounds, inquiring of everyone, *"Ce soir?"*—did they want to stay again that night?

"Now you take those smells, those sounds, and the special order in which they happen," Robin tells his pupil patiently and systematically, "and once you recognize how they fit together, you know right where you are and you can get in step, see?" He pauses to measure Andy's comprehension and sees from his blank stare that his buddy doesn't understand. "I mean, if you don't put the kitchen noise and the toilets flushing and the coffee smell together the right way, you're not part of it—you're on the outside, not in, get it? Just like with the furniture they move around and the *"Ce soir?"* which means "This evening?" or "Tonight?" which even if you don't know French you can figure out what she's talking about, unless you just want to stand there completely out of it and never know what the hell's going on."

At this Andy brightens. "Yeah!" he offers, "I know what you mean. Like all those things first time 'round you never notice."

"Absolutely," Robin jumps back in, "absolutely. Like when you were there the first day, those things were happening, but you didn't notice them. Then, after you wise up to what's going on, you wonder if you were really there that first day at all. And the answer, man, is that you weren't—because you were not part of the ambience."

"You bet—just like sky boxes!"

"Like what?"

"You know, sky boxes, those glassed-in, air-conditioned suites they got hanging off the roof in the bigs. Like they started in Houston"—Andy grimaces with distaste as Robin picks up his reasoning and follows it along, scowling himself—"with fat cats sitting up there with nothing to smell but their margueritas and nothing to hear but TV!"

"Buddy, do I hear you," Robin laughs along.

"One time on 'Game of the Week,'" Andy adds, "I think it was at the Hump in Minnesota, they showed those sky boxes during the game, and all you could see through the windows were the backs of everybody's heads turned around to watch themselves on TV, watching TV!"

"Perfect metaphor, man," Robin agrees, and adds a few more

thoughts from Paris because it feels nice being there right now. How he'd sit for an hour in a little square, or even in a busy park, just taking in the smells and feeling the air—breathing Paris, he called it. "The traffic's mostly diesel, even cars and taxis," Robin remembers, "and to this day when I hear that ticking diesel sound and catch a whiff of exhaust. . . . "

As he speaks the two friends smell it, and with this even Andy is carried off to the Luxembourg Gardens, traffic noise from the Boulevard St. Michel, and the happy feeling of a breakfast just consumed at the Hotel du Panthéon. Neither is surprised or anxious to note that it's just the team bus from Quad Cities pulling up to the side gate. They'd rather stay abroad for at least another minute before the park fills up with ballplayers and the ambience turns American once again.

⊖ Release ⊖

Dick Hillier has not been part of the Mason City Royals' pennant drive, and the team's progressive good fortune has been a nasty commentary on his own bad year.

It started with high promise with the young shortstop coming off a great rookie season at Elmyra, where the Royals had assigned him two weeks after the June 4 draft.

Some said he was foolish to take their first offer, or to sign at all this first time around. High-school kids have all the bargaining chips, so why not play a few of them now, his coach had reasoned. You get a bigger bonus when they think you might go off to college instead, and if big bucks aren't invested there's no guarantee a club won't put you on their back burner. And now it's to the back that Dick's been shoved.

It began in spring training. The eighty games he'd played at Elmyra were kid's stuff—spoiled kid's stuff where all the little bonus babies were left to act like mamas' boys their first time out. An easy schedule with occasional days off. No real backbreakers of bus rides, just a few quick zips across and back on the Dewey Thruway. And lots of patient instruction, clearing up potential problems before they had a chance to take hold. Such as his nervous double pump before throwing to first—a former big leaguer straightened that out in the first week, teaching Dick to pace himself on the runner's progress and not the ball's bounce. Doing that made him much more fluid, and he took delight in keying his throw to the same steady motion as the batter's dash toward first.

But in Florida he found himself neglected. Even in the parking lot, where he learned what bigger bonuses could buy. A Datsun Z, several Mazda RX-7s, and the perennial favorite Camaros and Firebirds. Dick had no car at all, just an underpowered motorbike at home, and he felt belittled riding the dinky shuttle bus from motel to training complex twice a day with the nonroster players down here on a prayer.

This second-class status followed him right out onto the field. A kid from Panama, Ed Sanmarda, started out quiet but soon was getting all the looks at short. Dick had been the star in high school and a prima donna in upstate New York, but here in Florida he felt like he was always waiting for the bus—outside the motel each morning, at the stadium gate every night, and even at the shortstop position itself, where with five other prospects he stood in line for a chance to catch grounders.

The first bad sign was when he didn't go to Mason City as he expected but was instead held back for another month of spring training. This was the biggest sham he'd ever seen, and it introduced him to the tacky world of baseball politics. Extended Spring, as everyone called it, was for no one's benefit except some witless assistant farm director up north who'd found himself overstocked at certain positions and needed an extra four weeks for things to sort themselves out. In the old days, he heard from some old-timers among the coaches, scouts wouldn't even file a kid's contract until it all panned out, and there was always the chance some young hotshot from Lackawanna, Pa., could find himself ditched in Florida without his month's pay and with no ticket home. That was one of Branch Rickey's tricks, a veteran hitting instructor told him, and for the young shortstop one more baseball legend bit the dust.

That wouldn't happen to him, but as the weeks went by "release" became a factor to consider. There were some kids worse off than him, including a good-looking young right fielder who'd nixed a fancy scholarship to Texas A&M for a small bonus with the Royals, ten thousand less than his even though he'd been a higher pick. After two weeks in camp the kid began to fade and no one was there to pick him up—the instructors were drawn like flies to jelly around the hundred thousand plus numbers—and Dick received his first lesson in comparative economics. The last day of regular camp there were two lists posted for the A-ball squad: Mason City or Extended Spring. Those not on either list were handed envelopes, which Dick had been told contained release papers and an airline ticket home.

On May 15 he found an envelope in his own mail slot at the camp office, but he knew nobody got released after the expense of Extended Spring. As suspected, it held assignment papers to Mason City and an airline ticket several coupons long, running Sarasota to Atlanta, Atlanta to Kansas City, K.C. to Des Moines, and Des Moines to Mason City, half of them on airlines he'd never heard of. All super-saver tickets purchased over a month before, which told Dick just how early his fate had been decided. About the time that Panamanian kid started hitting breaking balls, he recalled.

His first week in Mason City was spent as a nonentity. As a non-roster player he didn't even have a number, and he felt like a bat boy in his blank uniform top. His locker was an extra one way down at the end, and soot from the oil-fired water heater stained his street clothes. Because no one had a spare bed in their shared apartments he stayed in the distant Motel 6, watching trucks rumble by on the interstate and breathing exhaust fumes around the pool each day till four o'clock, when he'd find a traveling sales-man checking in who'd give him a lift out to the ball park for a pass that night. Then after watching nine innings from the bench he'd flag down the same guy for a quick ride home.

He'd always take a full set of warm-ups with the club, including infield and BP, because "working out" was his official status. But their winning season had set the Royals' starting line-up in place and nobody wanted to tamper with success. The manager ad-mired his fluidity in the field and thought his swing had promise, but said he'd have to see who was going to Elmyra and what turned up from the draft before making any promise about a ros-ter slot. Besides, that decision was made in Kansas City.

"But how can anyone in K.C. know what I've got when there's no stats on me?" Dick demanded, and Carl had to agree that with nothing going in on paper he'd remain pretty much a ghost. His high-school coach's worry about the low dollar sign on his muscle was bearing out, and Dick figured he wouldn't be surprised to stop seeing his reflection in mirrors. When he caught Lynn Par-son whistling the old Beatles tune "Nowhere Man" he knew that his sense of things was shared.

What spooked him most was the way the regulars kept their distance both on and off the field. The manager and coach of course had no interest in him, but he thought at least one guy off the twenty-three-man roster might want to pass the time of day.

But the starters were all obsessed with their stats and the second string spent all its time trying to be first, so nobody had much time for lonesome Dick Hillier at all.

The intensity these guys poured into the game surprised him. His own days were pretty vacant—this was the first time he'd ever been involved in organized sports without having to worry about school. But what studies had taken out of these other players' lives was replaced with paper work on themselves, and the trade-off was far from equal in time. Each pitch would be charted— Dick knew that, sure enough. But the manager and coach also kept elaborate records of hitting, running time to first, and every conceivable game situation, including batting averages with men in scoring position and ratios against right- and left-handed pitchers. Copies of the figures were left in the trainer's room for everyone to study, and before games the percentage hitters would crowd around a fan who used his son's Apple computer to work out even more elaborate analyses.

Dick was sitting on the bench one day in the dead minutes before game time, abandoned once more while the starters poured over the fan's computer printout, when the manager came back from his office phone with several pieces of good news.

"Hillier!" he called, and Dick jumped out of his skin at hearing his name called for the first time in weeks. "You're getting some company and a place to live, so write this down." So perhaps the paper work on his career was about to start.

Dick grabbed a pencil from the trainer and on the back of last night's line-up card took careful note of all the happy details. Two regulars were going up to Chattanooga—Double A—and the lease on their apartment was his if he wanted it. Plus a nonroster kid from Batavia, part of a throw-in deal with the Indians, was flying in tomorrow, so they might as well be roommates. Best of all, a roster slot here in Mason City would be open by the month's end, since the two Double A replacements would free things up. Carl was already shaking his head at all this paper work, but invited Dick to make the most he could from these vagaries of organizational politics.

The next morning Dick thumbed a ride to the ball park so that he could join the GM for his trip out to the airport. The kid from the Tribe was due in at 10:06, and Dick wanted to be the first to see him.

"His name's Chief Simpson," the GM said, and for a moment Dick was panicked—an Indian, not just from the Cleveland organization, but a real live one? But the letter from Kansas City explained the kid was a navy brat, son of a warrant officer who'd named him after his own aspiring rank. So now Dick expected a butch-cut he-man off a marines poster. As it turned out, Chief Simpson was as normal-looking as anyone on the team.

First stop was the Thunder Ridge apartment complex, where a harried manager was supervising moving men, a telephone repairman, and the meter reader from the utilities. There was some business about a security deposit, but the GM talked him into waiving it because these kids were taking over an already secured lease. "Look at them," he chided the guy, "do they look dangerous? Ballplayers aren't destructive types." What about after a bad loss? the landlord wanted to know. Don't worry, the GM told him. These guys are nonroster, they can't lose because they never get to play. "Then what you got 'em here for?" the guy wanted to know, and the GM said he figured that was a pretty good question.

It was a question Dick and his new friend Chief would ask themselves as they set up housekeeping here in Mason City. "I been nonroster all my life," Chief Simpson confessed as they hauled his suitcases up to the second floor. "My old man liked lots of transfers, always looking for a promotion. I've lived in three countries and eleven states, man, and I'm only eighteen years old."

So for starters Dick can tell him what a normal American childhood is like. He runs through the facts of life in Canton, Ohio, like an anthropologist, and for the first time notices how special it is to have gone from sandbox years through high school with the same group of friends. Chief's single question about this phenomenon strikes Dick as odd, only because it never happened. "Did any of them ever die?" he wants to know, and Dick finds it strange to consider that his tight little world has never been so disrupted.

Despite their different backgrounds, Dick and Chief hit it off good. The high-school shortstop who'd been turning to a ghost up here in A-ball now has someone to relate to, and as Dick and his buddy kid around on the field a subtle domino effect takes over, as one by one the other players accommodate the pair. Even the coach and manager are giving them some attention, and Dick realizes that two is the magic number when it comes to starting a community. But without Chief here he knows for sure he'd once more be the odd man out.

Comfortable on the field, the roommates set themselves the goal of sharpening their skills to the point some roster slots will just have to open up for them. At night they talk baseball, running through the league's top hitters and discussing how they should be played at short and in the outfield. Then hitting strategies for the pitchers they'll face once they're on the team. Dick fancies himself a number-two man, dependable for making contact yet keeping out of double plays and always with a great on-base percentage. Chief's been tabbed a power hitter, a doubles and triples man you like to have hitting third, so a lot of their talk is about timing the hit-and-run plays and how to anticipate pitchouts.

Afternoons they head out to the ball park early, turning down a ride in Andy Thompson's van from Thunder Ridge in favor of hitching. At one o'clock they'll rouse the grounds keeper from his sack lunch and thermos to pull out the batting cage, and as one takes his turn pitching the other will spray all eighty practice balls around the field, each hit to order for a specific game situation. Neither throws like a starter, but they're not weak batting-practice lobs either, and in a few weeks they are proud enough to invite Carl's look at their skills. He's sufficiently impressed to call Robin Haas over to burn some good stuff past them, but even against Robin they get good wood on the ball and, more importantly, place their hits just about where they say they will.

When the ground's too wet for Jack to drag the cage out early they practice their fielding specialty, relays. There's a neighborhood kid who loves to hit flies and liners out to Chief in left. There he'll grab them and rifle in a throw with Dick lining up as the cutoff man. Just like their situational hitting, these outfield throws soon begin to sparkle.

"Runner on second, a rabbit!" Dick will call, and signal the kid to drop a liner twenty feet to Chief's left. As it takes off over his head Dick moves a few steps onto the infield grass, watching Chief's run but also stealing a glance at home to get himself in line for the throw. Chief grabs it on the first bounce, takes one more step to set himself, and rockets it in to make the play. It's just high enough that Dick can leap to snare it for a toss to second or let it sail on toward the plate. Twenty of these each day for two weeks makes them perfect, Chief's throw landing just a foot or so to the left except when Dick spears it to cut off the imaginary double at second.

When Carl is shown the play he admits it looks impressive, but when challenged for the roster spots gets a bit defensive. Who should he cut—Sanmarda, whose hitting leads the league? Thompson, good for three home runs and ten R.B.I.s this week? Top to bottom they're hitting well, that's why they're in first. Why should he mess with a winning machine? But Carl does promise to give the farm office a full report.

Dick knows that Lynn Parson, who starts in left, has been watching them, too, but with a scowl of disapproval. Is he worried for his job? That can't be, as Lynn's an easygoing type who's always supportive of the younger guys, even if his Berkeley hipness makes him seem a little too smooth at times. But Dick's been uncomfortable with the way Lynn keeps staring out at him, so he uses this break to approach the left fielder and feel him out.

Lynn is direct and blunt. "You're doing it all wrong," he says quite simply, "and it's never going to work."

This stuns Dick, who's figured everyone's impressed with his and Chief's hard work. Never one of those "practice makes perfect" Yo-Yos, Dick subscribes to the more solid theory that "perfect practice makes perfect." Branch Rickey said that. Or was it Connie Mack? Make it the latter because Dick's still smarting over the tarnishing news that Mr. Rickey never filed contracts until rosters were set.

But Lynn's statement has his cheeks burning. Two weeks' labor is being tossed aside like it's nothing at all, and Dick is determined to stand up for all he's done.

"What's the matter," he challenges Lynn a lot more brashly than he'd meant to sound, "we got the wrong angle on the plate? We sure could use some help from the coaches and you roster guys, you know!"

Lynn spits in the base-line dust to punctuate his point. "Okay," he says levelly to counterpoint Dick's excitement, "I'll tell you what you're doing wrong. You're tying yourself to this guy in left and him to you."

"Hey," Dick objects, even closer to hysteria, "we're great! Didn't you see all those moves we've got?" And check out our hitting, man—I bet we can score more runs than all the fancy averages you and Sanmarda and the others got!"

"That's it, boy, right there," Lynn concludes with a sorry head-shake. "You got us a two-headed, four-armed ballplayer here, and that's not how K.C.'s building teams. One slot, one guy—and you guys are two. No two slots going to open up both at once, no way."

Dick is livid as his and Chief's planning is so casually dis-missed, tossed right out the window by somebody who's not even bothered to look around and see what they've done.

"Look at Whitaker and Trammell," Dick implores. "Those two were put together in the rookie league and moved up together all the way!"

Lynn's not impressed. "And who put them together? You think they decided it all themselves? That move was made in Detroit, boy, and no one up in Kansas City's put you kids together. Hell," he scuffs and spits again, "nobody in K.C. even knows who you are. Not a thing about you in the evening papers"—he's referring to Carl's nightly reports to the farm director—"so all this hustle-hustle stuff don't count a bit. Wise up, and stop wasting your time making me look slow!"

Dick wants to keep on arguing but a stronger urge makes him glance back at Chief, who's stayed out there in left to clear away some litter while his partner's talked with Carl and Lynn. The smooth veteran catches this immediately and compliments his pupil, saying now he's learning and maybe stands a chance.

"Just remember that number on your uniform," he tells Dick, who looks confused, since for now it's a nonroster blank. "It's the number you gotta keep looking out for," Lynn continues, and when the prospective shortstop's still looking perplexed he holds up a big finger and waves it in front of his face. "Number one!" Lynn emphasizes, and Dick finally nods that he's got the message.

Over the next few days Dick slowly makes a change. He starts shaving three or four relay plays off each session, and soon sug-gests limiting their swings to regular BP. Chief takes it all as a sign of achievement and success, agreeing that overpractice might dull the competitive edge. All in all, the two don't spend that much less time with each other, but in a subtle way their paths begin to split. Each day Dick is careful to get himself in-volved one way or another with the team, even if it means just hitting fungos for the outfield or shagging pitchers' BP. With this Chief holds back, sitting on the bench to watch Dick hit and field instead of getting in there himself.

The bad news, as usual, comes from the GM. He's in their locker room for two reasons only—handing out meal money or sending down paper work from Kansas City. When those papers involve a promotion to Double A or even reassignment to the rookie league club at Elmyra, Carl usually lets the cat out of the bag a day or two before. But anything more serious is left to the impersonality of the mails and the managerial distance of the GM's office.

The GM has walked in with a handful of envelopes, all but one of them the short brown affairs containing meal money for the Quad Cities trip. Three days out, thirty-nine dollars, which Jeff has parceled into daily amounts of thirteen dollars so that the guys won't even have to make change. But he knows their three tens and nine singles will be blown before the second day's over, and the trip back home will be made on a stomachful of popcorn and fries. One guy won't be making the trip, and as he fingers the long white envelope sitting on the bottom Jeff regrets having to bear the news.

The meal-money packets have names on them simply for Jeff's accounting when he fills them. After that, he treats them all the same and passes them out at random. Thompson may get Pedraza's—"Hey, I gotta buy tacos with this?" Andy will shout—and Billy Harmon winds up with Lynn's. Today everyone's eyes are on that bottom envelope sticking out beyond the rest, though nobody's got anything to fear except the nonroster Bobbsey Twins, as Jeff calls them. He sees both Dick and Chief stealing looks at him from opposite ends of the clubhouse, Chief down near his locker while Dick's up at the trainer's door getting help with some twisted spikes. Chet's room is really the social center, its scissors and tapes and bandages attracting all the guys instead of scaring them away as it does him, so Jeff starts handing out the envelopes here.

Sanmarda, Thompson, Escobar, Mueller, and Moore grab the first five, and Jeff's wondering if he should show his hand now by giving Dick his money when Andy shouts out, "Hey Hillier—I'm eating on you!" He's no sooner said this than the room's dead-quiet and everyone's aware of Chief Simpson sitting down there on the end. Yet nobody will look that way.

Jeff feels trapped, and wonders if the kid will walk up to him now and take the long white one he's fingering at the bottom. But Simpson just sits there, staring across the room where nobody's gaze dares to meet his own, and for the longest time there's nothing said at all. Finally Lynn stands up halfway down the row of lockers and swears a blue streak, banging the door for emphasis. This prompts some curious chatter above which he can boom, "I'm hungry as an armadillo! Let's have some dough!"

"Armadillo?" half the room is asking and Lynn treats them to a story he heard playing Double A ball in Texas, all about those little rodents doing head-ons with redneck pickup trucks and eating away the wreckage. "Bab-*eeee!*" he shouts again, "Ah sure could eat some a them *greasy wheels!*"

This keeps the team laughing long enough for Jeff to quickly hand out his envelopes and leave. Like a coward, he's thumbed right through them to the bottom, making no distinction for the big one, tossing it to Simpson with the same easy manner as he's given the smaller brown ones to Naboa and Pedraza sitting nearby.

He's out of the room and back to his office in a flash, cranking up the phone to the Howe News Bureau and reading off a long list of stats so that he's safely in another world, the paper reality of this Mason City Royals' team. But on the line's other end the guy's asking if there's any roster change, so Jeff's stuck with it at last.

"Yeah," he reports matter of factly as he pauses to light a cigarette, "Simpson—released."

☺ Nicknames ☺

Any number of nicknames for the new right fielder would be better than the one he's got, and the fact that he played his first week in minor-league ball simply as "Frito"—his real last name—suggests he'd be better with none at all.

They could have called him "corn chips" or "bandito," his name was rich with possibilities. But the team responded to his strange aloofness by sticking to what the trainer marked on adhesive tape above his locker—"26, Frito"—and after eight days of lusterless play he's remained a nonentity, a nameless shadow lost among the colorful locker-room crew of "Piggy," "Guags," "Bonzo," and whatever. To the players Frito's a sluff-off and he just doesn't exist.

But the fans have noticed his slew-footed play in right and his awkward, half-hearted swing at the plate. "What's with this guy?" they ask, as a soft liner drops a few long strides away from where he's been standing. "Who paid this guy a bonus?"

"There's no bonus deals for Latin players," the GM tells them. "They're not eligible for the amateur draft, so there's no pressure on the clubs to sign them. Some are even here without professional contracts. Guys like Frito do it for an immigration card."

"I'll bet!" a fan laughs back. "I think his bonus is that he doesn't have to run more than twenty feet to catch a ball. I'll bet he's got that in writing!"

The GM ambles off as the team trots in—a pop-up to short has let the inning end without Frito's sleepiness costing more than a hit in the box score and an easy left-on-base. But the fans give Frito a hoot nevertheless, while the other players leave him alone in the dugout, happy in his nameless world.

A short road trip to the towns in their state—Cedar Rapids, Bettendorf, and Dubuque—doesn't improve Frito's fielding or his status with the team. While the rest of the guys joke, drink beer, and clutter up the bus with boom-box sounds of competing radios and tape players, Frito sits alone up front, staring through the windshield as the Iowa countryside unwinds.

"They grow corn down in the Dominican?" the driver turns to ask. Frito's lack of response chills him—it's like talking to a ghost. So this is how Kansas City stocks their low minors, he mutters to himself.

But back in Mason City Frito has become a hot topic in the box seats. Next home stand the group of regulars behind the screen are buzzing, close enough to the bat rack to be heard, not that Piggy, Guags, and the other full-fledged players care. As for Frito, nobody's heard a word from him in two weeks, so the fans assume he speaks Spanish and nothing else. But even their chant of "hijito" when he takes a childish swat at a lazy curve doesn't seem to register with the wraithlike man from right. "This guy's not from the Caribbean," a fan complains, "he's from Mars."

Because the town's sportswriters hang out in this same box when they're not scorekeeping or off covering a high-school meet, they've become party to the chatter about the mysterious Frito.

"It's organizational politics on Kansas City's part," a fan explains to one of them, the *Courier*'s first-stringer, Dick Crews.

"So what's politics?" Crews asks. "The new ownership wants Democrats?"

"Come on," the fan replies. "You know how many real prospects the Royals can afford to sign. One, maybe two of these kids will ever make it to the bigs. So they cheap it out by getting flunkies like Frito here to play catch with their future stars for a season, just to see who's good enough to make it up to Double A."

When Crews runs this by the GM all hell breaks loose. "For crying out loud, Dick, don't print that!" he implores. "Ink like that will have K.C. out of here overnight. Those screwballs down in box 28 are just writing stories for you, so lay off!"

The reporter is miffed, but next night behind the screen he greets the grinning, expectant faces with a story better than anything they could concoct.

"I asked Jeff about your man Frito," he begins, and everyone turns around. Even the bat boy, just a yard beyond the screen, stops to listen, because every time Frito bats or lopes in from right these guys cause a minor commotion.

"Turns out he's got real talent, a great personality, and a terrific nickname with the team," Crews announces. Nobody will believe him for a minute.

"He's what. . . ?" Two of the fans say this together while the third just slaps his program on the rail.

"That's right," the reporter insists. "They're keeping his good stuff under wraps because there's so many scouts around."

"Dick, that's a bunch of baloney," the third fan scoffs. "But I want to believe something today, so give me something I can check out with the boys down there. Now what did you say his nickname was?"

Crews smiles broadly, savoring their anticipated response.

" 'The Cat.' "

Way out in left some players doing stretching exercises before the game turn to look as box 28 erupts in laughter.

"That lazy bum? That lead-footed bozo? 'The Cat'?" The guys are howling. "Crews, you're out of your mind!"

"Not for his speed, not for his agility, you idiots," the writer protests. "Don't you know anything about his background?"

"Yeah, he's from the Dominican," one of the younger fan admits. "But what's so special about that? So's Pedraza, so's Roman last year. My aunt used to go there for vacations."

Crews now turns instructor. "Boys, in Frito's part of the Dominican—a little jungle island named Saona—a cat is a great delicacy."

"A what?" the older fan scowls in disbelief.

"A fine culinary specimen," Crews adds with satisfaction. "A rare gastronomic treat!"

For the home stand's balance the guys in box 28 bat around Crews's screwball information. Frito's performance in the field shows no improvement, and at the plate he's still the world's worst sucker for a change-up or an easy curve. But he's suddenly become more colorful, a real character out there between the lines, as even his teammates pick up on the horseplay spilling through the backstop screen.

Angel Naboa, who hits two slots ahead of the lowly Frito, perks up when he hears himself compared. "Angel's from downtown Mexico," a fan's exclaiming, "he doesn't eat cats." When Herman

Escobar's in the on-deck circle, he finds he can't ignore the questions from the box—"Hey Herman, ever had lunch out on that Saona Island?" He finally asks the bat boy what's this all about and is told Crews's story verbatim. By the next day it's spread throughout the club, with only Frito remaining oblivious to it all.

There are still the fly balls dropping into right unchased, and when Frito's surprising, out-of-form dive for a sinking liner is scored an error the guys in box 28 turn back to shout at Crews in the press box that he's wrong, that ball was twenty-two feet away. But cat stories give an added luster to Frito's at-bats. "Too much fat on his cat last night" they jeer when he overswings on a change-up and dribbles back to the mound, "Frito better start eating some lean ones!" "He's a big star back home," the older fan counters, "Mama sends him the very best farm-fed." One night when Frito startles them all by sharing a few words with Manny Hernandez in the on-deck circle, Crews stops by to say he's promising Manny a prime piece of cat that night if he gets on and scores.

"He's describing the hindquarters, offering him a rear leg," Crews points out.

"More meat?" a fan plays along.

"Yeah," Crews answers, "but the best parts are the hind claws, the big ones. They make great toothpicks."

Whether Frito hears this banter is debatable. And his teammates, while aware of it, never rub it in. But as simple shorthand they've been calling him "The Cat" among themselves, and on Tuesday night the Latins cheer Frito into waiting out a walk and then stealing second on an inattentive pitcher. Rising from the dust he's seen smiling to himself as Pedraza, coaching at first, shouts a string of Spanish in which "gato" figures prominently and the guys behind the screen break into a spontaneous "How 'bout that Cat?"

That night the team busses out for a late-nighter to Eau Claire, and first baseman Andy Thompson tells the guys to deal him out and please keep the music down for a while, he's sitting with The Cat.

"Ey, Gato," he smiles, settling into the first-row seat above the door, Frito lifting off his gear bag and acknowledging him only with his eyes.

Andy tries to start a conversation in Spanish—he's majored in it at college after growing up in Ybor City—but he's painfully aware of sounding more like a literary critic discussing Cervantes than a teammate on the bus. So he switches to English, seeing again that Frito's eyes are taking note.

"My street talk has gone to hell," Andy begins, speaking slowly with the hope that Frito may understand. When his words draw a soft chuckle from the right fielder, he talks on. "My dad's an Anglo and my mom's a real assimilationist," Andy continues. "They wanted me to study electrical engineering at school."

"I didn't know South Florida offered that," Frito says in disarmingly perfect English. "Do they stress mathematics?"

Andy feels a happy laugh building up from tbe bottom of his stomach. You shrewd Dominican, he wants to say. You've been hosing us all, even taking all this cat nonsense, because you're here to study. But he keeps this to himself and cheerfully fills Frito in on just what his university requires and how eager they are with athletic scholarships. The radios are booming again and no one but Earl, the driver, is aware of what's going on, and to him Andy and The Cat's talk is schoolboy stuff, about as boring as Frito's customary silence.

On the road trip nothing much changes as Frito takes it easy on the field, the manager accepts his time-clock attitude and minimal competence as he concentrates on developing Ed Sanmarda and Johnny Mueller, the club's real prospects, and the rest of the team works on sharpening its skills. Even Andy leaves the right fielder alone, waiting for the anonymity of late-night travel for his businesslike talks with The Cat. He fights off curiosity about Frito's background—is Saona really that primitive, and where'd he learn such great English?—and sticks to shoptalk about required hours and NCAA eligibility. But at least one question has been answered.

"Hey Cat! What ya saving it for?" A noisy bleacher bum has picked up the fiction all the way from box 28 and degraded it into a sexual rag. "Your girlfriend's back home," he razzes Frito from the right-field corner when a ball is allowed to drop in, "she don't need you tonight. Let's show some hustle! This is Mason City, Iowa—you don't want to prowl here!"

Like everything else, Frito ignores it. English-speaking or not, it doesn't register, for it's a world apart from where he really lives. Andy has called his coach back home, who's promised to bring South Florida's athletic director to the series in Peoria, where Frito's promised to finally pour it on.

"You say they call this guy 'The Cat'?" the coach asks Andy. The prospect of recruiting an unsigned Latin with both college eligibility and academic smarts is tempting. And such a name implies this guy is finesse-city on the field.

"You bet, Coach," Andy tells him, signing off the clubhouse phone and heading through the tunnel toward the dugout, from where he can hear the evening's chatter in the box seats warming to its pregame pitch.

☹ The Swoon Wagon ☹

Mack Ptaszynski has been a pitching coach long enough to know the telltale signs.

The Mason City Royals have been in first place since the third week in April. That's one sign: too long. No sense of a fight to keep his throwers lean when the going's been easy. Seems like half the dates before mid-May are always lost to rain or cold, and the first-half schedule has been loaded up with no-contest games against such perennial losers as Eau Claire and Dubuque.

But now it's July and his staff's diminished sharpness is showing up all over. Those games lost to Midwest spring weather are coming due as doubleheaders in the steam bath of Iowa's late summer, making a five-man rotation with four days off a thing of fantasy and fond memory. Plus the weaker teams—and that's just about everyone else, thanks to the Royals' overbearing 56-23 record—are loading up with sharp-eyed hitters from the June draft. Peoria's got the Rangers' number-one pick, a career .485 hitter from Oklahoma State, starting in their three spot, with a power-hitting high-school kid drafted seventh in the nation coming up right behind. For the five-game, three-day series this weekend Mack's starters are all grumbling about tired arms as they whine around the trainer. So far they've kept it quiet in front of Mack and Carl, but the signs are clear.

"Here comes our swoon," Mack sighs from the broken-down couch in Carl's office. He sounds tired himself and looks it, stretched out in his exercise top and jockey shorts, the sprung and tattered sofa cushions arching up from where he's propped his hairless old man's legs.

"You don't mean that?" Carl asks him in protest. As manager he has plenty of real and immediate things to worry about without getting philosophical.

"It's coming," Mack sighs again, "I tell you, I can see it coming." From the half-open door they can both look into the trainer's room, where Billy Harmon's sore elbow waits while a crowd of pitchers bothers Chet about this and that, hoping he'll intercede for a few days' rest.

"These babies don't want to face Peoria," Mack tells Carl. "They're playing angles with the schedule, acting like they're not ready for the Rangers, holding back till those stinkers from Dubuque come in."

"You want me to remind them we've got a rotation?" Carl asks, but Mack has gathered up his legs and is rising with a cautionary, hold-off motion. Times like this, he figures, Carl is showing his relative youth. Forty-two years in baseball—ten of them in long relief with the laughable Washington Senators—have taught Mack that there's more to running an effective minor-league club than rules and regs and hard-nosed discipline, and now's the time for a bit of teaching. "Let me handle this," he tells the manager, and flips on his shower clogs to shuffle through the door to the trainer's room.

"Hey Chet!" he calls through the crowd of starters grouped around the rubdown table, where Billy is perched and still waiting for some tape. "These young ladies looking for some help?"

The pitchers grumble. Children of their age, they're firm believers in the miracles of sports medicine. Mack's okay for rotation on a curve ball, but Chet's the guy they like to question for hours about tendons, muscle strength, fat counts, and special diets for fitness and performance. For the old war-horses of Mack's generation, beer-swilling and steak-eating and out of shape for practically any other sport but golf, they have nothing but disdain. He may know the mechanics of pitching and the psychology of working on a hitter, but their bodies are their own.

They've got a point. Robin, Freddie, Al, and Keith and the others are physically resplendent next to Mack. Tanned from late mornings on the apartment sun decks and around motel pools on the road, they glow a healthy bronze. Their training-room costume is socks, stirrups, and clean white uniform pants, their upper torsos bare and muscular for Chet's attention. Old Mack, standing half a foot or more below them, looks ragged in his work-out jersey and worse in his undershorts, the sunburned ring from his neck around his throat and back making him look for all the world like a fresh-plucked turkey.

"These puppies are talking to the wrong person," Mack objects as he steps in front of Chet. "I never seen such healthy specimens hanging around a doctor's office so," he scoffs. "You girls should be out there on the field, running sprints so you don't lose your wind!"

"Daddy, that went out with the St. Louis Browns!" Freddie laughs. "With the Philadelphia Athletics!" Robin adds. "With the who?" Keith interrupts. "Don't you mean the Kansas City A's?" His question stops Mack for a moment, a sad one. This boyish-looking pitcher is a decade off and doesn't even know the Oakland A's once ruled the American League from Philly. But the St. Louis Browns! Mack thinks back to '53 when he pitched the last AL game in Sportsman's Park. As a Senators' reliever he finished lots of seasons in ball parks no longer around, including some magnificent duels in Connie Mack Stadium with Bob Trice, Bobby Shantz, and Art Ditmar. Then Shantz and Ditmar were sold to the Yankees, new ownership started moving teams west, and baseball soured. Now it's all Gatorade with salads for lunch and dinner.

"Sports medicine!" Mack shouts to bring himself back. "Don't you boys know what really needs doctoring this time of year?"

"Arms!" two or three of them chorus. It's time to level with the coach, so they dare getting feisty.

"Balls!" Mack growls, shutting them down like a garage door. Keith blushes in surprise at this first vulgarity he's heard from the gruff but clean-mouthed old man who's been a father figure since the first day of spring in Florida.

"Baseballs, lunkhead," he barks at Keith. "You gotta doctor baseballs come July. Everybody's seen your stuff twice by now, so give 'em one more look and it's good-by!"

"Homers?" Keith worries aloud. Next to Freddie, he's served up more dingers than anyone else on the squad.

"No sir," Mack levels with him. "Good-by to you and back home to Talahassee. You children know nothing good but fastballs, no wonder you're hurting with ninety innings on those arms. It's about time you learned some finesse."

The pitchers are now exchanging worried glances, avoiding Mack's icy, instructorlike stare. But the old man stays firmly in charge.

"The Skipper's given me his okay for some morning sessions"— Carl in his office is startled to hear his name invoked and the whole crowd in the trainer's room groaning—"and I want to see you fellas out at the equipment gate tomorrow at ten."

This sends the pitchers back to their lockers, leaving Chet to wrap Billy's arm and clean up before the game. That night the bull pen's quiet as a more serious Al Elgin bears down on the Burlington hitters and goes the distance for a 5-2 win.

By ten the next morning the pitching staff's waiting at the gate, watching for Mack's car, when a battered old Plymouth station wagon comes rumbling across the lot. Only its Florida plates keep the guys from thinking it's a beater from the poor side of town. Windshield glare hides old Mack till the last moment, but before he can switch off the ignition and climb out the guys are pressing him about his sorry wheels.

"My Buick won't hold all the stuff you guys need," he tells them. "This here's my swoon wagon."

"Looks like it's swooned already," Freddie teases, but Mack is all seriousness.

"I'm looking right now at what's swooning," Mack says as he surveys his mound staff gathering around the wagon. "Your ERA's up half a point, you're walking lousy hitters and giving up the long ball two, three times a night, and pretty soon you won't be in first place at all."

"So why the wagon?" Freddie asks. "What's a heap like this got to do with good pitching?"

"Everything, son," Mack announces with grave authority, "everything. Now sit down here."

As he flips the tailgate and takes a seat, the pitchers hunker down and sit cross-legged on the ground, looking like a Boy Scout troop ready to learn some new knots. And Mack is dominant above them, reaching back into the wagon's cargo hold to find a box of stuff he takes the whole next hour to explain.

First comes a satchel of tubes, jars, and dip-sized cans with brand names covered up by tapes and homemade labels.

"Oh no, Mack," Freddie protests, "you can't be having us put foreign substances on the ball!"

"You're damn right I can't," Mack agrees. "I don't mess with any of those foreign substances. Everything I got is made right here in the U.S.A. Now pay attention."

For the next hour he runs the boys through the predictable assortment of grease, oils, resins, and jellies, plus some talcum powder to throw off the hitter's sense of their release point.

"They'll keep looking at the little puff of white when you snap it off," Mack explains, "and next thing they'll hear it popping behind them in Smitty's glove." The pitchers laugh because they like this, and Mack makes a mental note to have Jim Smith sponge down his catcher's mitt between innings, out of sight in the clubhouse, to give it extra pop and boost the staff's morale.

The guys stretch while Mack rummages around for his file case. The little metal strips are small enough to slip inside a glove's webbing, and Freddie tells everyone these are also standard tools of the locksmith's trade.

"Where'd you study locksmithing?" Mack asks him skeptically, and the guys hoot about Freddie's more apparent skills at breaking in. "Where'd you think he got the scratch to buy that monster Lincoln with the FONZ plates?" Keith teases, and Freddie whirls to argue about his three winters' hard work in the wax and trim shop. But Mack calls for order and then it's another hour, this time on scuffs and scratches and what they'll do to a game ball.

By noon the guys are hungry—some have skipped breakfast—but Mack won't let them go until they've seen the ball in action and learned where their greases and jellies can be hid. Al and Keith have headed in through the gate, but Mack calls them back to the parking lot.

"Stay off that playing field," he cautions them. To their questioning faces he replies, "You wouldn't want me to be doing anything illegal, would you boys?"

"So what's with all this junk you brought?" Keith objects. "If this stuff's not legal to use, then. . . . "

"Then I guess I got to tell you," Mack sing-songs back, "that there's nothing against the law about us having a little catch out here behind the dumpster."

"Mack's right," Freddie explains to his sometimes stupid college-boy friend. "There's no rules at all about loading up the ball out here."

With that he squats down to play catcher as Mack positions himself on the slope behind the garbage bins. Torn-up popcorn boxes and beer cups litter his makeshift mound, and the breeze kicks up a few peanut shells as the old pitcher scuffles around for a toehold in the shifting gravel. He's never thrown a ball except for BP lobs and the guys are momentarily awed as he sets up to pitch. Even Keith, not yet born when Mack was out of baseball and the Senators long gone to Minneapolis, knows that when Mack was his age he'd already faced Joe DiMaggio, George Kell, Vic Wertz, and others whose stats were intimidating then and awesome now. What Mack doesn't like to be reminded about is his footnote in every record book: the 564-foot tape-measure job he served up to Ted Williams. But even that was nearly ten years before Keith was toddling on this earth.

"Now watch this!" Mack is calling as he leans back and fires what starts out as a standard fastball. But ten feet in front of Freddie's glove it takes a downward dive and then slides sideways, bouncing a foot away from where Freddie's sure he's got it caught.

"That was the K-Y Jelly," Mack advises as Keith tosses him a clean ball and Freddie looks behind him, still surprised at where the first one went.

"Now watch this," Mack says again, and the pitch flutters like a knuckle ball but picks up speed in time to pop Freddie's mitt but good. "You throw it like a change-up, but flip your wrist a little when you release," Mack adds. "The Vaseline I put along the seams will keep it from cutting but you've still got all your speed."

"Hey Mack," two or three of the guys are interrupting, wondering what's going on.

"Watch this," he says again, as the ball comes in level but drops two feet before tagging Freddie on the thigh.

"Mack, where are you getting all this stuff?" Keith demands. "You got it in your glove? That won't work in this league!"

"Well come on out here, Mr. Umpire," Mack derides him. He hands over his fielding glove, then the batting glove beneath it. Then his hat, then the wristband on his catching hand. With a shrug, he turns his pockets inside out. Keith, Robin, and the other pitchers are perplexed, but Freddie's laughing from behind the imaginary plate, part of a pizza box that has blown away from the dumpster.

"Check his skin," Freddie calls to them.

"His skin? What skin?" Keith asks in disbelief.

"Go on," Freddie says, "take his forearm there and give it a little scrape."

Keith grabs Mack's glove hand and reaches up the old man's

arm. "May I have this dance?" he laughs at the embarrassed young pitcher, but Keith goes ahead and pokes him just where you'd take a blood test and jumps back as thirty-weight machine oil dribbles out.

"What the. . . ?" Keith is asking himself as Freddie shouts the answer.

"Hollywood skin, that's what old Mack's got!" Keith now studies the arm and notes the high sheen and telltale pockmarks where Mack's already reached for the jelly and Vaseline. He's used a trick the movie stunt men invented to keep blood flowing in bar fights and brawls: a thin, clear layer of soft adhesive plastic, under which they hide their stage blood, covered by a bit of makeup or pimple screen. A twenty-minute lesson in cosmetics follows, with Mack reminding them how to kid off any inquiring umps.

"Make 'em feel like queers out there, wanting to feel you up on the mound," he advises, prompting a few more jokes about the K-Y Jelly and the spermicidal foam Freddie's heard can be kept underneath a class or wedding ring. By half past twelve the boys know quite a bit, and Robin—the team historian—no longer wonders how Mack could compile a winning record with such a perennial losing team. The man's a walking drugstore!

No longer in a hurry for lunch, the guys hang around Mack's wagon, gossiping about doctored balls. But Freddie's been nosing around behind the back seat, pulling at an odd contraption of springs and levers attached to a ragged extension cord.

"What's this," he asks, "an electric jack or something?" when Mack cautions him away.

"You boys don't want to mess with that," he growls, "and God help me if I ever have to use it." He makes it sound like a torture instrument, but as the swoon wagon's ultimate piece of junk it has the players buzzing.

That night ends the three-game series with Burlington, last of the easy teams they'll face for over a week. What Mack's swoon wagon has to back them up gives the pitchers a new confidence, and Keith throws a strong seven innings, allowing just five hits, before Carl calls in Freddie for the last six outs, four of which are strike-outs. But Freddie's fastball is hopping all over the place, and his curve drops even more than its customary load of expectorant should allow. Now that the bull-pen bench is clear and Mack's with him in the dugout, Carl asks his pitching coach what's up.

"What've you got Guagliardo throwing out there?" Carl asks, and Mack just laughs.

"He's showing the college boys some engineering with aero-dynamics, huh?" Carl prompts, and to this old Mack responds.

"You want these Eagle Scouts going into Peoria buck naked?" he chides. "You want Al and Robin throwing straights to that .485 hotshot they got from Okie State?" Mack pauses for effect. "You want to win some ball games there?"

"I want to win some games," Carl replies, and takes himself out of the conversation. He turns to where Chet is packing up his gear as Freddie faces his last 0-2 count. Chet wipes off his jar of Vaseline and looks ready to make a joke, but Carl says he doesn't want to hear anything about it. He turns to Robin, who'll open at Peoria, and hears more things that aren't music to his ears. How is he supposed to chart those crazy pitches, Robin is asking—his clipboard sheet looks like the record of a drunken Risk game at three in the morning. Carl just takes it from him, wads it up, and tosses it in the trash. He'll doctor the mound report for Kansas City himself.

As they load the bus for the overnight to Peoria, Carl sees Mack taking his bags out to the Buick parked across the lot just out of foul range. He thinks to ask but doesn't, and is rewarded for his right guess twenty minutes later when the old pitching coach returns in time to meet them with his battered Plymouth wagon.

"Old Juney Swoon wants to make the Rangers series, all right?" Mack is asking across his rolled-down window.

"You bet," Carl has to laugh, and asks if Mack wants some company along the way.

"Nah," Mack declines, shaking off his offer of a chatty pitcher or two. "Juney's got a radio and it's clear channel all across Illinois," making Carl jealous of the fine late-night music Mack will have while he suffers through the punk-rock tapes on half a dozen ghetto blasters.

"Besides," Mack adds, "I don't want nobody going through my stuff while I sleep between Dubuque and Ottawa."

Seven hours later, at nearly six in the morning, the team bus pulls into Peoria's Travelodge Motel on Eighth Street to find Mack's old wagon parked by the door, the coach himself catting out in the front seat. Neither the bus's air brakes nor whooshing front door has wakened him, and one by one the young pitchers see him and grin as they climb down the steps and get their gear from Chet, who's tossing out the baggage. Keith is the last, and when he sees there's no one left he leans down to the open window and gently touches the sound-asleep old man.

"Hey Dad," he whispers, "time for bed, huh?" Mack's eyes open and he smiles, and in a moment is joining Keith as the last players file in to the desk.

⊖ Metaphors ⊖

Dick Crews is a man of metaphors. Covering nearly all of the Mason City Royals' games for the *Courier* presents a constant challenge to write new stuff with fresh angles, and early on he's decided vivid prose is the way to go. Since mid-June his stories have been rife with violent comparisons, and his lurid account of the 16-12 slug fest with Quad Cities earned him a corral of horse-laughs from his buddies in box 28.

He still has the clipping from that game, which a fan under-lined in colored ink—red for overwriting, green for comparisons running out of control. "We need a metaphor-abuse hotline for guys like you," the fan advised, since his pen work with Crews's column made it look like a Christmas tree afire.

By early July Dick's writing has hexed a player. Big Mark Wig-gins, a power hitter born to play DH, had lost thirty points off his average since the end of May, but when he turned this around with a solid five for five against Dubuque, Crews was ready with a flashy simile.

"Mark Wiggins, with arms as big as Popeye's," the story began, "had not been eating his spinach lately." Interwoven with the de-tails of the Royals' win and Mark's big night came extended meta-phors for how the slugger's success must surely be attributed to his getting back on the garden greens. Problem was, those five hits were all Wiggins would get for the next three weeks, prompt-ing the fans to lay the blame on Crews.

"You've put the whammy on him, Dick," the older fan is saying. "He's no good now till you take it off!"

"What do you mean?" Crews protests. "I just said he's got arms like Popeye."

"It was the spinach that did it," a younger fan explains. "Spinach makes him sick to his stomach, and now that's all he can think about when hitting."

Crews tries laughing this off, but as Wiggins nods weakly at a biceps-high fastball there's nothing he can do to quiet down the fan, who's now claiming Wiggins is turning green.

Eddie Sanmarda's up next, and for the strong but little short-stop the fan's in full voice as Crews turns red with feigned shame.

"Eddie Sanmarda!" the fan shouts, causing Eddie to steal a glance back as he steps in to hit.

"Eddie Sanmarda, who has arms like broomsticks, has not been eating his lentil soup," the fan continues, until Crews swats him with his scoresheet and the box settles down to watch Eddie take three called strikes.

"Hey, watch those metaphors," Crews warns as he leaves the box and makes his way through the two sets of bleachers to the bull pen, where he hopes to sneak an on-field interview with Freddie Guagliardo. The wild assortment of misbehaving pitches he and the staff have brought back from Peoria has Crews wondering, and the locker room's no place for candid, off-the-record talk. With Mack still in the dugout this early and Freddie with a good six innings from his customary mopping up, Crews figures now's the right time for some investigative reporting. But first, just like a bull-pen catcher, he has to loosen Freddie up.

He starts by rattling off some neat-sounding Spanish names, as the uncomprehending Costy Pedraza stares blankly from the bench he shares with Guags.

"Miguel Diloné!" Dick shouts. "Uribe Gonzales! José Deleon!" He loves the music of these exotic handles, a whole new romance to compensate for the lost glories of his baseball childhood—Kluszewski, Harvey Haddix, Hamner, Schoendienst, and Spahn. "Porfi Altimerano!" he sings out, puzzling Pedraza even more, who wonders if this crazy writer is talking to him. Freddie stands up and for a moment acts serious, telling Dick that Costy speaks no English and will think he's being teased. Pedraza's a hot one, packing a knife in his gear bag, Freddie explains. So for the moment Crews cools it and settles down to talk shop. But his clowning around has done its job, and Freddie's been enlisted as advisor and trusted confidant even before the interview's begun.

"Julio Cruuuuuz!" Dick shouts out just one more time to keep new ice from forming, and Pedraza gets up angrily and stalks away. "Nice talking with you, Costy," Crews calls behind him and Freddie says come on, you gotta watch it with some of these Latins, especially those that can't talk.

Crews agrees, recalling that in his own youth big leaguers had names to match their styles. Mantle, Berra, even Kubek—those sounded like Yankee pin-stripe titles, and the Dodgers all rang true to Brooklyn. Furillo, Campanella, Pee Wee Reese, Big Don Newcombe. Even the expansion Mets had names with class. What does a championship pitching staff sound like? How about Seaver, Ryan, Koosman, and McGraw? But today the names are comical to Crews's Anglo ears. Except for "Roberto Clemente," which looms larger than life and also sounds Italian, their litany is stuff for laughs.

"Costy Pedraza!" he yells, loud enough so that the pitcher turns to look back from the dugout. "Carries a knife, huh? He from the Dominican like Frito? He eat cats, too?"

Dick's finally got Freddie laughing in spite of himself, and from the dugout Pedraza's glaring at them both and exchanging a few words in Spanish with Herman Escobar. Freddie hopes this doesn't lead to trouble later, but Crews just cracks him up.

"Dick," he motions over for Crews to join him on the bench, something Crews hopes the umpires and stadium cop won't see, "we had a kid from Venezuela down in spring training you would have loved."

"How's that?" Crews asks, eager for another fancy Latin name.

"Well, the trainer told Keith Henley first day that this guy's name was José Puerco de Esmarelda, and Keith believed him."

"You mean Keith doesn't know any Spanish? Even I can figure out that means 'Esmarelda's pig.' "

"Yeah, and when Keith started calling him that the whole squad went nuts before Porky even noticed."

"Porky? You mean that really was his name?"

"No man, that's the nickname he picked up from the whole deal. He thought it was funny, especially 'cause he's such a skinny little guy."

"That's great!" Crews agrees, and rolls out the new name so loudly it echoes back off the fence signs in left field. "Puerco de Esmarelda!" and Freddie notes some more activity down at Pedraza's end of the dugout.

"Okay, Dick, I know why you're down here," Freddie says once Crews calms down, mostly to keep him shut up before Costy's on both of them with a switchblade. "You've seen all that junk we're throwing and think I've been teaching the guys some tricks."

"Guags, would I ever think that? Why, that's illegal, and playing games with the law just isn't your style." This cracks Crews up again, prompting another "Puerco de Esmarelda!" from the doubled-over sportswriter.

"Well, it's not my idea and it's not me teaching it," Freddie insists, the image of schoolboy innocence as the teacher asks who broke the window frame.

"And I didn't say so either," Crews points out. "Your curve is too good for that already, you don't need that cheap carny stuff."

"Carny?" Freddie asks. "What do you mean by that?"

"You know," Crews tells him, "the kind of stuff you see in traveling carnivals, the things a carny hand would spread around to sucker the locals. People living in cheap houses down in Florida all winter, hanging out and goofing off, then making their bucks up here each summer, following the show from town to town in beat-up old station wagons and campers."

"Hey man," Freddie objects, "you don't want to go talking about old Mack that way! He's the best pitching coach in A-ball and K.C. pays him twice what they give Carl. There's nothing shabby about Mack at all."

"Did I say a thing about Mack being shabby?" Crews inquires, a bit put out. "I just said he's like those carnies sometimes. Just look at how he's got you guys out doctoring the ball."

"I didn't say a word about Mack doctoring the ball," Freddie insists.

Crews feels it's time to make his point. "Look, I don't care about Mack's doctoring. What's neat is how he keeps you guys pumped up. He's got these carny tricks to make you think the whole deal's bigger than it is, and look how it's working. I'd say this pitching staff's *possessed!*"

"So Mack's some guy, huh?" Freddie asks proudly.

"You bet," Crews agrees. "I'm just worried about what's his second act."

"Huh?" Freddie is mystified.

"He's pulled you guys out of that midseason swoon, but what's he going to do when things go flat again? Set off fireworks?"

Freddie argues that their staff's the best in the Midcontinent League and that they're so far up in the win column nothing can catch them now, not nothing. The Royals are headed for a Northern Division title and their pitching will never let the club down.

Crews laughs and says he'll be back to hear some more inspiring talk during the next blowout, and for that he doesn't have to wait too long. The two-game series goes easily enough with a shutout and a 3-2 squeaker, but the opener against Wisconsin Rapids starts badly. In the first inning Robin Haas is shelled for six runs—all unearned because the scoring starts after Andy Thompson's two-out, bases-loaded error on an easy grounder to first. When Robin walks his first two batters in the second, Carl lifts him for Pedraza, lately consigned to long relief, and though Costy gets them out of that jam his next inning is a nightmare. Dick Crews has been yucking it up with the guys in box 28 behind the plate, and while he hasn't trilled out any Spanish names Costy still resents his earlier teasing. The first man up is walked, then Costy boots what should have been an easy double-play dribbler back to the mound. Next pitch is a flat hanging curve, which goes out over the left-field wall, and before he knows it Pedraza's got the Royals down nine to nothing with no outs in the third.

As Mack visits Costy on the mound with Eddie in from short to translate, Crews picks his way through the overflow free-night crowd to the bull pen, where Freddie's been joined by two starters who at any moment may be called on as Pedraza's own long relief.

"Cookie Lavagetto!" Crews calls out in greeting to Freddie. "Mookie Wilson!" Freddie sees that the writer's on a roll and wonders how far he can go before he's got everyone laughing along. One more name does it.

"Pookie Bernstein!" Crews is howling and the bull pen picks it up, the sportswriter complimenting their decorum and taste.

"Why not," he tells them, "this game's a real laugher. How you expect to win with Wisky Rapids playing football out there?" Freddie glances at the scoreboard and sees it's still nine-zip, but Pedraza's put two more on and Carl's sending Mack down to warm up Al Elgin.

"Hey Mack," Dick calls to him as he passes the bull-pen bench, "I think the umpire better check that ball." For a moment Mack looks worried, but quickly realizes it's another Dick Crews joke.

"Yeah, we think it's made of pigskin," Freddie chimes in with the punchline. But the question of what to do when the opposition puts up a touchdown, extra point, and safety still needs to be answered.

As Mack stands off to the side behind the warm-up mound, watching Al take his first throws, Dick leans over to Freddie for some analysis. Crews may joke a lot, but he's a serious student of the game and loves its fine points as well as all the high drama.

"Look at Pedraza," he indicates with his folded scoresheet, "look at him come down with the pitch."

"Yeah," says Freddie, "I'm looking."

"Now watch again and tell me if it's any different."

Freddie concentrates on the delivery and picks it up right away.

"His legs are bending and his foot's coming down someplace different each time," Freddie reports with brightness and satisfaction.

"You bet it is," Crews emphasizes, "and that's why ball one was high outside and ball two inside in the dirt. Costy's tired—he might as well be groaning through the fourteenth inning out there. He's got to come out."

With that Crews turns to look back at the dugout, and sure enough Carl is leaning out and gesturing with a quizzical look to Mack out here in the pen. Al's not ready—he's scarcely thrown ten pitches—so Mack shakes his head and makes a talking gesture with his hands. Carl picks up the sign and relays it to the catcher, who turns to face a dugout of eighteen grown men leaning toward him with their arms outstretched and hands miming quack-quack beaklike sounds. What the hell am I supposed to tell Señor Pedraza, catcher Jim Smith wonders to himself. He'd love to trot out there and run Costy through a German lesson—"Ist das nicht ein schniztelbank?"—but he knows the temperamental pitcher would never stand for it. So he motions Eddie over and tells him to waste some time in Spanish, French, or any other language both of them know.

In the bull pen Mack now has Al throwing harder, but Crews is summing up the situation's hopelessness for an attentive Freddie Guagliardo.

"Al's a starter, and so are the other guys Carl can use before we get to Guagliardo time in the eighth and ninth." Freddie nods, knowing that the regular relievers burned their arms out sneaking fastball after fastball past Cedar Rapids last night, too proud to use Mack's junk and also intimidated by the league president sitting there in box 36 right over their dugout.

"You're right," Freddie agrees, "guys like Al and Keith need twenty minutes plus a day before to think about it." Freddie's proud to be the archetypal fireman, ready to pitch at a moment's notice, into the game in a clutch situation with just a dozen warm-up throws. Of course he's only primed for three to six outs. Carl once made the mistake of putting him in the seventh, and the extra inning proved costly indeed.

Mack now tips his hat and Carl thankfully heads out to the mound. In a moment Costy's gone to scattered applause and Al lopes in from the pen. Nobody out here has much faith, and as Mack passes the bench he's got a sorry nod for Dick Crews.

Al's a disaster and so are the other two starters who follow him. The Royals have scratched out a few runs with singles and sacrifices, but the 18-3 tally is a humiliation. They've left Keith Henley in for six of those runs—four on homers—and Crews is keeping Freddie's mind off his eventual date with slaughter.

"Keith's stuff's not shabby, man," Freddie is complaining, worried for the first time tonight. He's jealous of his ERA—one bad inning can knock it out of whack when all he throws is one or two—and he doesn't relish facing these Wisconsin Rapids hitters, who've been seeing everything. "I guess they ate their Wheaties today," he offers lamely, but Dick misses this invitation for a hex and leaves Freddie on his own.

Top of the eighth comes like clockwork and Freddie's sent in with a slap on his butt. The bull pen's now deserted, but Mack stays over at the wall with Crews—no sense joining that depressing bunch in the dugout when his pitchers have so miserably let them down.

"So what's next, Mack?" Crews asks him, expecting a joke. But Mack is smiling at something all to himself, and Crews goes crazy trying to draw him out. In desperation, he tries candor.

"The reason for all that junkyard stuff," Dick begins as the old veteran returns his sideways glance in kind, "was to beat off that swoon we all knew was coming." Mack laughs, admiring Crews's knowledge of the real game being played out here. "I know how old-time carnies like you operate, I've even seen what you've got left in the back of your wagon."

Now Mack rewards him with a full grin and some inside information. "So you've seen that old contraption," he says. "These children can't even guess what it is. Guagliardo here thinks it's an electric jack."

"An electric jack," Crews chortles, "that's great! Freddie Guagliardo thinks it's an electric jack!" What Dick and Mack are

talking about is an ancient batting-practice pitching machine, a
tripodlike affair strung with belts and levers like a Rube Goldberg
invention. There's one at Cooperstown, and a few more in the
back seats, trunks, and cargo holds of cars and station wagons
parked here and there across the minor leagues. Mack is one of a
dying breed.

"You're just like an old carny, Mack," Crews tells him with an
affectionate laugh. "I was telling Freddie all about you guys—
wintering on the cheap down in Florida, packing it from park to
park up here in the summer, teaching kids like these your grizzly
tricks."

"Well, we need some tricks tonight," Mack agrees. "I had these
babies loose again with all that medicine, but when you get blown
out this late in the year you need something else." He motions to
where his second car, the battered Plymouth wagon holding his
supply of junk, is parked beyond the equipment gate.

"You're not going to bring that old contraption in?" Crews exclaims, but Mack just stares out at Freddie struggling with the
Wisky Rapids line-up hitting like a house afire.

"That's what Mr. Griffith said it would be for," Mack sighs
quietly, and Crews is suddenly all questions. Does that old machine date back to Washington Senators' days? Did he really get it
from old Calvin Griffith himself?

"He wasn't old then!" Mack objects. And neither was Mack himself, Crews realizes, though even on the baseball cards he has
from that era Mack Ptaszynski looks like an aged man at twenty-
five.

Mack has leaned out from the wall to search the stands down
behind the dugout and around home plate. Crews asks what's up
and learns Mack's worried that the league president's still in
town. He's willing to risk a twenty-dollar fine from the umps, who
if he tickles them right may not even report it, but pulling a stunt
in front of the league boss could cause repercussions all the way
to Kansas City.

"Nah, Williams is back in Madison," the sportswriter assures
him, and Mack hops over the wall and heads out toward the
wagon.

"Mack, I don't believe you're going to do this!" Crews is laughing, happy that he'll be privileged to see a baseball legend acted
out before his eyes.

If all goes according to plan, Freddie will finish the eighth and have himself and all the staff fearful for the ninth when the Twins are sending up their heavy hitters. But by prearranged signal Carl will hold him in the dugout and give old Mack a dramatic two or three minutes while the whole park's attention is focused on the empty mound.

At that point, Crews knows, old Mack will stride out on the diamond and unravel a bright yellow extension cord, the line running from the dugout edge to the pitcher's rubber. This will start the crowd buzzing and send the home-plate ump over to question Carl.

Playing his role, Carl will divert the ump's attention until Mack can get back, feed the crowd's love of suspense with another minute's pause, and then dramatically wheel out his Katzenjammer Kids contraption, a batting-practice machine to face the Wisky Rapids line-up in this madly concluding frame.

☻ Sweet Home Chicago ☻

For more than a week before the All Star break, Freddie Guagliardo has been singing up a storm.

He loves to hoot and holler in the dugout, where the resonance is good as on any Motown single, but the promise of a few days off has him singing even in the flat acoustics of the trainer's room and clubhouse. Three teammates—Ed Sanmarda, Jim Smith, and Robin Haas—will be playing on the Northern Division squad, and today they're Freddie's special targets as he bops from bench to locker with a tag line for each friend.

"Goin' to Chicago," he sings for Eddie, "sorry but you can't come too!" This is older American blues, Ed can tell, but he doesn't know the song or who did it—the only way such music gets down to Panama is with the Rolling Stones or on old Yardbirds albums. But he recognizes the tune Freddie's singing now for Robin and Smitty, the All Star starting battery, and when Eddie joins him in the lyrics half the clubhouse chimes in.

"Come on," Freddie beckons, "Baby where you want to go?"

"Come on," the guys answer back, overdoing it on the gusto but what the hell, "BABY where you want to GO?"

The Mason City Royals' collective answer resounds through the bowels of the stadium so that even the grounds keeper, who's cut the engine on his tractor after pulling out the batting cage, can hear them from the field.

"Back to that same old place," they're all singing, "sweet home Chicago."

Less than half the guys have been there, even though they all know Chi-town lore from watching Cubs baseball on the cable. To them, Freddie's as much Chicago as Jack Brickhouse and WGN, though only Freddie knows what those letters stand for. "We Got Nothin'," they spell it out for Guags, kidding him about the hopeless Cubs, but Freddie comes back with a lecture about how it stands for "World's Greatest Newspaper" and how everything there is tops, number one.

"You ever had Deno's pizza?" he asks the pitchers, and Robin says he's heard about frat houses three hundred miles south in Carbondale ordering five-hundred-dollar taxicab deliveries of the stuff.

"That's my cousin's place," Freddie says proudly. "You ever hear of the Taft Hotel? That's where my old man runs the bar. You ever heard of the Berghoff? On West Adams? Fantastic place to eat!"

"Your family run that too?" Robin asks.

"Naah," Freddie replies, "that's a bunch of Germans. But they've got this great schnitzel with cheese inside and fried egg on top and big steins of dark beer. . . . "

The guys cut him off before this goes on for hours. Freddie's married to that town, and if he isn't eventually traded to the Cubs he'll never die a happy man. He's got family life in Franklin Park, a thoroughly urbanized suburb on the near northwest just before O'Hare, all planned out. In May his girl friend Mary had joined him in Mason City, and even their breakup in June didn't change the face of Freddie's future one bit—by July 1 he had Carmen in town, a letter-perfect replacement from the suburb of Elmhurst, and as a dead ringer for the unlamented Mary she was the image of Freddie's future Mrs. Guagliardo.

But having a Chicago girl in town is not enough for Freddie. When the team's in the Quad Cities or Madison he'll jump on the expressway after the game and drive all night to some after-hours place and party till tomorrow. Or he'll help his dad close up the Taft and be dealt a poker hand with the old man's staff, then roll down Division at four in the morning to catch the street action on Rush. From time to time he'll meet a major leaguer breaking curfew, and there's always guys from the press and broadcasts falling out of bars that time of night. As his manager Carl doesn't like it a bit, but Freddie sells these trips to the Skipper as a filial obligation. His mom's been sick this summer and having Freddie back to joke with her, mow the lawn, and chase to the grocery store and bakery cheers her up immensely. He really spends all morning with her, not heading outbound on the freeway until noon or one. What amazes Carl is that his young reliever is always back on time, stronger and fresher despite the lack of sleep than he was the day before.

Carl attributes this to the city's wild energy, hits of which he figures Freddie needs from time to time. But Freddie explains it all with his car. That block-long Lincoln in which he looks so ridiculous tooling around in Mason City like a misplaced Mafioso is a dreamboat on the highway—after six hours on the road Freddie feels better than when he left, soothed by surround-sound stereo and massaged by plush upholstery. Power everything, plus dashboard readouts on miles per gallon and temperature inside and out. When he's in that Lincoln Freddie's got life arranged just as as he likes it, and touching base with home makes everything perfect indeed.

He's got his All Star break planned out to the hour. He and Carmen will have his cousin's apartment up in New Town off Broadway and Belmont—a gorgeous, woody set of rooms in an impressive stone-front building on West Briar Place just a half-block from all the action. He'll tell his folks they're staying at Carmen's parents, and she'll say they're at his, letting both families think the two of them are chastely separated by bedroom and couch, when in fact they'll be at each other like rabbits after their nights on the town. No more boring bedtimes after quiet late nights of popcorn, beer, and TV movies in that Godforsaken Iowa burg.

By ten each morning they'll be fresh for Mama Guagliardo, who'll give Carmen recipes and coupons she's clipped while Dad gasses up the Lincoln on his credit card and shows off Freddie to his friends at the little shopping strip around the corner from their home. After lunch an obligatory game of catch out back, Freddie trying out the fancy new stuff the Royals' major-league instructor taught him down at spring. Then back to New Town for some time in the sack before a pizza at Deno's and another night on the street. The Cubs are in Philly and no one in Freddie's family would be caught dead at Sox park, but other than that this little vacation promises to be pretty nice.

For the last game before the break Freddie leaves his wheels back at the apartment, parked out beyond the last building away from the little kids playing ball, sap and bird dirt from the trees, and the other nuisances that would spoil his immaculate wash and wax job. He and Carmen have worked five hours on it and the car shines like an auto-show centerpiece. Carmen's even used her nail polish to sharpen up the license plate's letters—DA FONZ—

and she's ready to try the "Land of Lincoln" motto when Freddie tells her enough's enough, that lettering's so small she'll muff it. He steps back to snap an Instamatic wide shot of her perched atop the Lincoln's front fender, hot to trot in her skimpy shorts and overfilled halter top. "Mama mia!" Freddie sighs to himself, savoring equally both chick and car. This is what life's all about.

Four days later he's back, but not the Freddie everyone's come to expect. The die-hard minor-league baseball fans have filled the home-plate boxes an hour before play begins, and here's where players kibitz with the locals when the mood strikes them. Freddie—along with Keith and Billy, who've come to view these regulars as family—is usually all jokes and smiles. But this time, when the fans least expect it, he's all sour and serious.

He barely manages a "Hi Lew" for the old retired grocer who's usually got an Italian joke for this spunky little favorite who reminds him of his own days working wholesale produce in Freddie's hometown. To Lew's inquiry about what's eating him, he just replies with a question about where's Lew's friend the prof.

Lew's box-seat mate teaches communications at the local junior college, where he's also assistant baseball coach. Freddie likes him because their backgrounds touch at all the important points, including a love of quality automobiles. The prof drives an old Mercedes, and that's what's on Freddie's mind right now.

"He's on a beer run," Lew says, but just then the bearded and spectacled professor comes wobbling up the ramp, sloshing brew across his bare legs and sandals from the tray of sixteen-ounce draws he's balancing with three brats and a scorecard.

"Hey man!" Freddie greets him and motions down toward the dugout where there's a break in the screen. Freddie's wearing his serious look, a better job of miming heavy business than the prof has seen in movies like *The Godfather* or on old "Untouchables" reruns, so he parks his food and beer and follows Freddie on down.

"So how's Chicago?" the prof asks and Freddie just shakes his head.

"Not good, man, not good," the young pitcher complains, pushing out a sunflower seed between his teeth and lower lip to look even more Brando-ish. "That's what I got to ask you about—who works on that old Benz of yours?"

"My Mercedes?" The fan wonders how this relates to Chicago. There's a guy over on Cleveland Avenue, he says, who's good on all

imports except Volvos, which he hates—owns a 230SL plus an
MG roadster, really loves cars as much as Freddie and himself.

"Do you think he could do me a favor?" Freddie asks, and from
the way he lowers his head while keeping his eyes level and focused the fan knows Freddie's not talking about a tune-up check
or a break on parts.

"He doesn't work on American cars, as far as I know," the fan
hedges, not wanting to get involved, but Freddie interrupts with
enough subtle passion to make it clear only he can help him with
his problem.

"I don't have an American car anymore," he says quietly, and
the fan is as dumbstruck as if Freddie'd changed his nationality.

"The Fonz-mobile? You don't have it? What happened—repossessed?"

"No way, man," Freddie perks up. "I paid cash for that car. It was
all mine and Friday night it got ripped off!"

"Oh, christalmighty," the fan laments, sincerely touched by
Freddie's loss. "That baby's one of a kind. You kept it showroom,
inside and out, I know. Don't you think the cops will find it?
Doesn't your family have some pull?"

"Yeah, my uncle knows who did it"—Freddie's uncle, the fan
now recalls, is an actual mobster living like a king in River For-
est—"but the car's gone, there's nothing he can do."

"Gone," the fan ponders. "Out of town? They still run cars up to
Rockford?"

"No man," Freddie regrets, "in pieces. These guys sell it to a
chop shop while the starter's still wired. Maybe I could get the engine back, but the rest of it. . . . " Freddie looks pretty sad.

"But what's with my mechanic," the fan asks to get him back on
track, "you want him to sell you something he's rebuilt? He's
working on a Datsun Z and there's an old Mercedes diesel he
wants to get to yet this summer."

"I already got a Mercedes," Freddie says a bit more quietly.

"You bought another car already?" the fan asks.

"No, I got mad and went out and tagged one. But I don't want to
take it out of state until I get a license and the numbers changed.
All I got's a title now and the car don't match."

"Tagged?" the fan is asking. "What's that mean, stolen? You
stole a car? Freddie. . . . "

"Hey, they stole mine so why can't I steal back theirs?" Through
Freddie's self-righteousness the prof can spot his Chicagoan's

lack of fine discrimination, right to his use of pronouns. But after all, the city is pretty much a case of "you" and "them," so how can he object? But what's this Freddie wants his mechanic to do?

"I gotta have somebody fix the numbers," Freddie explains, telling how the morning when his Lincoln turned up gone he walked the streets around the near North Side until he found something worth taking. The Mercedes was just too tempting, even though such an upscale car would be hard to tag and hide.

"Tag and hide," the fan remarks, "you make it sound like a kid's game. Freddie, won't you ever grow up? You remind me of this guy I knew in high school—he'd always be sauntering up and asking, 'What do you need?' So you took this car right off the street? In daylight?"

"Nah, out of a lot," Freddie tells him with a smile. "I seen the line-up at the Apco lot off Michigan and Huron, and there's this sharp-looking Benz just purring like a cat. A bunch of Arabs were parking them and those guys don't care. So I told the supervisor someone wanted him at the Erie Street gate and parked the car myself!"

"Parked it?" the fan wonders, and Freddie grins with pride.

"Yeah, and I kept the ticket. Gave the driver another stub, the schnook. At noon with the supervisor out I came back, paid the three and a quarter, didn't even tip the Arab creep who brought her down, and I had myself a brand new Mercedes-Benz!"

Now all Freddie has to do is get the VIN number to match the title he bought to a wrecked Mercedes later that day—that's the tagging he's talked about, a more sophisticated and serious way of stealing a car and not getting caught. Then he'll apply for plates and bring it out here and be cruising in style again. But for now he's carless, bumming rides to the park with Al Elgin, since Carmen doesn't like to come out with her sister's old Chevette till game time. Plus can you see Freddie Guagliardo coming down the street in a little red Chevette?

The fan admits he can't but wonders why Freddie's so protective of his stolen wheels, here so far from the nearest Chicago cop.

"Listen," Freddie emphasizes, "they catch you with a car like that you tagged, they take it away from you!" His eyes widen with the gravity of this consideration.

"I guess they would, Freddie," the fan agrees. Freddie Guagliardo never ceases to amaze and amuse him. But at least he can offer condolences for the spoiled trip home. Which Freddie appreciates, as there's more bad news to offer and help to request.

Turns out Freddie's lost the team ball signed by an overlapping crew of four years' worth of Mason City Royals teammates, a slowly evolving roster in which Freddie's been stuck since his first season in pro ball.

"Did you leave it in the Lincoln?" the fan asks, "I'll bet it turns up in some used-parts catalogue along with your engine and transmission." But Freddie says it's a whole different story, though it surely hexed the visit and cost him his precious car.

"I'd brought the ball back home so my folks could see the new guys," Freddie says, and tells how his brothers grabbed it and started tossing it around the yard. Worried that it would scuff, Freddie lunged to catch it. He did, but as he pivoted to toss it to his dad for safekeeping the throw took off and sailed across the hedge and through a neighbor's window.

"So you're still breaking windows at age twenty-three!" the fan laughs, but is again puzzled why Freddie needs his help with this.

"The neighbor's an English teacher just like you," Freddie explains, "but he writes books, too."

"Oh yeah?" the fan notes with interest. "What's his name?"

"O'Brien something," Freddie says. "I never got it straight. All I know is he writes books all summer and was always telling us to shut up. And all those years he never gave back any of the balls got hit in his yard, but we never broke a window, I swear, and this time it wasn't even my fault!" Freddie's indignance is a sight to behold, and the fan loves every minute of it. This O'Brien guy should know what a character he's got next-door, a true original—*there* would be a book to write.

"So how can I get this ball back for you?" he asks, wondering if someone in the neighborhood could go to O'Brien and explain.

"My Dad went over that night to apologize and fix the window, but the ball wasn't there. That jerk had mailed it off."

"Mailed it? Why? Where?" The fan thinks Chicago now has a chop shop for baseballs, too.

"To this guy he was writing, this guy he's doing a book about," Freddie complains. "Some moron in France. Was writing him a letter and sending him part of the book and so when the ball flies in he puts it in the package and sends it off. So now my ball's in France! I figured since this guy's a writer maybe you know who he is and could ask him for the ball back. It's pretty special, you know—half those guys are out of baseball now."

"Freddie," the fan demurs, "I don't know French and I don't know much about French writers. I'm afraid your ball is gone just like your car. Geez, I'm sorry. . . . "

"The guy's not French, he just lives there," Freddie hurries to add. "My Dad says he's Irish just like that damn O'Brien."

"Samuel Beckett?" The fan is dumbstruck. "Samuel Beckett's got your baseball?" He struggles to say more but can't.

"Yeah, that's the bozo. I bet he's got part of my car by now, too."

⊖ Hot Dogs and the Sox ⊖

Buddy Knox was thin, trim, and athletic in high school. Dyersville East voted him the "All-American Hot Dog" senior year and even the Dubuque papers picked it up. Playing their team in the state finals made him a six-county celebrity at the age of seventeen.

Now he's twenty-one, in his third year of Class A baseball, and nobody's about to vote him anything. Since leaving school he's put on thirty pounds, all in his belly. His legs are still good—he's a sharp defensive third baseman—but his nerves get edgy when he passes lunch without a beer. That was part of his famous hot-dog routine: once on a van trip to see the Minnesota Twins he put away sixty-five cans, all before they'd flipped shut the tailgate and staggered into the Met. On the ride home he drank another thirty-five, "just to make his hundred," for he was still underage and couldn't fool the stadium vendors. Now he's old enough to drink anything he wants, but more than a few beers make him sick and he can't hold the hard stuff. But he still needs to drink.

Beer and baseball, they've been wedded in his life since childhood. In the backyard playing catch, his father would snag the ball barehanded so he could hold a Pickett's in his other. During vacations the old man would take him to Chicago on the bus to catch the Cubs on a Sunday as they closed out a home stand, then stay the week for two series with the White Sox, his father's favorite team, in the stadium that smelled of beer and stale cigars.

Those had been basement years for the Sox—they were again now, rest his father's soul—but the old man liked telling him about the glory years of Luke Appling, then the *Go! Go!* team of

Luis Aparicio, Minnie Minoso, Nellie Fox, Sherman Lollar. There was a catcher's name: Sherm Lollar.

He'd always felt superior to the other Dyersville kids, knowing the South Side of Chicago as he did. Head east from the station for a bit to Clark Street, or was it Dearborn, catch the bus to Archer Avenue, transfer then get off at Wentworth and walk past the line of bums a block long to Comiskey Park.

First time he saw those bums he emptied his pockets before his dad could stop him. Blind guy playing the accordion, stump of a black man with no legs, propped up on the pavement begging, pleading, "Just a penny, just a penny." That's part of his baseball nightmare, too, which reminds him that he needs a drink.

Inside Comiskey he loved the vendors, old men with sometimes just the rasp of a voice who'd probably been selling their beer, popcorn, and scorecards since the park opened in 1910. Such a stern, severe old park. Straight upright seats, steeply raked, chairs actually behind posts, all of them in cool dark shadows. Field a perfect hexagon edged in startling white gravel, stands two-decks high, even round the outfield where nobody sat. Home-run balls from years back still lay up there, Buddy thought, but his father wouldn't let him look.

He would send him down for a beer though, when he wanted a draft. A ten-year-old kid buying beer. The first times Buddy would ask for an unwanted pop so he could lamely add, "And a beer for my dad," but pretty soon he stopped. In Chicago nobody cared.

There was no Little League in Dyersville even by '72, but Buddy played with the Cub Scouts, AmVets, Jaycees, and finally the American Legion three nights a week in Epworth, a hawkish post that prefaced each game with a prayer for "our prisoners and missing in North Vietnam." At Dyersville East he knew he'd letter in baseball, but once the football coach saw his lateral moves he was on his way to another at defensive back. Track was his baseball coach's idea, mainly to build up his wind and keep the weight off. No sprinter, Buddy ran cross-country, where he had the time and space to think.

No pro scouts ever came to Dyersville, and the gung-ho letter-men had to ride the bus to Big Ten schools or tryout camps for walk-ons. Buddy's father died in 1975, but he'd followed the Mason City club in its Three-I days with the Sox and so the day after graduation Buddy borrowed ten dollars for gas and fifty for food and a motel and drove the two hundred miles to Mason City, where the A-ball Royals had the franchise. For two nights he sat in a $2.50 box gauging the worth of these players and decided he was their match. Approaching their manager as the third day's practice began he introduced himself with the challenge, "Mr. Peterson, I'm Buddy Knox from Dyersville, that's over toward Dubuque, and I think I play better ball than your man at third." "Well, hot dog," laughed the manager, but Buddy was told to take infield practice just to see. He did his act and after a call to the farm office in K.C. Buddy was signed.

That year he hit .250 and fielded errorless ball in twenty-five games, reserving for Freddie Hernandez, whose hitting was taking him straight to Triple A. The next season Buddy started, raised his average above .300 and still fielded cleanly. But the loneliness of half a summer on the road with Spanish kids and Johnny Rebs and California hotshots signed right out of junior college spoiled his fun, and soon he started chasing brandies with beer, tequila with beer, even a boiling Greek liquid called Ouzo with beer, simply for the rush. By August he was missing games for the sickness, and when he did play his hitting and fielding languished. Carl Peterson would have canned him then and there but for the lack of a replacement, and next March at camp the manager's eye was pealed for someone new at third. Johnny Mueller, a nineteen-year-old from Georgia who hit like a charm, took Buddy's job without a fight. "You'll reserve Johnny," Carl told his down-faced former starter, but through April and May Buddy was such a wreck he never played a game. When Johnny's mother took sick and he flew back to Valdosta, Lynn Parson came in from left to play a barely adequate third. By late August the minor-league season was ending, and Buddy's junior year in professional ball had come to nothing flat.

Yes, the season is ending, and Carl is looking over his team. 80-51, tops in the league and better than any major-league club— they're sailing. Power down to the bottom of the line-up, and a .280 hitter on the bench; plus the ERA is best in the minors. But there are problems. Not baseball hassles, but player problems just the same. Carl is tall, lean, and younger looking than his forty-five years, but inside he's getting old. His daughter just about grown, he sees these kids as his own, the sons he would liked to have had, and so many of them are in such sad shape. Take Buddy.

Buddy has a drinking problem he doesn't even know about.

He's the only Iowa kid on the club, and you'd think staying near home would stabilize him, but it's those habits he's stayed close to. Country kid, worse, small town, hot rods and beer bars, probably drank his stuff from quart bottles since junior high. His street clothes look like all the rest, but Carl still pictures him like the kids he sees clustered on the sidewalks outside bars when he drives back from each game. DeKalb Ag and John Deere Implement caps, red beery faces, hair long but greasy stringy, never washed. Wrinkled sports shirts unbuttoned over the belly, already a beer gut at eighteen. Web belt, heavy work pants. Wolverines.

Jacked-up Camaros and Trans Ams at the curb, polished like pinball games. No girls, this is a gasoline crowd. A few bikes: big ones, Nortons and 1200cc Kawasakis. An ump who coaches high school during the year once told him a good tenth of these type kids will never see out their twenties. Most go out in glory, 120 miles per hour leaving the blacktop and taking out a barn, usually five in the car with them. Others in job accidents. An occasional suicide. Some just disappear.

One night he stopped in a beer bar, "Ratso's" they called it, to get a line on these kids, try to figure Buddy out. He kept on his Royals hat and dragged an old sweatshirt from the trunk, looking like a corn farmer come back to his high-school hangout.

Eight kids to a table, three pitchers passed around, all talking about the relative speeds of turbo-charged engines. "Mo-Par," one fat boy kept saying, and Carl never found out what it meant. But one phrase that kept coming up again and again he recognized, for Buddy used it once at lunch, trying to explain the joy of high-speed chasing in these hot Iowa cars. "The float," they called it, what happens to a big overpowered American car when it cranks up past 100 on level road. Something like hydroplaning without water, Carl figured; the outstretched rubber forms an airfoil and the car practically flies.

How can you steer a car when there's no rubber on the road, he felt like asking. You idiots, you want to kill yourselves. Just then the fat kid throws up, right across the table, tries to rise and drops into the muck head-first. Oh no, Carl thinks, he's going to be sick himself. This may be why the cool clean death at 120 miles per hour looks so good.

The next day is August 10, and for the rubber game with Cedar Rapids Johnny Mueller starts at third and plans to play the whole game—they'll need his bat right down to the ninth, for the Giants are one team against whom they can never roll up enough.

At 4:30 Buddy does not report. He's rocking on a barstool at the Dugout Lounge, drinking the six-pack he won way back in June with his fluke inside-the-park homer, watching the cable pickup of Chicago's game with the Yanks. It's the top of the ninth, the Sox have blanked New York and sit atop a six-run lead, never looking so good. A rookie kid named Thomas is pitching, called up from the farm last week. He's younger than Buddy. They faced each other once in the state finals and Buddy nearly drilled his teeth with a liner through the box. The kid left the game at once, "because he had to change his pants," Buddy always said.

Right now the Thomas kid is doing well, two outs, but for Jackson manager Don Kessinger calls a conference on the mound and the director fills the gap with crowd shots. The white gravel track sparkles in the sun, fuzzing out the color. Stern Protestant chairs sit rigidly in the lower deck's gloom.

The camera tracks a vendor foolishly selling scorecards in the ninth, a very old man who likely can't carry anything else. Buddy remembers him from the old days when he and his father would talk inning after inning about even older players from days back while the Sox lost and the scorecards went unsold.

Not waiting to see what Reggie does, Buddy shoves the rest of his six-pack down the bar to the crippled geeze who's been watching along, jumps into his Camaro and wheels across the street to the carwash for a fill. "Gotta check the tires," he tells the attendant, "goin' to Chicago, see the Sox."

He loves baseball, and in Chicago baseball may once again love him.

⊗ Adolph Menjou's Tryout Camp ⊗

Of all the regulars who congregate in and around box 28 behind the screen, Hal Woods is the one who has the most to say.

If it's about minor-league baseball, he's the world's authority, subscribing to several trade papers and keeping elaborate track of the Mason City Royals' alumni as they make it up through higher classifications toward the bigs. Chattanooga and Tacoma are Kansas City's AA and AAA clubs, and Hal knows their rosters up and down. Not all their players started at Mason City, but how his hometown boys make out against the top draft picks and veteran acquisitions from other clubs is his constant source of pleasure.

Some day he pictures the Royals' starting line-up on the "Game of the Week" as being Mason City graduates to a man. Better yet on "Monday Night Baseball," where he can hear Howard Cosell's raspy voice-over as the smiling faces of those once-familiar kids flash by.

Ed Sanmarda, Billy Harmon, Angel Naboa, and Robin Haas—Hal's seen them all, many of them in their first professional ball game on a cold and often snowy mid-April night when, fresh off the plane from Florida, these kids open the Class A Midcontinent League season. For seventy home dates each year he'll watch them grow into smoothly competent ballplayers, and for their road trips he'll clip box scores and chart their averages against the other clubs both home and away.

With guys who share box 28 he'll create a running narrative of the team's progress and individual fortunes within it. Eddie's flirtation with that little Jolene, the shagger. That lazy kid Frito who passed through here in July. Costy Pedraza's fight with Eddie on the mound. It's like an ongoing narrative, a serial of short stories, and Hal is pleased to read and sometimes write a little bit of it each night.

This afternoon, however, he's stepping into the pages as a character himself. Manager Carl Peterson's said sure, he doesn't mind if Hal brings his glove and shags BP with the pitchers in the outfield. Carl finds it hard enough to get his rotation and the relievers out there—seems like everyone's got an excuse when the late-afternoon temperature and humidity top ninety and there's a doubleheader up that night. All those lazy rainouts from April and May, he recalls with displeasure. But Hal's all spunk and polish, since his own season's just beginning.

First thing that hits him is the heat. The turf's baked solid and sends up waves of radiant warmth, and as the sun sinks lower it's just to blast his face directly out here in left. Sunglasses and his New York Life gimme hat don't help a bit, and he wishes he were back along the base lines taking warm-up tosses with the team.

He'd stood alone on the field, waiting for the guys to come up the clubhouse tunnel, hoping Freddie Guagliardo—with whom he has a joking sort of acquaintance—would come out first. But first man out was Herman Escobar. He had wondered what to say—should he try something in Spanish?—when Herman simply waved his glove to invite Hal's first toss. Soon Angel Naboa joined them and they played an isosceles version of three corner, Hal grateful for getting twice the throws, since his arm was plenty stiff from twenty years' disuse, but soon the field was crowded with light-blue workout jerseys and Hal could share some throws with Guags. Lynn Parson had joined them just before and was throwing a spooky knuckle ball that Hal hated to catch—he could see the league stamp between the seams as it floated toward him without a spin—and he didn't trust this cool left fielder who often seemed superior to everything. But with Freddie it was fun, particularly when this tough little Chicagoan saw Hal was a lefty like himself. They talked about all sorts of things just like before the game through the screen, but this time Hal was part of the action and not just its audience. Warm-ups were pretty nice.

But out here shagging is work. Just standing in the face of this sun is draining, like watching eight dozen loaves of bread bake in the oven. Hal wonders what the ball will be like when it comes sailing through this incredible heat.

Like a rocket, that's the answer. Like standing downrange for a fireworks test and measuring the Roman candles as they speed toward you, arching maybe twenty feet off the ground at most and dipping back down to whistle past your head. The pitchers have always made it look so easy, but today is Hal's day for another of life's surprises.

Andy Thompson has been first up in the cage, and Hal's waited professionally while the big first baseman lays down several bunts. The ball jumps off his bat a half-second before Hal hears the little pop, which should warn him that for the serious stuff due next there might be some recalculations needed for space and time. But Hal's just cooled his heels as Andy settles back in the box and reaches around to send his first liner screaming out to left.

Hal sees him turn with the bat swung around before he hears the solid crack that sends the ball out toward him. He picks it up right away, but it looks so different than from the stands. In box 28, line drives sail out in a comfortably blossoming trajectory, usually to fall easily into the fielder's glove and other times bouncing up against the wall with all the vigor of a Nerf ball. But out here it looks so different. What starts off as a tiny dot soon becomes much bigger, like a subway car coming to fill the tunnel before you. And also faster, for what begins as an easy loft soon accelerates until it whizzes past you at the speed of light. The ball thuds behind him at the wall before Hal can ponder what to do.

This time Andy slaps a grounder between short and third and Hal's convinced it will be an easy pickup. But he reaches down to find a powerful snake wriggling by at top speed—the hard field's let it gain momentum with every top-spin bounce, and Hal can't even put a glove on it. He blushes red and looks around to see if anyone's been watching, but the other fielders are off in their own little worlds, content to let him have the action whether he can handle it or not.

He's hoping for some easy flies when Andy sends one over his head. Another comes right after and Hal misjudges it, breaking forward only to see the ball take off and land twenty feet behind him. This is embarrassing indeed.

Several low liners hit on either side of him, safely out of range, and Hal sees Andy's spraying them to all fields, going with the pitch as he might in situations meant to advance the runner. This means his swings are coming to an end, leaving Hal with hopes the next batter up will have less power and determination.

It's Ed Sanmarda, which gives poor Hal no chance at all. For several minutes he watches balls fly out, and has to dodge a liner landing at his feet which burns, too hot to handle, across the grass.

Finally Angel Naboa steps in, hitting poorly since coming off the DL. Hal sees that here's his chance to shine. His own meticulous stats remind him to play shallow, and sure enough Angel's first swing sends a lazy Texas Leaguer out to left. Hal's played it right—"Hey, I'm a pretty good scout," he chuckles—and takes two steps to get underneath. Closer it gets, however, the faster it comes, until the amateur fielder has to drop on one knee to settle his catch. With a pop in his mitt he has it, and proudly flips the ball over to the pail behind second. Hal feels just great and trots back into position, looking all the way a pro.

This catch, however, is the only one of the day. Eventually he runs back for a few liners that have gone wide, but retrieving balls along the fence is hardly fielding. Everything else is over his head or beyond his reach. Soon Robin Haas comes over to play against the wall, a mute comment on the fact that Hal's been too timid to venture back there where the really hot ones have been hitting.

That night Hal's late showing up in box 28, coming up the ramp and down the aisle just in time to see the managers and umpires meeting at the plate. His friends have heard about his shagging—Dave Alpert, who usually doesn't have too much to say, has had a picnic giving them the rundown on Hal's struggles in the field. So when his friends ask him how it went, their tone is patently rhetorical.

"Fantastic!" is Hal's word to say it all, and when they laugh in disbelief he immediately sees the need to embroider whatever account they've heard. "Really," he continues, "I put on quite a show out there"—he ignores their cries of "Laugh-in" and "Bozo's Circus"—"and impressed a lot of important people!"

"Let's hear it, Hal," his box-mate says in a gesture of surrender, and the guys lean back with their brats and beer to take in Hal's story as the field's prepared for play.

He treats them to some razzle-dazzle talk about warm-ups—how he tossed a few to the pitchers and had them asking how to throw such stuff. Then the points on hitting he gave Ed Sanmarda, the league's leading slugger through most of August. Finally the full story about his debut in the field.

"Sure, and they're all applauding as you mosey out to left, just

like the great Bambino," his friend kids, and Hal sees the need for
some credibility. No, the players didn't take too much notice at all.
After all, shagging BP is pretty routine stuff, not the place where
any special talents are displayed. And for the first several balls hit
out there, he recalls, things were handled pretty routinely, pock-
eting the easy flies and tossing them over to the guy collecting
them behind the little screen propped up at second.

But with the solid-hitting Andy Thompson stepping in, things
warm up, and soon Hal is prompting "oohs" and "aahs" from the
other fielders as he darts in to snag a sinking chip shot off the
grass and then at once turn back to pull down a long high one
over his shoulder. He's running full-tilt across toward center and
reaching out to grab a twisting liner when in the corner of his eye
he notes that old Mack has drifted down the line to watch his play.
Mack stands there, hands on hips and with his sunglasses and
hat brim leveled straight at Hal, studying his smoothly effective
moves. Pretty soon he waves Carl out from the dugout to come see
what he's found out here shagging in left.

Carl joins Mack to watch a few more sparkling plays, capped by
Hal's climbing the fence after a dead run to pull down an Andy
Thompson drive with "home run" written all over it. "Lord Almighty," Hal hears Carl mutter to his coach as Andy leaves the
cage and the manager calls him over.

"Hey kid," he says to Hal—the image of their middle-aged
buddy standing there in his gimme hat, Bermuda shorts, and
tennis shoes has the entire box howling—"you think you got it in
you to play this way in a game?" Turns out the center fielder has a
groin pull and his backup's down with the flu, so rather than risk
a utility infielder out here Carl thinks it may be smarter to acti-
vate Hal and be sure the ground is covered.

"You bet, Skipper!" Hal agrees, and Carl likes his feisty spirit,
which matches his sharp play.

Because he hasn't seen Hal bat, the manager inserts him
ninth. The first innings go smoothly—an easy fly to center, then
a sinking liner that Hal spears with a dive looking much harder
than it really is. But the guys still crowd around him in the dugout, slaps and high fives all around as he laughs them off and
struggles to take his seat down toward the end.

He hasn't figured to bat this early, but in the bottom of the second the Royals have a rally inning, two singles and a walk loading
the bases for their number-nine man, Hal Woods. He strides to

the plate amid a mixture of cheers and murmured questions—
who is this new kid?—and as Hal looks to the third-base coaching box he sees the half-worried, half-hopeful look on Carl's face.
We're in a pennant race, boy, the look tells him—don't let me
down!

And Hal doesn't. The first pitch is a high fastball, which he
rockets over the scoreboard. The stands erupt and before he
rounds second base the entire dugout's on the field, heading toward the plate to sweep him away when he touches it to complete
his grand slam. Even the opposition players are nodding their ad-
miration, and as he's carried back to the bench Hal sees Carl has
walked over to the owner's box to confer with the GM. Jeff has a
phone plugged in, and after a few shared whispers he hears Carl
—"who by this time is being played by Frank Sinatra," Hal reminds his friends—asking for Tom O'Reilly, the Royals' farm director in Kansas City.

"O'Reilly," Carl says with unrestrained excitement, "I think
we've got something here!" O'Reilly is played by Adolph Menjou,
sitting there in K.C. in his double-breasted suit, toying with the
old fashioned two-piece phone as he puffs thoughtfully on a
smooth cigar. Meanwhile back in Mason City Carl is covering the
receiver to ask to jubilant Hal if he's free to fly to Boston that night
on the red-eye. The Royals are battling the Red Sox and they need
Hal's bat as well as his glove in treacherous Fenway.

"You bet, Skip!" he says again, and baseball history's rewritten
once more.

Hal's about to continue on right through the World Series when
his friends remind him he's way ahead of things, that mythical
night game where he starts in center is not yet even underway.
Besides, the regular man in center, Dave Alpert, has finished his
warm-up exercises and is coming over to the screen. Maybe this
is part of the story too, Hal's friend wonders aloud.

"Got a groin pull there, Dave?" he asks, which puzzles the shy
outfielder.

"No—am I walking funny?" Then he blushes and starts to turn
away, but checks himself when he remembers what's in his hand.

"Mr. Woods," he calls, at once adding twenty years to Hal's age,
"you forgot your hat this afternoon." He's got the battered New
York Life freebie cap Hal's worn in BP, and accepting it around the
screen at once puts him back in the world of hard fact.

"You feeling all right, sir?" Dave questions. "Carl and Mack were afraid you might collapse out there," he says sheepishly. "Our trainer was looking up the number of the inhalator squad."

Box 28 isn't laughing. To tell the truth, it sounds more like a warm-up for Sunday choir practice, as one friend hums a bit and another whistles, all of them glancing up and around here and there in different directions as Hal stares downward quietly.

"I'm sorry you had so much trouble," Dave says to resolve the matter. "One thing," he adds, "Carl says he's not risking anybody off the team shagging BP again. You scared that man to death! Nobody, he says. No one, never!"

⊖ The Language Game ⊖

When Carl stops by the GM's office for his mail, the bright-blue logo of the Kansas City Royals stands out amid the quieter envelopes.

They're using the expensive stationery, he notes, and that always means trouble. Routine farm-club business almost always rates just the black-stamped, cheap paper wrapper, stuff like you'd buy at Woolworth's and send through Insty-Print with all the class of some tacky direct-mail offer. But the thick bond envelope and embossed lettering tells Carl that this comes not from the player-development staff but from the chief executive offices, and how can that be good news for him?

It takes him the long walk back to his office to get the thing undone, and thank God old Mack's sprawled there on the couch when Carl reads the news.

"No more Spanish," he tells his veteran pitching coach, and tosses the letter aside in frustration.

"No Spanish?" Mack asks, stretching forward to reach the letter, which has fallen at his feet. "We're not getting any more Spanish players? That's okay with me."

"No, no *Spanish*," Carl emphasizes as Mack finds his place in the letter and gives a little grunt of understanding. "*English* only on the field, starting tonight!"

Turns out the home office is distressed that a Latin kid can spend any number of years in the minor leagues and never pick up enough English to get by on his own. This keeps the Spanish-speaking players together, forming cliques, which are against club policy and good managerial sense. Moreover, the directive suggests, having part of your team carrying on in a foreign language isolates the English-speaking players from the game and builds new allegiances based on language rather than on club.

"I've always suspected that," Mack agrees. "You get a Latin kid or two on base and the Spanish-speakers in your infield shift to their side. Remember that bandit with the Cubs, whispering when a pick-off move was coming? For two years the Cubbies never got a Hispanic leaning the wrong way at all!"

"You think we got some of that here?" Carl asks suspiciously.

"I'm not saying anything like that's going on," Mack says with the back-off motion used to keep him out of minor-league politics, "just that this directive may not be all the horseshit you think it is."

"Then you tell 'em," Carl says, and turns to his other mail.

Okey-dokey, Mack thinks to himself, I got myself into this one so I'll do it to get myself out. He makes his way through the trainer's room, where Chet's just setting up and turns into the locker room. All heads look up, for this is usually bad news when management comes into their territory. New training rules for sure is their common belief.

"Okay, fellas, listen up," Mack calls, which is hardly necessary as things have hushed once he's passed through the door. "Mr. Sulzburger up in Kansas City wants the Mason City Royals to play baseball in English, so that's the rule once you're out there on the field."

"English?" Johnny Mueller questions. "What kind of ball we playing now, Japanese?"

"You got a Japanese glove, moron," Jim Smith chides him. "You know what the Case Equipment workers in this town think of that!"

"Yeah, we're getting cricket bats so we can play English," Andy Thompson laughs, and Mack stands back a while to let this horseplay run itself out. His silence works, and soon the guys are asking him seriously what this new directive means.

So Mack reads them the whole thing, with its elaborate philosophy of team unity and the linguistic integrity of purpose. This prompts a short debate among the players as Keith Henley admits he feels put out of it when people speak Spanish around him.

"So what you think we feel like, man, when you talk Anglo?" Herman Escobar objects, and the six other Hispanic players agree—except for Costy Pedraza, who's not sure what Herman has said.

Some fancy chatter breaks out in Spanish, and as the American players look around uncomfortably old Mack interrupts to say this is just what Kansas City means. Up and down the farm system, from Triple A to the rookie league, Royals teams are being alienated from themselves by language. And a team that doesn't feel like it's together won't play together well.

"Now maybe I shouldn't bring this up," Mack adds, slowing down to wonder about it himself, "but we went through something sort of like this in the early fifties when major-league organizations started bringing along Negro players."

"Dinosaur time!" Johnny Mueller breaks in, and laughs break out all over.

"For Chrissake, Mack," Jim Smith begs him, "at least say 'black' so we know what you're talking about."

"Okay, black players," Mack gives in, and continues with his story about the way some squads got split in two, all quite unintentionally but divisive nevertheless, as black ballplayers began to cluster by themselves.

"We had to step right in and break it up," Mack recalls, and Lynn Parson cuts in on him to imagine how. "Yeah," he says, "I've heard these old-time Negroes tell how they had to learn whitey habits, like eating frozen waffles for breakfast and singing Perry Como tunes and stuff," and the clubhouse breaks up in laughter. Mack's glad Lynn's said it, for things have threatened to go tense on him.

What they have to do is really easy, he explains—just learn the good old American words for baseball action and stick to them on the field. Same for those little calls of encouragement, which should be easy enough. Mack will be in charge and he's designating Lynn as co-captain for organizing language drills, since that's what they'll do today instead of infield and BP. No hitting or fielding, just a run-through of every basic play with an emphasis on Yankee phraseology.

For starters Herman's put at second base, with Billy Harmon moving over to Eddie's slot at short. Johnny stays at third while Andy takes their throws at first. Mack's special wrinkle is to have four more Anglo players standing just behind Herman, and as the ball comes toward him they're to shout appropriate words and phrases such as an American player would use. That way Herman will start to think baseball in English like Kansas City wants him to.

"This creates a new language environment," Mack explains, wondering if he needs to say more, but Andy does it for him. "You mean psycho-generative, like we study at South Florida," Andy chimes in, and Mack tells one of the pitchers to grab a bat and psycho-generate some hard grounders to second base.

As Herman crouches forward, Donny Moore leans toward him for a quick whisper, and the second baseman nods and calls out to the batter, "Heet eet to me, souckar!" Al Elgin has been ready to slap it out, but at this he drops the ball in laughter. Donny whispers again and Herman shouts "You out, baby!" and everyone agrees this is better as a smiling Herman scoops up the ball and makes his phrase ring true.

Mack has taken two other Latins—Angel Naboa and Manuel Moreno—out to center field, where he plans to show them how to call for the ball. The Royals' starting outfield is all Yankee—Lynn Parson, Dave Alpert, and Donny Moore across from left to right—but when one of those guys is down Angel or Manuel is put in on a utility basis, so they'll have to know the words for covering things from all directions. Robin Haas is waiting in the fungo circle, and Mack signals him to send one out.

"Say 'your ball,' " Mack yells to Angel as the ball drifts away from him to Manuel.

"My ball!" Angel calls and the fly drops weakly between them.

"No, no, no!" Mack chants as Angel eyes him timidly. "*You* say '*your* ball' to Moreno because it's *his!* Got it?"

Angel nods yes and the old coach calls for another fungo. This time it's headed toward Angel, and Mack urges him to claim it. "It's your ball, son, so make the call!"

"Your ball," Angel yells in a panic, and the liner drops untouched.

Mack is livid, dancing around in circles as he repeats "Mine! Mine! Mine!" When Angel asks if Mack was supposed to catch it all hell breaks loose and Ed Sanmarda runs out from the dugout to see if he can help.

"Eddie, you ever see that TV show 'Sesame Street'?" Mack asks him in great exasperation, and Eddie's grin says "Sure." It's how he's learned his English this summer, and so straightening out possessive pronouns for his Latin brothers is an exercise easy as pie. For a few minutes he looks like the puppet Grover as he dashes back and forth between his teammates demonstrating "my" and "yours," tossing in a "here" and "there" for good measure.

Meanwhile Carl has come out on the field to see how drills are going and soon wishes he had a videotape to send those idiots back in K.C. Costy Pedraza's having one hell of a time telling Herman Escobar who's to cover second base. It's supposed to be a simple matter of signaling to second or short, which in the past has been accomplished by Herman drifting in behind the mound and picking up the news from Costy. But all that fluidity is lost as the two Hispanic players stop and wait on each other's cue, just like two school kids in a shabbily rehearsed class play. First Costy laughs, then Herman starts to say something but breaks off in a giggle. Carl can just see this happening in a game.

"Shortstop covers, shortstop covers," Carl yells at them, pointing to Billy. Herman stares blankly even though he knows enough English to get himself around. Around town, Carl figures, the guy can order himself a hamburger easy enough, but on the ball field it's still all Español. How anybody can change this overnight escapes him.

Mack now joins him from the outfield for a strategy meeting at second base. Does Carl think one day's drill will do it for the dozens of situations coming up in every game? They've got no choice, the manager replies, as the farm director's planning a visit before the month's end so he can see the new plan working.

"He's even asking Jeff for a list of all the big promotions," Carl adds, shaking his head in exasperation.

"What's he want, to win a bag of groceries on A&P night?" Mack's laughing at this just as much as anything this afternoon.

"No," Carl replies irritably, "he wants to miss the promo nights, doesn't want any crowds. Wants to be here when we got two hundred people so he can hear Sanmarda and Escobar out there talking English on the field!"

"Talking just like two professors, huh?" Mack laughs again, but adds he's got a way to keep any language problems from disrupting play. If they start their regulars, there's only one danger spot and that's with Sanmarda at short when Pedraza's on the mound. "When you pitch Costy," Mack deduces, "just send in Knox to third, move Harmon over to short, and switch Mueller from third to second." The outfield, they both know, is okay as long as Parson lays off the jive talk.

Carl's still shaking his head. "I don't think that's what the house cats up in Kansas City have in mind," he objects, "but until we get this language business down let's do that."

What Carl's unprepared for, however, is the horseplay all this language business has generated. With his attention given to the Latins, the manager hasn't noticed what his all-Anglo outfield has been doing. That night, however, the crowd's predictably small, and from the dugout he can hear the trouble Lynn's inviting from left field as Dave and Donny trot out to center and right for the national anthem.

"Buenas noches, señores," Lynn's calling to them in flawless, finely inflected Spanish, with just a trace of California accent. "¡Bienvenido al jardín!"

"Thanks buddy," Dave calls back, but Lynn objects to his English, insisting they conduct business tonight in Spanish. Dave's had just a year of it in high school, but that won't dissuade Lynn, especially since Donny's had none at all. So as the first batter fouls off a few and takes a ball low the outfield tosses back and forth the Spanish words they've picked up in the locker room. At short, poor Eddie Sanmarda looks confused, perplexed in fact at the cacophony of language he hears behind him.

For the first two batters up the outfield's left to itself, untroubled by the soft grounder to second and the strike-out on a full count. But the third batter's got power, and after ripping a long foul down the right-field line he lifts a towering fly to right center. It's anyone's ball, but before Dave can make the call Lynn's running over threatening serious reprisal if there's a word of English said. Lynn's felt sorry for the Spanish players who've struggled with these silly drills all day to the detriment of their performance, and he figures this is one way to put such nonsense to an end.

"Es tu pelota," he calls to Dave, prompting him with the proper line for taking a ball himself. But Dave thinks this is what he's supposed to say, and so instead of yelling "Es mío" to call off Donny he simply repeats Lynn's line, making Donny think the play is his.

The ball has reached its apogee and is arcing downward toward them as both Dave and Donny circle underneath. They look like dancers in a folk pageant as they complete a circuit, then reverse direction and do it again. All the time they're chattering in broken Spanish, possessives as footloose as their ragged play.

"¡Es tu pelota, idiot!" Dave is screaming as in contradictory fashion he reaches for the ball himself. Donny's calling "¡Mío, mío!" to no effect. With seconds remaining Dave runs through all the Spanish he knows, a ninth-grade semester that has now boiled down to a few frantic cries as the ball rockets down the chute toward them.

"¡Hola! Me llamo Paco," he shouts, and when Donny fails to respond he follows quickly with "¿Cómo estás?" and "¿Dónde vives?" But it's all too late as Donny lunges forward, their legs entangle, and the two confused fielders tumble together with a shuddering tear of muscles and twisting of joints. The ball bounces free and dribbles back to the wall, where Lynn retrieves it.

With the batter standing safe at second, time is called. Carl runs out with the trainer and finds that neither player can make it to his feet—Dave's pulled a hamstring and Donny's ankle has collapsed nearly sideways. But neither is complaining. "¡Hola!" Dave says weakly, and Lynn decides to lay it on the line.

"Buenas noches, señor," he greets the Skipper. "Bienvenido al jardín."

As his two starters are helped off the field Carl hurries back to the dugout, where he can survey his active roster in the flesh. But there's not much choice, and Herman Escobar's already warming up with Angel Naboa down the line.

"Tell them the outfield's speaking Spanish tonight," he calls to Mack, who keeps his face straight as long as he can.

"You telling Kansas City their plan is nuts?" the old coach asks him.

"Parson's going to do that for me to earn back his hundred-dollar fine," Carl reports, glancing out to see his new outfield taking shape with Lynn struggling to understand the captain's calls from center.

⊗ Mack's Stats ⊗

By the middle of August Eddie's teammates are socking so many home runs that the meat of the line-up can virtually live off the free pizzas and six-packs they win with each round-tripper.

Plus there's an occasional prime-rib dinner from a restaurant downtown, based on a scam worked out by the bull-pen crew. A coupon in each scorebook invites the fans to guess the answer to the night's baseball trivia quiz. Some are easy, like Which club has three MVPs among its starters? Boston—Rice, Lynn, and Yazstremski. As the season wears on the trivia get harder, sometimes impossible to guess, but one night while the bull pen loudly debates the answer a fan watching warm-ups offers to turn it in for them on his card.

Question: Which major-league pitcher had the worst losing record in 1978? Hint: He's with the Cleveland Indians. Mack, who's been complaining how during his one stellar year with the National League he was passed over in the All Star selection for three pitchers with inferior records (Don Sutton, Don Drysdale, plus a third he's forgotten but also a Dodger—Walt Alston managed the Nationals that year), insists it was Rick Waits, "if he pitched." "No," Freddie Guagliardo argues, it had to be Rick Wise. The pitchers turn thumbs down on their coach and side with their short reliever and send the fan down with "Rick Wise." Three innings later he's back with a gift certificate made out to "Billy Poobah," whose name when announced sends the bull pen rollicking off their bench, since that's their nickname for any dead-blind ump. Freddie and Robin Haas, who was also dead-sure about Rick Wise, agree to split the meal. And the fan promises to come back tomorrow with an even better fake name, "Napoleon St. Cyr."

"Sandy Koufax," Mack yells with a vengeance. "Whaa?" the crew asks back, still thinking of Rick Wise and those nineteen losses. "That's the bum who beat me into the All Stars," Mack reiterates. Freddie cracks up. "You're right, coach," he mocks, "stats don't mean a thing."

So the food has been coming fast and good, and by the month's last Sunday Eddie has four five-spots from meal money tucked away. Donny has been saying that he misses the old Panama Pizzas Eddie cooked up in leaner days, that next year the little shortstop is sure to make it to a better league—and so maybe for old times' sake they should have a last cheap-food celebration, spending the extra bucks on beer.

Sunday noon the team troops in to find little finger-sized tortillas set out on the coffee table, replicas in miniature of the whoppers Ed prepared all summer, his Latino approximation of American junk food. But there's so much noise coming from Angel and Herman in the kitchen that everyone knows at once what's up. Latin music pounds from the stereo—Mongo Santamaria, the closest K-Mart can get—and Angel, tuxedoed, walks in stiffly with a huge platter on each arm. Fried bananas, refried beans, and mounds of steak in rice sprinkled with green peppers and peas. "¡Cuba libre!" Andy Thompson shouts, remembering such meals at the Columbia in Tampa's Ybor City, but Angel counters "¡Hey no, man, viva México!" and enters with a stolen bar tray ranked with the finest beers: Carta Blanca, Bohemia, Indio, Dos-Equis dark, Tres-Equis light, and his father's own Tecate. A pile of lemons, a salt shaker, and a tall bottle of tequila stand at center. Now Eddie's back with another tray of the Cuban and Mexican food Herman's been preparing.

Eddie has reminded his compadres to go easy on the hot end of their old family recipes, and hence the food is tasty and appealing to their Anglo teammates. The guys eat up, pacing the tequila and knocking off the Mexican beers. They've never drunk before game time, but they're still feasting when the Cubs come on at one o'clock and so the prospect of settling down before the TV looks good indeed. Billy, Buddy (who can hardly stand), and Andy offer to clean up so that their friends can catch Rick Reuschel's first inning against Atlanta. Donny likes the ambience of Wrigley

Field, though he's never been there and never will unless he makes the Royals and Chicago meets them in the series. But he's seen Jack Brickhouse on the telecasts all across the Midwest network, knows about director Arne Harris and his hat shots, loves that low brick wall behind the plate, the bleacher bums, the stone apartments across Sheffield Avenue with the fans perched in windows and on the roof. Ex-Cubs fill the majors—Kessinger, Madlock, Sutter, Morales, Trillo—and every time he hears their names it's in Jack Brickhouse's voice.

Reuschel looks good, striking out five batters through the third. But the Cubs have trouble hitting, and when Buckner sends a low liner out to center Dale Murphy can only dive to trap the ball. The second-base ump, however, calls it an out, and to a man the Mason City Royals scream their hearts out. "Hey Blue," Donny yells, "what was that? You working for the Braves?" Andy, who's in from the kitchen, is furious. "Great call, Blue," he screams at the set, "gonna give him some help on the strike zone now, too?" They're all debasing the ump, pummeling his image on the screen as the Cubs' manager argues—these are the things they'd like to say in their own games and can't. Plus some choice words for the Braves now loping off the field. "Murphy, you're a cheat," Billy Harmon is yelling, and addresses his next remark to the whole Atlanta team, breaking up the room. "You glamour boys, this time next year you'll all be working in a car wash!"

Commercials settle them down. A shot of bubbles rising in a fresh Budweiser draws a heavy belch from Donny. A boring ad for yard fences. Then something about land buys in Arizona, "forty minutes by jet from Tucson." "Hey man," Billy exclaims, "*we're* forty minutes by jet from Tucson!" Back to the ball park, but Atlanta is slow in getting their batter up to the plate and Milo Hamilton fills in with some trivia stats. "Dave Kingman has the longest ball hit out of Wrigley Field," he's telling Lou Boudreau, "but do you know who's hit the longest one anywhere else?" "That's easy, Milo," Lou replies, "Ted Williams, 564 feet in 1949." "But who was the pitcher?" Milo Hamilton prompts, and Boudreau doesn't have the answer. From the truck, Arne Harris flashes the answer. A rookie pitcher for the old Washington Senators, relieving for Bob Porterfield on opening day: Mack Ptaszynski. Around the living room the Royals are up and shouting. Pity poor Mack in the bull pen tonight.

Reuschel has more good innings—will Chicago trade him, too,

Donny wonders? But after nodding off for a while in contempla-
tion of all those vagrant Cubs he snaps awake to the face of Lee
Smith staring in for a sign. "Huh?" he asks himself, and rises to
the snores of twenty-two teammates sprawled about the room.
"Fourteenth inning, and we're going to have to call this game for
darkness pretty soon," Jack Brickhouse is telling his sidekick,
and Donny feels his stomach sink way down. "Oh, mama!" and
the phone is ringing off the wall, their trainer pleading that the
umps will call a forfeit if the team's not there in fifteen minutes.
Carl and Mack are too mad to talk. "Lay out the duds, we're coming," Donny yelps, rousing the players with kicks, shoves, and
curses. But he's laughing and they laugh, too. Twenty-two of
them roar off toward the stadium in Andy's, Donny's, and
Johnny's vans, leaving Buddy sick on the bathroom floor.

☻ The Squeeze Is On ☻

It's minor leagues for umpires, too, Carl keeps telling himself. But bad umping is the one aspect of A-ball shabbiness he simply can't abide.

There'll be bonehead plays in the infield, balls lost to outfield sun and misjudgment, and pick-off plays that backfire and put the runner safe on third. Carl imagines himself up in the stands and frames the perfect picture of Class A minor-league baseball: the first baseman scrambling after a runaway throw while the runner rounds second, heading for an unprotected third.

Sometimes it's even worse, as the first baseman rockets his throw across the infield only to have it skip past his teammate at third, the pitcher, plus the catcher backing up the play. It's happened once this year already, and will surely happen again, including the nightmare of a runner who just a moment before had scratched out a cheap single now ambling home to cross a totally deserted plate, while what looks like half a dozen Royals swirling down the left field line in pursuit of the ball.

But worst of all is the apprentice umpiring. Carl's coached or managed at the A level for six years now, and while he's patient with the eternal ineptitude of his youngsters reporting in the spring, the undying incompetence of these umpires drives him batty every year.

He can be lucidly philosophical about it, patiently explaining how unfair it is to let these rookie umpires butcher the game. Sure, a young shortstop might boot a grounder or strike out with men on base. But what they're aiming at is an unattainable perfection. Nobody's ever fielded 1.000, let alone hit it. Yet as they mature, their numbers will at least rise toward that impossible goal, a Zeno's paradox of fielding numbers in the nine hundreds getting closer to a thousand with every proper play but never fated to reach it at all.

And look at hitting. .400 seems an absolute season limit, just like a 3.6 mile. Try as you might, you just can't get any better than that, and what does that give you except missing out six times for every ten? For thirty-five home runs a hitter will gladly accept a hundred strike-outs. There are sacrifice bunts and flies that don't even cost you a time at bat, and sometimes even a double play is worth it when it scores a run. On the playing side of it there's ample room for failure—in fact, it's built into the game.

But umpiring, based on the authority of rules, is an entirely different matter. Safe or out at first is not a case of unattainable perfection—it's just safe or out, yes or no, with nothing in-between. Same for balls and strikes. It's either in the strike zone or out of it, not .997 in or .328 out. Same for foul or fair. It's a binary system, Carl likes to explain to sympathetic listeners all summer as the bad calls mount, a set of lucidly simple oppositions. And so there's no excuse whatsoever for fouling them up.

But foul them up they do, as a perennial crop of rookie umpires makes mayhem of the struggle for perfection Carl's boys are waging. Rookies or rums, that's all this league gets—raw amateurs or guys who even after a year or two can't seem to get it right. Out East, down in Florida, or up in the Northwest there'd be an honest-to-goodness rookie league for cases like this, but here in the Midwest A-ball is the lowest classification for fifteen hundred miles either way. And so his players, most of whom have shaken the wool out of their own play in competitive college ball or at Elmyra in the New York–Penn, are stuck with game officials less adept than themselves.

It's a rotten system, Carl complains to all who'll listen, and it's the cross he bears each year from mid-April to the end of August with the Mason City Royals.

At least he has some allies in the stands. Crowds in general will howl when any call goes against the home team, but watching the strike zone and keeping an eye out for balks remain the specialties of a loyal hard core. One of them sits at the grandstand's edge just above third base and the dugout. He's football coach at the high school, and his strong voice carries well across the field. He even cheers the team when they change positions between innings—"Let's show some hustle out there!" he'll bark—but like

Carl his personal issue is the state of umpiring in this league.

"I think it's awful," he'll complain to friends passing by who've heard him berating the umps. "These young men are working hard and the umpires are hurting them, hurting their careers. It's awful!" The home-plate ump is over at the dugout collecting more balls and he glances up at Coach, as everyone calls him, letting him know he hears. "That's right, buddy," Coach says sternly, "I'm talking about you! Where'd you learn your strike zone, at barber college?" Burned as he is, the ump is forced to laugh—at least old Coach's lines are original, night after night— which might as well be kerosene tossed on his fire.

"Go ahead and laugh, you dummy," Coach calls down to him. "This time next year you'll be detassling!"

Carl has the feeling this game won't be a good one, and the night's events soon bear him out. The umpiring crew is particularly bad, two awkward guys who were rookies last year and who if anything look worse now. For Carl they've made it a rough year from the start. At the plate tonight is the poorest balls-and-strikes man Carl's ever seen, a lumbering giant they've nicknamed Lurch, whose overbroad shoulders, high forehead, and hobbling gate make him look like Frankenstein's monster. He really does lurch around there behind the plate just like a top-heavy sailboat. His inability to bend down means he has no sense of the strike zone's bottom at all. Carl swears he calls the pitches when they're still at eye level twenty feet out from the plate, and for a curve-baller like Freddie Guagliardo there's no fair chance at all.

It was a disputed call of Lurch's on one of Freddie's curves which got Carl ejected in the last inning of the season's final game a year ago, an important one where the team was fighting for a first-place tie with the Muskies. Arguing a strike call is an automatic ejection, and Carl knew he was asking for it. But Lurch escalated the affair into a near brawl, and before the shouting was over he'd tossed three players who'd been cheering their skipper from the dugout. So Carl's season ended ignominiously, and also expensively, because he felt responsible for his boys' league fines as well as his own, which was double that of the players.

And then this season opened right where the last ended, with the same crew umping the April 13 opener at Mason City. Even before he'd changed to blue, Lurch was over at the dugout, smiling at old Mack but glaring at the manager.

"Well, Peterson," he sang with mock exclaim, "so the Royals decided to keep you!"

"I see you're not up either, Dufus," Carl muttered back, and Lurch promptly challenged him to say that in the game. "You don't learn to keep your eye on a low strike, I'll tell you worse, loud enough for your mama to hear it," Carl told him, and Lurch just spun around and kicked his way back to the visitors' dugout in that stiff-legged way that gave him his silly nickname.

Lurch's partner last year and this has made them a true Mutt and Jeff team. He's a short, baby-faced kid named Will Cleaver, and from the start the fans have called him "Beaver." From the boxes he's quite a sight, especially when Lurch looms behind the plate and Cleaver disappears in perspective, his diminutive size making it seem he's standing out in deep center field instead of just inside second base.

What a pair, Carl has to admit. These guys already have two strikes against them even before they take the field.

What a crime, Coach is telling his cronies up in the stands, running through all his arguments why the league should keep at least the same standards for its umps as the ball clubs do for their players. If the Royals fielded a team as bad as these umpires, the Coach is fond of saying, they'd never get out of an inning. That these umps can get three outs counted straight is a miracle, and most nights he'll yell himself hoarse disputing their calls.

Tonight the first inning goes smoothly, thanks to Al Elgin's good control and the way his fastball sinks. No count runs past a ball or a strike, and all three batters hit sharp grounders so there's no chance of any close calls at first. Cleaver is pretty good on the bases, losing it only when there's two men on and he has to cover all three sacks at once. As umps work up the ladder their job gets easier as another man is added to their crew at each classification. But here in A-ball they've got the absolute mimimum. Carl can't think of any game where there's less than two—in the rookie leagues, Legion ball, Little League, or even Cub Scout softball, where he once found himself umping for his nephew.

"Cub Scout" is one of Coach's favorite goads, and everyone knows how close to the money he is. There are certain things he can say, and others that he can't really get away with. With the umps controlling the game he really should be more careful than he is, but seeing better officiating in his own high-school conference, where neighbors work for twenty dollars, has blown his patience with these bums who are earning a thousand per month plus a better meal allowance than the players.

Quad Cities is throwing their junk-ball artist tonight, Stu Maddigan, and Carl worries for the frustration everyone will suffer. His power hitters go nuts, watching Stu's assortment of palm balls and knucklers dance past them like wounded sparrows, and the fans always get antsy with his infuriatingly slow pace. Old Mack has set aside his bull-pen duties tonight to spend some pregame time with the line-up, telling them how to spot Stu's stuff and the proper rhythm for hitting it. But how long this impromptu discipline lasts is anybody's guess, and Carl's hunch is that it won't be long before his hotshots like Thompson and Mueller get exasperated and start swatting wildly at Maddigan's offerings like a bunch of gnats.

Sorriest of all, however, will be the home-plate umpiring. If Lurch is a failure at calling curves, Stu Maddigan's knuckler will make any notion of a strike zone totally inconsequential. Old Son of Frankenstein likes to call them well out from the plate—Carl sees him make the commitment and cock his arm that far ahead —but where a knuckleball floats that early has no relation to how it lands. And sure enough, the first pitch Ed Sanmarda sees is called a strike even though it bounces just behind the plate.

Eddie takes no notice, but Carl runs in a few feet from the coach's box at third to challenge an already defensive Lurch. The manager knows better than to say something, since arguing a call's an automatic toss, but Lurch is ready to give Carl a healthy piece of his mind.

"I'm calling this game, Peterson," he shouts at Carl, holding his mask as if it's a weapon. "You plan to call it, I got a fifty-dollar shower all set for you!"

"Did I say something?" Carl asks, and at once has the crowd behind him. That's the classic mistake fools like Lurch make every time, getting the whole place against them from the start.

"You are now, buddy, and I don't want to hear it!" Lurch pulls himself up into his stare-down stance, which makes him look like a comic-book Mussolini. The crowd's laughing, but Carl doesn't want to precipitate anything without cause or benefit. A late-inning ejection in a tight game can fire up his team, but to be booted on the first pitch would just make everything go flat. So he turns around and heads back to his coaching box, tossing a few words over his shoulder to Eddie, but really just to look like he's having the final word with Lurch.

Maddigan's second pitch is a straight change, and the umpire calls it fairly—chances are it is a strike, but it's hard for anyone to be sure whether it's caught a corner or not. Carl makes no objection, but the crowd's primed and they jump right on poor Lurch. First there's a general groan, then some scattered insults, and finally the distinguishable lines from the deeper-voiced fans.

"Bad call, Blue!" a fan yells from the boxes. "That was way outside!"

"You dummy!" calls a hoarser voice, which halts for the want of anything intelligent to add. But Coach has plenty to say, and does.

"What do you think this is," he demands, "a four-strike league?" The crowd picks this up and cheers along. "Next year you guys'll be calling girls' softball," he adds, and gets a hand from the crowd for his sentiments.

Off-field action Lurch can ignore as he's trained to do. And as long as Carl stays put off third the game's still in control. There's a bit more hooting from the stands, but down at first little Cleaver gives the umpire salute—a muscle-flexing sign of solidarity—and Lurch happily flexes him back. Over in his coach's box Carl stops to think how isolated these guys really are, how vulnerable it is for just the two of them to stand out there between fifty players in front of two or three thousand fans. Maybe that contributes to the inconsistency, not that anything should excuse it.

With his third pitch Stu Maddigan establishes a rhythm of sorts, and once the hitters and Lurch have made their adjustment to a steady diet of junk the whole park finds it easier to get on with the game. With the knuckler not working at all, Eddie draws a walk and steals second in the ample time provided by a change-up. But Billy Harmon's mystified by Maddigan's circus stuff and can't even get a bat on the ball. His third swing comes on a pitch that's bounced a foot outside, and he looks shamed walking back to the dugout. But power-hitting Johnny Mueller does the same thing, lashing away at two balls in the dirt before Carl gives him an emphatic take sign. Probably too emphatic, because the catcher signals a straight fastball and Maddigan's first one of the night splits the plate.

Now it's up to Andy Thompson, the first left-hander in Mason City's order. Carl knows his hitter likes to pull the ball, but against junk like Maddigan's that means patience, lots more than this big fun-lover usually shows. And to no one's surprise he turns way ahead of the first pitch, lining it over the Dodgers' dugout.

Carl flashes a take sign so that Andy can get some sense of Maddigan's speed, or rather lack of it. It's a low ball anyway, and Lurch calls it right. But then Andy lunges at a dancing knuckle ball nearly two feet high and tops it down the first base line. The catcher dives for it but it rolls foul, and Carl wonders what to flash his power hitter when he's down 1-2 to a junkyard artist.

Green light, what the hell. If Andy's smart he'll hold off and stroke the inevitable change-up out to right. With Eddie's speed plus the lead he'll take on the hit sign he should score easily. That's it, Carl decides—hit and run. Andy's already set and may not have seen it, but it's worth a chance. Worst that can happen is Eddie being gunned down at third, with a fresh at-bat for Andy in the second.

Carl could call time and be sure his hitter has the sign, but that would be a dead giveaway. Better to take his chances.

Maddigan's setting his grip for the knuckler—by moving beyond the box, Carl can see him fingering the ball, but at this point there's nothing he can do. It's the worst pitch possible for a run and hit, but it's too late to change things now.

As the pitcher comes out of his set position Eddie takes off, and from his startled look of surprise Carl can tell Andy's missed the play. But the exaggerated motion the knuckle ball demands gives Andy time to organize his thoughts and realize he must protect the plate—otherwise, with the left side open, Eddie's a duck at third.

All these mischances let the play develop just perfect. The series of surprises and mental calculations have slowed Andy down, while the pitch has given Eddie an incredible jump. He's halfway to third when Andy's late stroke sends a soft liner behind him, and he's made the turn to home before the left fielder even has the ball.

Where Andy's liner falls, however, reverses the play's momentum. The Quad Cities fielder is rushing in full tilt, and when he grabs it on the hop he keeps on running to give the ball more pump toward home. His perfect strike comes in a hair's-breadth behind Eddie, who's almost nailed with an expert spin tag. But in the same motion their catcher uncorks another strike to second, where Andy's overrun the bag. He dives back, but directly into the tag.

Three outs, Cleaver signals. Run counts, Lurch waves. "Thank God," Carl says, cheered as much by the correct call as by Eddie's good slide.

The Royals' 1-0 lead holds up, and by the middle innings Carl has forgotten about the officiating, though Lurch has told him twice to stop making fair-or-foul calls when the ball goes down the line. He finds it distracting, the umpire claims. It's just a habit, Carl tells him, a bit of enthusiastic body language, but promises to break it right now. This contributes to the unspoken truce, and since that rocky first inning there haven't been any real sparks thrown at all. Lurch has picked up Maddigan's slow-motion rhythm and has a feel for calling his junk correctly, and the sinker ball Al Elgin's mastered makes each top half a routine matter of whether or not the ground balls get through—thankfully there's no way Cleaver can blow it, since it's not a call at all.

But a one-run lead is nothing one can be comfortable with, especially when the worst crew in A-ball is calling the plays and strikes. Just one piece of misjudgment could cost them the game, Carl knows, and through the middle innings he prays that Al won't allow a base runner. His low pitches usually draw swings, and his high ones are fat in Lurch's elevated strike zone. But the odds of getting anything more off Stu Maddigan are slim. Once he gets his junk working he's unhittable, and what they've managed since the first hardly counts, as no one's moved beyond first.

Until the bottom of the eighth, when Johnny pulls a hard one down the line, so close to foul territory that Carl hops back as it screams by. Involuntarily he makes a big fair sign, pointing at a right angle to the field just as Lurch is supposed to do from behind the plate. Johnny's safe with a double, but as Carl turns to run his signs past Andy he sees an angry Lurch stalking toward him in his stiff-legged manner, kicking up dust along the line.

The manager intercepts him with an apology, but the umpire's hearing none of it.

"All right, Peterson," Lurch fumes, "I'll take your guff on calls, you can argue if you want to, but you will NOT show me UP!" For this last word he's within poking distance of Carl, and the syllable is driven home with a sharp finger against the manager's chest. Carl would like to explain that he's intended nothing as a comment on Lurch's umping, that it's just his own excitement with the game, but there's no room to get in a single word.

"You want to squeeze me, buddy, just watch me squeeze you," and with that Lurch spins around awkwardly and hobbles back to the plate.

Squeeze—Carl's shocked to hear an umpire use the word, much less admit he's going to do it. It's the players' term for an ump's retaliation, squeezing the strike zone smaller when a pitcher's complained about a call or making it bigger when a batter's reacted too soon to a presumed ball four and started down to first. Each is an example of showing up, and if Lurch thinks that's what's happened here, Carl is sure to pay. Thank God he's got a lead, slim as it is.

Johnny's dancing around off second, so Carl calls time and warns him not to draw a throw, he'll surely be called out. He then flashes a string of hit signs to Andy, making it clear that his big first baseman should swing at everything. But Andy dribbles the first pitch down to first and ends the inning before anything serious can develop. So much for offense, Carl thinks—now for the top of the ninth.

Al's first pitch to QC's Louie Harriman is a swinging strike— there's nothing Lurch can do with that one—but when his second offering comes in at the letters it's called a ball. Al looks over to his manager, but all Carl can do is shrug and make a swinging motion with his forearms—make 'em hit. So Al tosses up a series of pitches too good to ignore, and soon there's two men on with none out.

As usual, Freddie Guagliardo's been throwing in the pen, so Carl decides to get him in here before Al allows a run. Freddie's a strike-out pitcher, Al isn't, and strategy dictates a clear out with no advance before one can hope for a double play.

Up in the PA booth Bill White puts on his *Godfather* tape as Freddie walks in from the pen. He's done this twenty times already this year, but apparently Lurch does not remember hearing it, for he spins around and makes a violent cutthroat gesture up toward Bill. For his point the announcer just shrugs his shoulders, but as Lurch continues motioning so emphatically Bill pops the tape in the middle of its tune, perplexing the crowd and surprising Freddie, who's just a few steps from the mound.

"Don't show me up," Bill can tell Lurch is saying to him, though with all the crowd noise it's a case of lip reading. The announcer shrugs his shoulders again and shakes his head, implying that's not been his intention at all. But Lurch is on a fine edge, there's no doubt about it.

"Don't argue any calls," Carl tells his pitcher, "Lurch has got a case of the weirds," and Freddie nods. He's roped in his curve lately, which makes it easier to call, plus he establishes each hitter with a fastball, so the umpire should have no problems. But Freddie isn't told the squeeze is on.

"Ball, high," is Lurch's first call on a pitch no more than belt level. Freddie's too startled to say anything, but the way Smitty shakes his head when tossing it back let's him know that getting the ball across won't be easy. For his second pitch he tries a slider, and though it nips the outside corner Lurch calls it a ball, too. At this Freddie just stares with hands on hips, and Smitty's return bounces past him on the side. Billy retrieves it and gives him the news about the squeeze.

Freddie has been through this before, not with Lurch or Cleaver but with other umps he or his teammates have crossed. No matter what he throws, the first three pitches will be called balls unless the batter swings. That's the psychology of the squeeze— start 'em out with a 3-0 count, then see how good they are. What comes next will be called fairly, partly to avoid the onus of a decisively bad call but mostly just to keep the pressure on. It's a hell of a way to play a ball game and an insidious style of torture to practice on a short reliever like Freddie, who's so proud of his rep as a stopper and so protective of his stats from K's to ERA.

So long as this third one is the ump's anyway, Freddie decides to have some fun. Hoping Smitty doesn't pull neck muscles snapping back to watch it sail over, Freddie uncorks one six feet high, still rising as it comes over the batter and heads toward the screen. Call that ball three and be happy, he intends, but it turns out differently. Committed to the pitch, the hitter has begun a high swing he can't hold back, tips it, and Lurch disgustedly makes the call. So with 2-1 Freddie decides to waste another. This one's a screamer high and inside which the hitter ducks, Smitty bails out on, and Lurch catches squarely in the mask. The mask comes off, the big ump staggers back a few steps, and the crowd roars its approval.

Freddie stands there grinning until his side vision catches the cloud of dust at third and then, as he looks there, another at second. He's forgotten about the men on base—a classic relief boner—and now there are two runners in scoring position with nobody out and a one-run lead to protect. This is where the squeeze will get you.

Carl calls time and joins him on the mound. What can he say? Throw strikes, take the bad counts, the disadvantage, his K-ratio is so good it doesn't matter if there's three balls on him to start. The scrappy left-hander nods seriously and Carl hurries back to the dugout, keeping his eyes off Lurch.

It all happens in the next half-second. Freddie delivers a straight-down-Main fastball he expects to have called a ball, but the batter's hitting and sends a sharp liner right past Freddie's ear. But luckily Ed's been shading over to hold the runner and walks right into the play. He reaches for the ball, steps on second, and throws quickly to third, and before anyone can stop to think it's three outs, side retired on a triple play. Even the crowd is silent until they see the infield head in and the outfield follow. For most of them this is their first triple play, and it's quite a shock.

But it's not to be, and that's the real shocker. There's Lurch over by the dugout calling the Royals back. He signals "two outs" to the pressbox, and in a flash Carl's all over him. Bill corrects the scoreboard and the crowd gets nearly as excited as their manager, who's turned beet-red and is circling Lurch with his complaints. Not that it helps at all. Lurch has just a few words with Carl, telling him that Johnny's foot left the bag at third, before heading over to the Dodgers' dugout to get the runner back on base. There's some confusion as to whom Lurch wants—the batter? the guy who'd been at third?—and while this gets sorted out Carl stands forlornly outside the dugout. With the crowd yelling and Lurch bobbing up and down, his temper has nowhere to go but the boiling point, and as soon as the ump heads back to the plate Carl's on him.

The argument looks best from thirty feet away, halfway up in the stands. From there the crowd noise smothers even Carl's harshest words, and his frantic gestures take on dramatic proportion. His jaw and shoulders work in unison, one can see from here, with five or six words for every pump of his arms. He circles the umpire as if this is an arena theater, giving everyone from the season boxes to the far bleachers a look at his climactic scene. At one point Lurch bumps him and his hat flies off. Carl doesn't stoop to retrieve it since that would ruin the blocking he's so effectively contrived. Instead he uses it as a prop, a bit of counterpoint to everything he's shouting at the unrelenting ump.

From this point the hat is part of the scene, absorbing all the violence meant for Lurch but also standing for Carl's role as manager. When Carl kicks it in the dirt he's showing what he'd like to do to Lurch, but also what Lurch has done to him. Soon the hat's indistinguishable beneath the dust, but that gives Carl the chance for some dust kicking on the umpire's shoes and trousers.

Lurch must want this to continue, because he's made no move to eject his nemesis. It even seems he's baiting Carl to keep things going, for when the manager pauses for breath the ump leans down to brush off the plate.

This begins another bit of drama, for once Lurch moves back Carl steps forward to kick some more dirt over it. The ump lets him finish, then cleans it off again, only to have the manager dirty it once more. Like foes in a Laurel and Hardy film they'll stop to eye each other between each move, and the crowd loves every minute of it.

It could go on forever—that's the beauty of it—when Carl breaks the pace, gets down on all fours and like a kid at the beach builds up a perfect mound of sand across the plate. He leans back to admire his work and then, smiling up at Lurch, places his battered cap atop the little hill.

Clean off that, his expression says, as he stands up and walks back to the dugout. But halfway there he turns to signal Freddie Guagliardo on the mound to take some warm-up throws.

As Lurch hulks beside the covered plate Freddie waits for Jim Smith to get his mask and settle into position. Then, with a puzzled look toward everyone, he leans back and throws a curve that breaks neatly over Carl's hat and pops in Smitty's mitt.

He's sure this will bring his own ejection, but as with his manager's antics it doesn't. Instead the scene rolls on in an eternity of motion, his curve balls sailing past the hat while Lurch stares at Carl walking slowly back to his dugout.

⊗ Road Work ⊗

Nobody knows why, but the Mason City Royals just aren't hitting on the road.

Up and down the line-up, Carl has found the stats fall off when his boys get out of town. Everyone's losing at least forty points, it seems, and some of the power hitters are down an even hundred. This defies all the baseball logic he's ever learned, for rule-breaking distractions such as wives, girl friends, and favorite bars are usually left behind when the guys play games away. Sure, there's some fall off when you lose the home-field advantage, but not a hundred points.

The more knowledgeable fans who clip the box scores for games both home and away have been kidding him about what pansies he's been taking on the road. "I think you should find out what Ed and Andy and the rest have got here in Mason City," one tells him, "and put it in a trailer for your next trip out."

"You want me to take these fences along?" he asks, gesturing toward the 360 sign in dead center, which marks this field as the league's smallest.

"Come on," the fan says, shaking this off, "short fences work both ways. More homers sure, but less doubles and triples, and fewer flies dropping in uncaught—and these guys hit lots more at 250 feet than 360!"

Carl admits there's some truth to this, and for the three-day trip up to Madison he decides to take careful note of what the guys do on and off the field. There's got to be a reason, he keeps telling himself, and this time he's bound to find it.

It can't be the bus ride. Mad City, as the players call it, is not quite two hundred miles—less than four hours on the road, which means they can leave as late as noon and still get to Warner Field in plenty of time for visitors' BP. The brutal nine-hour overnighter happens only with Peoria, and to Carl's recollection the team's hit okay there. Pitching's been a little thin against the Rangers, but what else are college batting champs supposed to do with a home-field advantage?

There's Earl's driving, but the trip to Madison is pretty enough that he doesn't like to rush it. Across northeast Iowa they've got steep hills, limestone defiles, and four-hundred-foot-deep hardwood forests down between the geological backbones, where the temperature will drop twenty degrees and the light darken to a cavernous green. Then across the Mississippi at Prairie du Chien, where they pick up the sandy Wisconsin River and follow it halfway through the state before turning down to Madison. Black Earth, Wisconsin, is one of Carl's favorite towns up here, named perfectly and reminding him how strongly natural most of this league territory is.

Any moment, he sometimes fancies, his outfielders might walk off into the fields and start plowing. When Al Elgin carries in the ball bucket for BP, Carl pictures him on a dairy farm. The baseball seems so natural around here, part of the landscape and the culture, as if the diamonds emerged naturally from the ground beneath and might turn back to prairie grass at any day now. So unlike his big-league days spent looking into apartment windows across Waveland and Sheffield avenues at Wrigley Field, or playing in a ball park afloat in the ocean of a concrete parking lot, Carl is enjoying this second career right here in God's country, like the beer labels say.

Back in Mason City there's a cemetery rising on a little hill just beyond the right-field wall where Andy Thompson likes to park his graveyard shots. For Andy, pulling the ball means waking the dead, and Carl suspects that ten years from now, when he's been slugging the long ball up in Royals stadium or on the road in California or New York for half a decade, Andy will use this phrase when he pulls one out.

As the bus swings up through Wisconsin, Carl pulls out his charts and sees that Andy has yet to hit one in Madison. He's socked just five of his twenty-six homers on the road, and three of those were in a doubleheader at Cedar Rapids, where the fine hitting background and big league—quality lights give him all the best conditions. So that's one thing to keep in mind tonight—

Why's Andy such a weakling when he's up in Warner Field? Background, lights, deeper fences in the alley and especially down the line? It has to be something, Carl knows, because these stats don't write themselves.

Who else tails off especially bad in Madison? The computer charts a fan has given him tell a pretty clear story about who's off up here, and Carl uses the empty seat beside him to lay out three such sheets—home stats, performance on the road, and how they've done in the games played up here in Muskie country.

He's surprised to see that Andy's not the worst: .350 at home, .258 on the road, but an impressive .283 at Madison's Warner Field. The fall-off is with slugging percentage. At home Andy's is a towering .725, but in Madison it matches his batting average, which means he hasn't had a single extra base hit. Tonight Carl vows to watch closely and learn why.

Eddie Sanmarda falls off in hitting but not so bad in slugging, so there's his control group. But worst of all is poor Billy Harmon, who loses 141 points, down from his season's .238 to a pathetic .097 in games at Madison. Something's scaring him, Carl decides—maybe just the brash hedonism of this horny college town. Billy keeps a Bible in his locker, on the same shelf where other guys park their monthly issues of *Penthouse* and *Playboy*, and one night when Andy snuck into the clubhouse between innings and wrapped a *Hustler* centerfold around it Carl was stuck till one in the morning trying to console his distraught second baseman. How do you average something like that? His charts tell the story on what pitches Billy can hit, but what about these wicked curves thrown by the culture he seems too tame for?

This kid belongs in the major leagues, Carl decides, since up there he'd find plenty of shelter. Down here in A-ball there's nothing to insulate him from nasty moments on or off the field, and Carl's always figured that's why organizations absorb such titantic expenses—close to a million apiece each year to operate a club through Double A, and well over a mil and a half for playing in the American Association, International League, or the Pacific Coast, where K.C. has its Triple A club at Tacoma. Billy would have no problems at all playing down in those instructional complexes where some clubs go through the motions of an A-ball season. But everyone knows those kids will need at least half a year of real A-ball before they can move up. Florida ball is just plain unreal—four diamonds back-to-back with games taking place on each, but no crowds or hometown loyalties and cross-state grudge matches, no all-night bus rides and searching out the area's cheapest restaurants and laundromats.

Carl thinks again of the real-world pressure up here in the Mid-continent League as they pull into Madison. Their late departure precludes a check-in at the Roadway Inn, so everything but field gear is left on the bus as they pile out at Warner Field. An empty ball park is always different from the stands at game time, but here in Madison the contrast is even more extreme. The manager always enjoys poking around the field while his boys are still down in the visitors' locker room suiting up. He walks out to the mound and surveys the empty acres around him. A sprinkler is gently swishing out in center field, and even at this distance Carl can hear the separate drops of water hit the ground. The sound of sparrows darting underneath the roof draws his attention, and from the shadows up beyond the press box he can hear the swish of swallows' wings as these delicate birds find their nests. There's some rustling around the bull-pen wall, and Carl looks quickly enough to see a gopher disappear down a hole, then pop its head back up for a look around.

It's all so peaceful, and all ending so soon. In the Royals' dugout Carl can hear that someone's opened the door, because the sound of Johnny Mueller's giant radio is blasting out a soul tune he's pulled in from the black station in Milwaukee, only place around the whole league where the guys can get such music. He knows Lynn Parson will be first out as usual, this smooth veteran who's played in Double A climbing up the dugout stairs to take sole possession of this ball field as he does all the others first day into town. Lynn likes the peaceful time as much as Carl does, so the manager wanders off to the equipment cage beneath the stands so that his left fielder can have this moment to himself.

Bits of sunlight filter through here and dust hangs in the air as Carl watches through the fencing to see his players take the field. Lynn has paused at the top, reached up to the dugout roof, and taken a liberating stretch, then relaxed to stare across the field in silence. He steps out on the gravel and all there is to hear is the crunch beneath his spikes. When he reaches the grass the sound of the center-field sprinkler takes over again and Carl sees Lynn walking out toward it.

So cool, so sophisticated, so downright smooth, Lynn makes sure no teammates have made it up the tunnel before he reaches the sprinkler and sets himself for a graceful leap. Like a kid in a summertime backyard he clears it, then turns to run and jump again. The sprinkler turns to spray behind him and Lynn disappears in a cloud of silver droplets caught by the sun. Only his shadow shows black behind him.

A rumble from the dugout turns both heads, as Carl and Lynn hear Chet dumping out a bag of bats. In a minute he's racking them up and Warner Field sounds like a league night at a bowling alley. From this clatter emerge the Mason City Royals in their traveling blues. First sight of these youngsters at the start of a road trip always gives Carl a little shock, since after seeing them in white for a week or more he has to sort out their identities from scratch in these new playing clothes. Eddie looks smaller in dark blue, Johnny bigger, and so forth down the order. No wonder they're hitting lower on the road, they look so absolutely different.

With twenty-three of them on the field the ball park takes on new dimensions. A few minutes ago Lynn seemed lost out there in center, dwarfed by the fence and surrounding stands as he frolicked with the sprinkler. The field around him seemed just a flat and empty table loomed over by the grandstand and bleachers. But now its character has shifted, brought to life by the players, who make it a living thing. There's so much movement and color, Carl reflects, as his guys in blue and white spread out across the deep-green surface and make it their own. One year at the league's All Star game Carl watched from high up in the stands as the teams broke from their line-up on the base paths to take position on the field, and for a moment all the different-colored uniforms made it look like a pool table after a sharp break. "Three ball in the side pocket!" he'd called to a friend as DH Cal Majek in his bright Dubuque jersey jumped down into the dugout and the rest of them spread out across the green.

For the next hour the field will be theirs. Then after BP and infield the fans will start drifting in, and slowly the balance will shift toward the stands.

Up here in Madison the Muskie fans have a way of keeping that balance in their favor, which convinces Carl his team's performance will be hurt. In the normal course of things the home crowd holds an upper hand, dominating the field like players leaning over a game table, until the inning's first play. That usu-

ally establishes a relationship between action on the field and response from the stands, which never tips too far either way. Except in Muskie country, where the town's combination of classy
collegiate and white-collar professionalism has embraced minor-
league baseball as the latest thing. Each night there's one more
excuse for the fans to act up, and each promotion's been zanier
than the last. The "three-thousand-voice kazoo chorus" happened earlier, as an overflow crowd rasped for hours on the tiny
noisemakers distributed free at the gates. Carl has no idea what's
planned for this series, but with no excuse at all the Muskie fans
can still drive players to distraction, as has been showing up in
the Royals' Madison stats.

Carl knows it's going to be a rough night when the place is half-
filled by the end of batting practice. Lynn's been up there hitting
last and the fans have razzed him each time his raps have failed to
clear the fences. But for infield practice it gets downright brutal
as the crowd rides each player who takes a grounder. First there's
a little bit of "whoop/whoooo" as Carl bats a ball to third and it's
thrown over to first. As long as the rhythm's steady this doesn't
hurt, but the fans know that soon the infielders will be keying
themselves off the crowd and not the ball, and that's when trouble
begins.

Billy at second is their first target, and as Carl knocks a sharp
one to him they reverse their little song, sounding out the slower
"whoooo" as the ball rockets toward Billy and then switching to
the brisker "whoop" as Billy makes his throw to first. The strategy
has blown his timing and his toss goes wild, Billy blushing as the
fans give him a cheer. Carl turns to hit a soft grounder to Eddie at
short, but when the crowd shuts up for the first time all practice
the little Panamanian stumbles and lets the ball roll by. This
effectively ends the Royals' infield and Carl forgoes the customary
pop-ups to the catcher just to get them off the diamond. That's
his first mistake, he realizes, when his ears burn to the clatter of
a standing ovation as he carries his bat to the dugout.

There's not much for the crowd to do in the thirty minutes between infield practice and game time, and Carl imagines the beer
bars do well during this break. But beered up for the line-up in-
troductions, they're back in full voice. He's seen and heard noisy
fans before, but Carl has to admit these folks in Mad City play
their rowdiness with style. Everywhere else the visitors' introduc-

tions are ignored by all but the diehard fans keeping score, but here at Warner Field the line-up card is a major event. It's starting now and Carl anticipates its rhythm.

"For the Mason City Royals, farm club of the Kansas City Royals," the announcer intones, "batting first, the shortstop, Eduardo Sanmarda."

"Who?" the crowd thunders.

"Number 28, Sanmarda," the announcer replies as he would anyway, but now as part of a dialogue the crowd's devised.

"Oh . . . " the fans sigh in a unison of disappointment. Then it's the announcer's turn again with Billy, who bats second, and so on down the order. Carl can't believe that this hocus-pocus really bothers his players, but it does get the crowd involved in things right from the start, tipping the energy balance slightly in their favor. From now on, he knows from previous trips up here, it will be a struggle between us and them.

To hear the response to the Muskies' line-up you'd assume the crowd's already won. The Madison players know it, and after their pitifully weak ninth hitter has received a standing O equal to anything Ted Williams ever got at Fenway, the team itself emerges from the dugout to applaud the crowd, which the announcer compliments as the team's tenth man.

Hitting first is not something Carl likes. Far better to have the home-field advantage, not just because you get your last swings in the ninth but because you've got that first half-inning to loosen up and calm down on the field, with the finely tuned point of your starting pitcher out there to penetrate the opposition's defense. That's also why he thinks this sport's superior to football. The offense doesn't hold the ball in baseball, the defense does, which is more like life and makes better strategic sense. But here in Madison his boys don't have the ball yet, and the only way to get a piece of it in this top of the first is to seize it from the Muskies's pitcher with their bats.

Because Eddie's expert at making contact with the ball and is fast on the bases, Carl's had him hitting first these past weeks, and the little bit he's lost in R.B.I.s is an easy sacrifice for the great increase he's made in runs scored. If he gets on—and his on-base percentage for starting games is nearly 60 percent, as his good eye gets him plenty of first-inning walks—you can trust he'll soon make second, either stealing it or having slugged his way there with a double. And with Billy hitting second, Eddie's sure to wind up on third, for the little second baseman's a genius at advancing runners. Billy doesn't have much of an average and owns very few R.B.I.s, but Carl keeps his own box score for placing bunts or grounders in the infield, which push Eddie on to third, where Johnny's long ball gets him home even if it's just a deep fly out. In 58 percent of their games, Carl knows, his Royals have put something on the board in the first. So there's his mean. Now he wants to see how playing the game up here in Madison makes for any deviation.

Thankfully, no one chants "Eduaaardo" as they've done at the Bettendorf ball park in Quad Cities. It still bothers Eddie to play down there, because he can't quite find the line between rowdy heckling and vicious racism. There's none of that in Madison, "the progressive cradle of midwestern liberalism" as Carl had seen it described in some old political literature, and he thinks it's corny and a bit ofay that the Muskie fans always take it easier on dark-skinned players. Eddie keeps his sensitivity inside, but poor Billy Harmon often wears it on his sleeve, and Carl regrets having to toss these lambs to slaughter. But the umpire's calling Eddie to the plate, so the Muskie game is underway.

For the first at-bat the fans behave as if it's baseball and not some athletic version of "The Gong Show," as usually happens up here. They cheer the pitcher's sharp fastball, which whistles in for a called first strike, and groan with displeasure when his lazy curve misses the outside corner. When a second curve drops too low Carl knows Eddie's chances are good for another fastball, so he flashes him an emphatic hit sign. Bingo, Eddie raps a sharp grounder just past the shortstop and he's standing at first, taking those little leaps that mean he's testing the spring in his legs for a steal.

As Billy steps into the box the crowd perks up. They've seen what the Royals' 1-2 combination can do before, and realize that here's where the Muskies need a tenth man. Their response is prompt and little short of overwhelming.

"Hey, section four," a couple guys above first base are yelling across the field to the fans sitting along the opposite base line, "Lite Beer from Miller tastes great!"

"Less filling!" the third-base section responds in a chorus of a hundred voices or more.

"Tastes great!" the guys above first yell once again, this time joined by the entire section behind them. And like a TV commercial, the challenge and response get rocketed across the diamond several times before they break apart in raucous laughter.

Carl's heard this routine up here before, but always between innings. He hopes Billy hasn't been upset, but knows that hope is futile as he flashes a sign down to the batter's box only to see the frightened eyes of a helpless little rabbit, crouching there beneath the dissolving laughter and waiting with trembling intentness for the pitch.

"Tastes great!" the first base section hollers as a fastball strikes the catcher's mitt.

Oh no, Carl complains to himself, as Billy springs a step backward as if bitten by a snake.

"Time," Carl calls to the umpire, and runs down to talk with his rattled hitter. Let's not make this any worse than it is already, Carl's thinking as he leans to counsel Billy, let's not say anything at all about this crazy crowd.

"Eddie's going on this one," he tells Billy, "but don't swing unless it's too good to refuse. Save your hit until he can score from second. Got it?" Billy nods yes and Carl hurries back to his third-base box.

From first Eddie catches the steal sign, and as the pitcher comes out of his stretch the little shortstop lowers his head and takes off. He's got a great jump and surely has the base stolen when the third-base stands erupt with a mighty "Less filling!" and Eddie pulls up ten feet short of the bag as the crowd behind him yells "Tastes great!"

Carl at once knows what's happened—while Eddie's feet have been gunning him toward second, part of his mind has still been on the first-base coach's sharply barked "Back!" which will abort a steal. All that clamor behind him, the manager reasons, has fouled up his base-stealing circuitry and in confusion he's running both ways at once. But there's not even a run-down as the second baseman dashes toward the stranded runner, the catcher leads him as in a pass play, and poor Eddie is humiliated with a tag-out in the top of the first.

Now Billy's left with an 0-2 count and Carl gives the sign to hit away. Fat chance, he thinks, as Billy's still shaking and now looks white as a ghost to boot. But the pitcher wastes two sliders outside before coming in with his fastball again, and Billy actually manages a hard grounder to third and get his color back running down to first. He's out by five steps, but the rhythm of his game is reestablished and Carl's happy that the contest is proceeding again.

The fans lay off Johnny, largely because the Muskies command this inning and there's no sense distracting their own pitcher. But Carl still notices a difference with Johnny, who pushes a grounder through the box, and with Andy, who gets a welcome first-inning at-bat. Back home these two are a natural 3-4 combination, as classic in their power-hitting tactics as Mathews and Aaron, Murphy and Horner, or any number of successful line-up pairs which always make a winning team. But up here in Madison Carl, who's looking for a difference, sees it from the moment Johnny steps in.

His motion in the box has been all different, Carl notes. At home Johnny is all smiles, forever looking over his left shoulder at the preteen girls who perch along the grandstand wall just beyond the dugout. Before the game they'll send him love notes, and while he's batting they're a steady cheering section. His stance includes them, which prompts him to lead the pitcher and pull the ball—just what a three-hitter with men in scoring position is supposed to do. But up here he seems painfully weak on the left side, closing in on the plate as if to shield himself from the pitcher. Half his strength has been taken away—those cute little girls, plus the sound of a supportive dugout right behind him. That's why Johnny's leaning in, Carl decides, since on the road their dugout faces first, not third. And the weakness of his hitting shows it. Properly pulled, it would have been a solid double down the line back home.

As Andy approaches the plate, Carl feels a more subtle difference. His big first baseman is a natural crowd-pleaser, always grinning and taking great delight in making the fans react. Even a long foul will stir them up, and there's no more pleasing sight than Andy pausing down the base line to acknowledge the crowd's roar when he lifts a long one over the right-field wall. At home there's always a deeper rumble in the crowd noise when he walks up to the plate, but here in Madison, of course, the fans could care less, and the quiet through which Andy must make his way drains blood and muscle from him with every step. Carl wonders if stirring up the dugout might compensate for this, but realizes how pathetic it would sound for twenty guys to whoop it up within this hostile silence. Better to get the big guy thinking game situation rather than crowd response—watch the field, not the stands! Carl yells down to him, but Andy just looks blankly out to center field as if a cat's got loose out there or something. The loss of concentration lingers and costs him a called first strike on a hanging curve he could have murdered.

An inside fastball wakes him up, but another one on the outside corner only prompts him to send a grounder straight to first. The first baseman's been holding Johnny tight and catches the ball right on the bag. Damn, Carl mutters to himself. If Johnny had pulled his hit he'd have been on second, and with the first baseman off the bag Andy's grounder would have gotten through and scored the run. So there's the difference—a one-run lead at home and still batting with a runner on second, versus a big zero up here. All that action, Carl ponders—two hits, two chances to get a guy on second—and nothing to show for it. No wonder they're unproductive on the road.

That night, in a clubhouse silent from their 4-0 loss, Carl asks his team to come out early next day for some special drills. Their road workouts are infrequent, limited to rare off days when the team's stuck out of town. But Carl has some strategies in mind to make these road trips more successful, and he needs them for an hour or two to work things out. Humiliated by their flat performance, the team lacks nerve to object.

The 1:30 practice session starts with a lecture on concentration. The game's on the field, not in the stands, Carl tells his players. They've simply got to zone out all that interference, especially when they're on the road. They think Madison is bad, just wait till their major-league club rolls into Yankee Stadium or Fenway. And what about being up there 0-2 against a fastballer who's been Cy Young once or twice and there's another fifty million watching you on "Game of the Week" or "Monday Night"?

The drills themselves are quietly routine, with just some new pointers on mental hygiene. He puts Eddie on first and stands behind him as his coach, chanting a rhythmic incantation of words that are to fill every crevice of his mind. "Stretch, set, rest, throw," Carl prompts him as his little shortstop takes his crow-steps off the bag, shoulders hunched and arms dangling like a video-game Space Invader facing the pitcher while he makes a crablike sideways motion toward second. Now, once Robin's committed to the plate, Carl shouts "Go!" This word's supposed to trigger another chant for Eddie, a sharply stuttered "safe-safe-safe" as each foot strikes the ground taking him to second. Carl's told Smitty to use his best throw, but even with Robin tossing high fastballs Ed can't be caught. Winded from his ten straight steals, he's sent off to the Gatorade cooler while Carl turns to work with his power-hitting team.

Getting Johnny to open up is hard, even in this neutrally empty field. There's nothing here to intimidate him except a bunch of loose candy wrappers blowing in the stands, but that's enough to make him hunch in protectively toward the plate—surely, Carl knows, feeling these are the few square inches of this field he can hope to control. And right there's the problem.

"Mueller!" Carl yells, and then his nickname, "Mule Train!" As Johnny stands there with his bat Carl gives him a little inspirational talk on the power of positive hitting. He's patient and specific.

"You got a thirty-eight-ounce bat there, Johnny," his manager tells him.

"You bet!" Johnny grins, proud of the weight he swings.

"And how much does that baseball the pitcher has weigh?" Carl asks him.

"Five ounces," the slugger answers matter of factly.

" 'Bout as much as a couple Crystal burgers, right?" Carl prompts him and gets a happy laugh in return, as Johnny thinks of those tiny hamburgers sold back home in Georgia.

"Now you mean to tell me," Carl begins to hector him, "your thirty-eight-ounce bat can't send his little five-ounce Crystal burger just about anywhere in this whole ball park?" Carl gestures expansively, then turns back to the plate. "So what are you doing huddled down all chickenlike around this little bitty plate?"

"Got ya, Skip," Johnny nods, and for the rest of his swings acts like he owns the plate.

But what to do for Andy? If any problem is psychological, it's his. His average sinks a solid hundred points on the road, consistently, not just in bull pits like Madison but in the tamer parks as well. What can you do with a boy who loves to hotshot for the crowd? He'll put 'em out in Mason City for the cheers, but when folks boo him for doing that his heart just can't get in on it. One hell of a clean-up hitter this guy is whenever they leave town.

So let's get him out of the clean-up spot. Carl wants to kick himself for not thinking of this before. Put Andy down to six or seven on road trips, where odds are he'll have a runner or two on base or else be a second- or third-inning lead-off man himself. Hit singles, get on base, advance runners, pick up an easy R.B.I. with a sac fly, maybe even bunt. All these things will get his mind back in the game. Plenty of chances back home in Mason City to let big Andy stand there at the plate and be thinking of clearing off the bases with one swing. For road trips Lynn will hit fourth—such a steady veteran is impervious to fish cheers, Miller Lite commercials, and anything else these Madison zanies can throw at him. Back in the dugout Carl's clipboard stats confirm it—.289 at home, .281 on the road. Carl wishes he'd looked this up before.

He leaves his pitching coach to finish out the drills in more routine fashion. Mack's such an old-timer that he'll have the pitchers running wind sprints and the infield playing pepper, but mindless stuff like that is perfect mulch to rake over the new tactical principles he's planted in their minds today. He'll be depending upon Eddie to keep his mind on base running and for Johnny to open up. With Andy thinking singles and Lynn hitting clean-up they just might get some offense tonight. Young Billy's asked him what his own new role is, and Carl hasn't had the heart to tell him just to stop shaking like a leaf. But surrounded by some strong hitters with their heads on straight, his two spot should be secure. "Just make contact, son." Carl's let him off, and the manager's amused to see his quiet little infielder repeating the words to himself as if hearing them the first time.

Up here in Madison the visitors' clubhouse is new, part of the stadium's upgrading when the Muskies joined the league last year. So there's even a visiting manager's office of sorts, a little alcove just beyond the tunnel with a small desk, steel chair, wastebasket, and even a calendar and league-rules poster tacked on the wall. Here Carl squirrels himself away for half an hour, spreading out his home/road stats and studying the separate print-out for games at Madison. Lynn isn't the only player who stays relatively level on the road—a few utility men claim the same distinction, and Carl finds that Herman Escobar and Angel Naboa hit Madison pitching best. That includes the ten games back in Mason City, too, but since there's been no appreciable fall-off here at Warner Field he decides to count their twenty at-bats each against the Fish as statistically significant.

So Donny Moore and Dave Alpert, whose Madison averages have been a disgrace for reasons Carl can't fathom, will ride the bench tonight while Angel and Herman take over center and right. This will give the added advantage of making Lynn happy out in left, since for some reason Latin players are more hip to his clowning out there. Having his fielders loose can't hurt.

Carl's putting Angel in the nine spot when the team starts trooping in, first the infielders fresh from pepper, then the thoroughly winded pitchers. Mack trots in last, beaming with satisfaction from the re-creation of a typical Washington Senators' weekday drill at Griffith Stadium. But nobody's stripped to shower yet, and Carl realizes they're wondering if it's worth it when BP starts in half an hour.

"No BP, just an easy infield," Carl shouts over his shoulder as he runs back down his line-up card, and the team cheers its approval. In less than a minute the quicker ones are in the showers, and Carl feels his paper work go limp as clouds of steam billow over his desk and struggle toward the cooler air blowing up the clubhouse tunnel to the field. He takes his customary perch on the first step down at the home-plate end. Looking back, he can see the steam clouds catching the afternoon sunlight, then dissolving into silver droplets that scatter out across the field. The grass is greener, he notes, along the path these currents take.

For the next hour and a half Warner Field is quiet. The batting cage has been hauled out, but it sits unused until the Muskies start drifting in at four o'clock. By five the Fish are taking their swings, with a few fans out here early studiously noting fine points such as the opening of a stance and the shifting of weight. When the park's this empty and the PA's not blaring rock-'n'-roll you can hear everything, and Carl listens to the intelligent conversations drifting his way from the boxes back behind the plate.

This could be just about any A-ball park in America at five o'clock, he thinks. What a shame that in less than three hours the place will be transformed into a madhouse.

To Carl's surprise it doesn't even take half that time. Their assistant GM stops by the dugout, where he's basked in peaceful sunshine these past two hours, sorting out his thoughts, with the rude awakening that tonight the gates will open a full hour early. When Carl asks what for, he's told it's a big promotion, "boom-box night," and they're expecting capacity, which is six thousand fans. Lord Almighty, Carl wants to say, but stops short of asking what "boom-box night" entails. Given Mad City's habits, he's sure he can't imagine anything worse than what will be, so better to rest easy with his more modest paranoia.

There's a quiet murmur of radios and tape players Carl can hear from the clubhouse, but soon he's aware of a more synthetic sound coming from out behind the stands. As it ebbs and flows a few times through the quiet stadium Carl's curiosity gets the best of him, and he stretches, shakes out the kinks from the late-afternoon inactivity, and climbs up the grandstand aisle to see what's up.

At the top, to the right of the press box, he can look down at the park's main gate. They haven't opened yet, and the fans who walked in early are being urged outside to wait, but at least a thousand more are on hand, lined up two abreast in kindergarten fashion and snaking back five hundred feet across the parking lot. Carl's surprised they're not holding hands, and notes again that only in Wisconsin could you find such perfect discipline in lining up for organized madness. He'd see it in his playing days when visiting Milwaukee, and also remembers that it was in front of the Shroeder Hotel that a traffic cop ticketed him for jaywalking. What a city, what a state. Pure looney-tunes, and he's glad they'll get home tomorrow.

What this line of fans is doing makes them ripe for a twenty-first-century panorama of America's Dairyland gone mad. They've all got gigantic radios, Carl sees, and there's a corny-looking guy in top hat and tails followed by a vaudevillian young woman in a skimpy- but flouncy-looking costume leading the line of fans in a weird electronic cheer. Carl recalls them from the "three-thousand-voice kazoo chorus" his team endured their first trip here in May —Ron Gold and his lovely assistant Karen, they call themselves, and they're the semi-official Muskie mascots who organize the club's wildest promotions.

Tonight it's got something to do with those huge ghetto-blaster radios, and Carl decides he's witnessing a warm-up drill of sorts. There's been a scattered cacaphony of broadcast noises as Ron gets organized, but as he holds up a large sign reading 108 FM a uniform sound emerges of an announcer reading farm-market reports. This is not to Ron's liking and so he tries a sign reading 98.6 FM, and when a Cars tune breaks forth from the thousand radios he smiles with satisfaction. His lovely assistant Karen then takes his cue cards and hands him two illuminated devices, what the airport ground crew uses to direct big planes.

With a flourish he points them straight up, then lowers them with a firmly authoritative gesture. Like magic—or, better yet, as if there are strings from his fingers to each of the thousand radios—the sound vanishes. He then points at the line's beginning and motions upward. Their radios come alive, and as he roller coasters down the rank and file the sound of FM 98.6 rises and falls like a musical snake. It's really a beautiful sensation, and Carl waves back to his pitching coach to come on up and see. Maybe tonight won't be so bad after all.

☻ Sweet Jayne ☻

When Dave Alpert introduced himself in spring training as coming from New Jersey and Lynn Parson asked "Which exit?", everybody knew they had a potential wimp on their hands when he answered, "Twenty-four, you from Jersey, too?" Through the end of camp Lynn teased him mercilessly, asking "You from Jersey?" every time they met and replacing Dave's locker name tape with "Exit 24."

But Dave's a good-hearted kid with solid talent even if he's small and underweight, and everyone—including Lynn—has wound up liking him. Especially when his wife, Jayne, joins them in Mason City once her college courses at Montclair State are done.

Jayne's a knockout in both body and mind. Small like Dave, she's got a punkish cuteness she plays up with clothes and cosmetics. And her personality is a shiny Jersey brass, Joan Rivers at a pert age twenty-one. She's got a comeback for every line and makes a big hit with the fans down behind the screen, who never know if she's crazy or for real.

One night she spends chattering about underweight players, including spindly Angel Naboa, who looks like he could stand a few more pounds. Jayne's tried for years to beef up Dave—milk shakes and grilled cheese sandwiches right before bed have so far worked the best—but Angel's wasted frame has her in a fit.

"Lew, I wish I could speak Spanish," she confides to the old retired grocer who treats the players' wives to bingo cards and lucky-number programs every night.

"Why's that," Lew asks, "do you have to study it at school next year?"

"No, Lew," she explains, stroking his pants leg so charmingly as she tells what's on her mind. "You see, Angel's wife is over there behind the dugout, and while she's visiting this week I could ask her if she's ever tried cooking Mexican for him. You know, that style of food can be quite fattening!"

Lew tries not to laugh as he says he bets Angel has run into some of that Mexican cooking before, that it's probably just his metabolism. He finds Jayne to be the wackiest thing he's seen in twenty years of sitting with the wives, but wonders if she's putting him on. She's certainly pulling his leg, but that's just because everyone out East these days is all touchy-feely, he's seen it on TV.

"Metabolism! Lew, that's it!" Jayne's all excited and decides to tell Andy Thompson, who speaks good Spanish and is pretty brainy and informed to boot, that Angel should spend next week on a macrobiotic diet to get things working right. She'll send along some rice for late-night snacks when they're playing up in Eau Claire, for Dave's heard the rooms have coffee makers which double as hot plates.

Jayne's outspoken about a lot of things, and never balks at dragging out the players' private lives, especially when another wife's involved. Scrapes and scuffs and other ball-game injuries are a favorite topic, with the girls as candidly physical about their husband's bodies as are the guys in their own locker-room camaraderie.

"Don't you just hate it when Al gets a strawberry?" she asks the pitcher's wife, and old Lew blushes to hear Jayne carry on for the next half-inning about how such oozing sores mess up the bed sheets especially bad when she and Dave have sex. Jayne's certainly of another generation, Lew keeps telling himself, but he loves her manners nonetheless. After all, it's to keep feeling young that Lew sits down here and treats the girls, and Jayne certainly has him feeling that.

Nothing fazes her, not Lew's teasing or her own untangling webs of stories from back home. She'll talk about how great the swimming and fishing are in the shallows off Wilson Beach. That's one of Lew's favorites, which he gets her to retell each time a different friend drops by for an inning or two in the box. Jayne will rave about the water temperature that feels like a bathtub and the fish Dave catches almost two feet long. "I know this sounds horrible," she concludes, "but it's right near this big nuclear power plant," and the fans crack up as she admits they've probably all been poisoned—but still Wilson Beach, New Jersey, is the greatest place to be.

Before games Dave will come over to the screen to see her and exchange a few words, but he keeps pretty quiet with the fans. He seems a shy type, to match his slender build, and everyone wonders how the two of them hit it off together. "I'll bet that young woman's got herself right in the driver's seat," Lew tells all his friends, and they all agree that Jayne's the one in control. Even on the field, where her husband seems content to be a wide-ranging center fielder kept in the line-up for his sparkling defense, popping out of the shadows to pull down everything hit his way and then eluding attention until the next great play. Jayne knows he'll never get above A-ball with a .235 batting average—center field is a run-producing position—and she's been working at his being more aggressive at the plate, meaning both hitting fastballs and eating good food.

What puzzles everyone are all the stories from the road. Up in Eau Claire, for example, the paper carried a report that Dave socked a homer over 450 feet, when at home most times he makes contact the infielders can handle the play. One of Lew's friends adds up the box scores and finds that Dave's hitting .320 on the road and only .110 when the team's at home. Lew tries bringing this up discreetly with Jayne, but discreet's a style she'll never learn.

"Why Lew, every time Dave and I make love I give him an extra milk shake right after!" she proclaims with a passion, and Lew blushes because she's not done yet. "And I double the wheat germ on his cereal next morning," she adds. "Believe me, Lew, sex has nothing to do with it!" All this has Lew red as a stoplight, but Jayne goes on a bit more until something on the field distracts her and she's off on another subject.

Next time up Jayne cheers Dave even more than her customary ringside manner, and Lew is frightened she'll start telling the whole ball-park what he'd only meant to imply. But her noise is just standard jock talk, and for all its static doesn't do her hubby much good. With the pitcher bearing down on Dave, his bat wobbles weakly and his front foot shifts around in the box, and everyone can see his concentration visibly wandering. Baseball's said to be a game of intangibles, but Lew can see the problem plain as day—Dave's not intimidated by this fastballer, it's living in the same town as Jayne that's got him timid as a mouse.

On the road Dave's stats pile up and so do rumors of his conduct. The fact that fans at home know only one side of this center
fielder makes it fun for Lew to tease his friends with stories. Days
as free as his nights, the old grocer hangs around town to pick up
talk, and afternoons he'll sometimes swing by the ball park to
learn what's new. The day the team's due back from a road trip is
the best, as the GM's office is usually full of problems to solve.

That night Lew sashays down to his box like the cat that ate the
canary. He's heard a dandy in the office and has decided to play it
out among his friends before the wives show up at game time.

"Seems we had some police business up in Madison, boys," he's
pleased to announce, his straight face feigning a seriousness to
which his story's end will give the lie. His statement stirs up lots
of hurried questions.

"Yep, one of our players got arrested—spent the night in jail
and would still be up there now if Jeff hadn't phoned the Muskies'
president and had him pull some strings with the judge."

Everyone wants to know who, but Lew says they'll have to wait
until he tells the whole story.

And a pretty good story it is. The guys and the positions they
play are a ready-made cast of characters, certainly plenty of them
for a good dramatic mix. No need to invent something for them to
do—as ballplayers they're doing it already, playing in a made-up
game that everyone pretends is real. Only reason first base is
ninety feet from home is because everyone agrees to put it there
and not somewhere else, but once in place you can keep a realistic
history of who gets there and how. Lew comes out here for such
stories and he makes no excuses for it. He just likes to keep the
stories good.

"Turns out Smitty has a lady friend up there," Lew begins, and
his younger friends translate his archaic thirties terms into con-
temporary fact, taking the gal Lew's picturing in a floral print dress
with red shoes and matching purse and putting her back in cutoff shorts and halter top and probably bare feet, as she should be.

"Seems the boys thought Jim was going to sneak her up to his
room"—images of house detectives in double-breasted suits lurk-
ing behind a potted fern near the elevator, with Red Skelton at the
desk in a bellboy's uniform. Through this fantasy Lew keeps an
eye out for Jayne as he weaves his story based on things he's
heard around the ball park earlier this afternoon. He even works
in an Abbott and Costello scene, with two players hassling Jim as

he brings his local honey up the back stairs—really the open balcony that gives access to half the rooms at Madison's Roadway Inn—which his friends transpose to the proper layout and a younger comedy team.

Lew proceeds with a *Phantom of the Opera*–style narrative as the displaced roommate climbs to the balcony and sets out across the coffee-shop roof, planning to do some peeking through the catcher's window and give the boys a blow-by-blow account next morning at breakfast. But some other guests spot him catting across the roof and call the cops, sure that it's a prowler. A plainclothes squad answers and the ballplayer is surprised not by Smitty and his naked damsel but by two tough-looking guys in sweatshirts, jeans, and sneakers coming up behind him.

They grab him, he resists, "and they whale the living bejesus out of him," old Lew laughs.

"So who was it?" his friends insist, and Lew makes them guess. They run through a half a dozen likely suspects—the team's cutups and comedians, then the party boys whose averages dip a hundred points on the road, and the notorious all-around high livers—when Lew stops them to say they will never guess it the way they're going.

"Dave Alpert!" he reveals with a guffaw, and nobody can picture it. Unless they do it as a Jerry Lewis role in a film comedy, and for once their fantasies all coincide. But when Lew tries to tell them about Dave's call home for bail money, no one can imagine Jayne at the other end of the line. How would she act and what would she say? For that they'll have to wait for Jayne herself, which is just where Lew has timed things to leave them.

He looks up to see the object of their wonder walking down the aisle. Jayne looks her perfect self, just enough makeup to sharpen her already acute features and give a hint of Jersey toughness around her pretty mouth and sparkling, playful eyes. If there's been trouble in the Alpert household she doesn't show it, but Lew has no patience for small talk tonight and pops the question soon as she's said hello.

She's flabbergasted that they've heard and is pretty embarrassed. The GM promised to keep the story quiet, she says, but like everything else in this little toy world out here. . . . Yet she can't stay upset because she's anxious to add her own two cents to the narrative, and these fans are such good listeners.

"There I was, after one in the morning, and I'd just put my bird to bed"—Jayne's the proud and talkative owner of a parakeet, which from time to time gets loose and makes for more good stories in the box—"when the phone rings and it's Dave calling from jail!"

Lew is smiling, his eyes flashing to match Jayne's as if they're in collusion.

"Now don't say anything, Lew!" Jayne warns him with a giggle. "Dave isn't like what you think at all! All the guys are calling him a voyeur, but you know as well as I do he's not the type to WP."

"WP?" Lew asks.

"Window-peep—don't kids do that out here?" Jane asks. "Back in Jersey ten-year-olds do that, the ones who turn out rowdy. So Dave's really embarrassed."

Lew now turns around to his friends for a bit of indirect teasing, his favorite way of having fun with Jayne. "Now wouldn't you boys say," he asks rhetorically, "that fighting off a squad of cops, being caught red-handed in the act, and calling to be bailed out of the slammer after midnight makes for rowdy behavior?" He gets the gang laughing and turns to Jayne as if to challenge her with this raft of facts.

"My God!" Jayne blushes, playing up the effect. "You know all that? Lew, if you spread all this around how can I face the other wives? It's bad enough for Dave with the guys!"

"Why, let the people—Dave included—know that there's no Jekyll and Hyde act he's pulling off when he's on the road. Let 'em know you're behind him 100 percent on this and everything else. Then maybe he'll start showing some spunk here at home! If you ask me, he's been holding back for fear of coming on too strong in front of you."

"In front of me?" she asks in disbelief.

"Yes, young lady, in front of you! Seems like he's afraid of making us all wonder who wears the pants in your family." Lew says this with a laugh, but there's a lesson there nonetheless. He makes his point with a question.

"Now Jayne," he asks her, "did you and Dave go together all through high school?"

"Absolutely!" she says with pride. "One and one, all the way."

"And what were you doing all that time Dave must have been the big star in sports? And I know he was if the Royals drafted him so high."

"I was a cheerleader," Jayne reports.

"Captain of the squad?"

"You bet," she nods proudly.

"And did your cheering ever become bigger than the game?" Lew's lowered his voice to a gentler tone for this, but the words still have a little bite. Still, Jayne makes sure to take it as a joke.

"You know me, Lew," she admits, "I really get involved in things, but. . . . "

"Were there more people watching you than Dave out there?"

To this Jayne just smiles, and Lew knows he's made his point. But the fact that she doesn't have a quick comeback bothers him, and when they finish the night without another word about the subject Lew figures that Jayne's got something in mind. Whenever she's quiet, he's learned, it means she's cooking something up.

What's cooking isn't clear until the next night. When Jayne's not there by game time Lew worries he may have stepped on some tender toes and hopes Jayne's not been offended. No, that wouldn't be like her at all. But he still wonders what's going to happen, particularly when he calls Dave over to ask where's his wife and he gives Lew that same pixielike smile Jayne uses when she's got a trick in mind.

Lew settles down to watch the game and has just about forgotten the business with Dave and Jayne when he hears her name mentioned on the PA. Bill White has begun his customary introduction to the third frame, "Wendy's Inning," which features free fast-food meals for fans whose names are drawn when each batter makes a hit, and adds that for this occasion the center fielder's wife, Jayne Alpert, will handle the duties of calling each at-bat.

Talk about Joan Rivers—Jayne takes over the mike like a pro and her voice booms through the stadium at a decibel level Bill White has never risked. At once the verbal action from the booth outclasses the action on the field, and Lew looks at his friends knowingly. So this is what he gets, his glance tells them, when he opens his mouth to Jayne. But something nice is happening, for just as the old retired grocer and his buddies animated the story of Dave's window-peeping and subsequent bust with images from movies and TV, Jayne's now bringing the team to life in a way the fans on their own could never guess. And as she does it a virtual novel in action unfolds, the saga of the Royals' A-ball team playing out their short season here in northern Iowa. Lew's especially tickled with how she pulls it off.

Nicknames—that's her secret. The regulars out here pride

themselves in knowing the more obvious ones, including "Guags" for Freddie Guagliardo and of course "The Cat" for that kid Frito who passed through at mid-season. But nobody could guess the bevy of names sweet Jayne now brings into play. Maybe she's making some of them up, Lew likes to think, approving because it makes a better story. Anything's fine by him as long as it does that, that's what baseball's here for.

Eddie Sanmarda's the new lead-off hitter—the manager has moved him up since Donny Moore's started hitting for power—and his popularity makes it easy for Jayne to start some by-play with the fans.

"Hitting first for the Royals," she announces, "is the pride of Panama City, little Ed Sanmarda! Let's hit one, Sticks!" That's a new one for the ball-park crowd, as is Billy Harmon's—"Monkey Nose"—with which she introduces him as he steps up to hit second. Shy Billy's blushing and he takes the first two pitches for called strikes. But Jayne urges him on and gets the fans cheering, and the second baseman finds some sudden power and drives the ball sharply to left. Solid-hitting Johnny Mueller—"Mule Train," as Jayne calls him, another the fans have never heard—intimidates the pitcher who works around him with an assortment of stuff just missing the corners, running up a 3-1 count, which Jayne mocks from the booth.

"This thrower's been watching too much 'Game of the Week' stuff with all that big-league finesse," she kids him, "he thinks he's Seaver or Carlton for sure," and as the pitcher steps off the mound the crowd begins to hoot. Up to Jayne's challenge, he uncorks one down the middle and Johnny tags it out.

This gives Jayne the chance to play around with the bulk of the Royals' lineup, each of which she identifies by his clubhouse name—"Piggy" for Donny Moore, who's earned it by having more clothes tossed around the floor than hanging in his locker; "Elmer" for Jim Smith, who the fans have known just as "Smitty," because when loaded down with all his catching gear he looks like Elmer Fudd and also because his hunting stories are always about rabbits; then "Romeo" for Andy Thompson, the groupie's favorite heartthrob; and "Slick" for fancy, hip Lynn Parson, who plays left field with a laid-back California style never seen before in Mason City.

Mark Wiggins, slumping since late May, has been dropped to the number-eight spot as DH, last before Jayne's own weak-hitting husband. Everyone's hoping Dave will get to bat in this fantastic inning Jayne's announced, but after she improvises the name "Popeye" from one of Dick Crews's sports columns Mark contradicts her by topping a weak little roller back to the mound. The Royals take the field with a commanding 4-0 lead, but the crowd's still anxiously waiting to see how Jayne will introduce her husband, Dave.

Will it be with the label Lynn Parson hung on him in spring, "Exit 24"? Or something personal of her own? As the top half of the inning concludes the fans notice Dave looking up at the press box as he lopes in from center. There's been nothing hit out there this game, so no one has a clue to what she'll say. Dave's in the dugout just long enough to grab a bat, and the suspense builds as he stands before the crowd taking practice swings and tarring the handle of his bat while the pitcher throws his eight warm-ups. Dave kicks the dirt, steals a look up toward Jayne, then shyly turns to fiddle with the tar rag once she's caught his eye.

She times it perfectly. With the pitcher ready and the umpire moving in to take his position, Jayne begins her intro. "Playing center field for the Royals," she intones, and Dave tosses down the rag, kicks away the weighted doughnut, and takes his first steps to the plate. "It's that phenom from New Jersey some call 'Flash' and others know as 'The Peeper'. . . ."

Dave isn't blushing but the fans nearby can detect a small, embarrassed smile while Jayne continues. "That future golden glover who feels if two-thirds of the world is covered with water, he'll cover the rest. . . . "

The crowd is now cheering Jayne as much as Dave, and she continues on her roll. "My husband"—at this the fans break into a long spontaneous roar—"who's come direct to us from the lockup at the Dane County Jail"—the cheers now crescendo into an ear-splitting yell—"who tonight will start showing us he can hit his bail money if not his weight, and show as much spunk on the field as off"—some laughs are now breaking out but the cheering's not abated—"that scourge of the plain-clothes burglary squad, Dave"—she makes a slight pause while the noise reaches a fever pitch—" 'Boom-Boom' Alpert!"

☹ Freddie's Up ☹

For all the petty discipline problems he brings about, Freddie
Guagliardo is still one of the manager's favorites, so when Carl
sees his name on the reassignment papers just arrived from
Kansas City he takes careful and immediate note.

He knows they're not a release. The season ends tomorrow, and
anyway Guagliardo's the most unreleasable guy on the squad. His
stats this year are awesome—1.91 ERA with twenty saves, plus
something no other pitcher from top to bottom in the Royals' organization can boast, which is more strike-outs than innings
pitched. No, the club will never release Freddie. Even without
such a good year they'd find a place for him, simply because of his
four years' service in A-ball.

He's been the bull-pen stopper while four classes of prospects
have done their time in Mason City before heading up or out, and
for keeping the team competitive all this while the farm office
owes him something. If he doesn't get promoted by his sixth year
and if no other club grabs him when he's unprotected, the Royals
will make room for him as an "organization man"—a player-
coach in Double A, teaching sharper prospects what he knows
but cannot execute himself, or a patchwork of assignments supervising pitchers in Extended Spring and Winter Instructional
Ball.

But Carl's way ahead of himself. The fact that it's an overnight
express-delivery man who's handed him the envelope is a pretty
good clue these papers are not routine, not when sending them
costs twenty dollars. And what about the handwritten memo
from Tom O'Reilly saying that if Carl needs Freddie for the championship game he can disregard that September 1 reporting date

and just let the young left-hander get in sometime late that night
or the day after?

Guagliardo going all the way to K.C.? To the bigs? Carl flips
hurriedly through the first several pages to the destination line
on page four, and there it is—Kansas City, Missouri. In six years
of coaching and managing Carl's never had a player jump straight
from A-ball to the bigs, and even though this is just a September
call-up, when the teams expand their rosters, it still gives him a
shiver of excitement. His own career in the Phillies organization
was a long, hard grind, stopping for a year or more at each of
minor-league baseball's four stations, until after seven years' service Carl was given a season and a half in Philadelphia totaling
just eighty-five at-bats. But even that last jump from Triple A to
Philly was monumental, and Carl can remember how awed he
was reporting to Connie Mack Stadium that first afternoon after
flying in on Allegheny. Now Guags will make the leap all the way
from Class A. Well, the kid deserves it.

It's still so early in the afternoon that Carl has no one to share
the news with—even Jeff is out of the GM's office, "buying popcorn oil," as the note clipped to his door says. So Carl wanders
back through the empty clubhouse and stops before Freddie's
locker. Unlike the others, it's neat and clean. This kid takes his
baseball seriously, and for all his off-field and pregame cutups he
sometimes reminds Carl of an altar boy—scrappy when he needs
to be, but a tough believer in the rituals he helps perform. Carl
makes a mental note to ask him if he's ever served Mass. He wants
to keep a clear and complete picture of this young man, especially
since tomorrow he'll take the first step that may put him forever
beyond reach.

He's not staying here for the league championship game, that's
for sure. Carl has Robin Haas all primed for that contest, and in
his last three starts he's gone the distance each time. But even if
Robin wasn't so reliable, Carl would never cheat poor Freddie of
even half a day in the bigs. His own days as a utility infielder were
so fast and few, and sometimes these September kids get just one
appearance. So let's give Freddie every possible chance. Besides,
his four years' toil have made him a local hero to these Mason City
fans. Letting them send him off to the big leagues on this final
night of the A-ball season will prime everyone for the championship game. Who knows, tomorrow Freddie could be closing out a
game in Kansas City while Robin's shutting down Cedar Rapids

back here. Who are the Royals playing? Carl reaches for a schedule he sees in Freddie's locker. Detroit. Yes, that would be something.

Carl puts the schedule back and brushes against the toy tractor some fans bought Freddie after that time he tore around the infield on the grounds keeper's rig. That's the one time Freddie really felt his wrath, both face to face and in the pocketbook. That crazy stunt lightened Freddie's wallet by a solid hundred bucks, and now Carl realizes the kid will miss out on a big haul when before the championship game all fines will be returned—a little gesture of thanks and reward from a manager whose stock will rise in the organization thanks to their winning play.

He'll mail the hundred to K.C., maybe asking O'Reilly to have George Brett pass it on to Freddie. That was Carl's own intro to the major leagues, when the first person he brushed shoulders with in the Philly clubhouse was Richie Ashburn.

Carl's returning the fines because the players have stuck behind him, not just because they've won. He knew he had a winning club halfway through spring training when Ed Sanmarda started seeing pitches and his power boys, Mueller and Thompson, began clicking together. For a while he thought he'd challenge the league with a power offense, strong hitting going 3-4-5 with Ed, Johnny, and Andy, but winning has become more intelligent since he switched Eddie to the number-one slot and played him on the bases strategically. Their percentage has jumped since then, and Carl thinks the brains have helped. Rather than just pounding it out like a bunch of flatfooted heavyweights, his hitters now function like a finely tuned machine. Do this, then that, and odds are what you want will happen. It's an instructional part of minor-league baseball which never gets the proper emphasis, but this year's team sure has it.

Among the pitchers, Freddie is the one who's picked up this style of thoughtful play. For all the previous years he'd just been breaking off those roundhouse curves—a good talent, but something he was running into the ground. He'd let it make him an A-ball fixture, his badge of consistent inconsistency. When it worked it was his out pitch, but when it didn't he'd find himself 2-0 or 3-0 and have to throw fastballs, surprising no one and often giving up a home run.

This year he's learned to pitch. As the short relief stopper he's strictly an eighth- and ninth-inning man—the full line-up never sees him, not even on consecutive nights—and so it's hard for batters to pound his first pitch, which this year has usually been a fastball or hard slider. Then something off-speed for strike two. The big curve has become a real out pitch now, something it should have been all along. It's what O'Reilly noticed when he came down here in July and asked Carl for more elaborate reports on—counts for each out, pitch positions, and so forth. So the call to Kansas City shouldn't be that much of a surprise.

But when the pitching coach comes in and sees the papers on Carl's desk, he seems plenty surprised. He's been around so much longer than Carl he can tell what they are just by the different color of the top sheet—shocking white, full bond, rather than the pressure-sensitive crap the farm director usually sends them. His first guess isn't Freddie.

"Who's going up?" he asks the manager. "Sanmarda? K.C. got an infield injury?" Short-term backup for someone on the DL is the only reason Mack can figure why one of their boys might be getting the big call. "Parson?" he tries again. "They short of jokes in the clubhouse? Need a deep baritone in the shower?"

"Guagliardo," Carl tells him and lets the old veteran react as he will.

"Well I'll be!" Mack chortles, but Carl's glad to see his smile is spreading and sustained—the coach is as happy as he is. For all the harmless trouble he's caused, everybody still loves Guags.

"You want him in the pen for Cedar Rapids?" Carl asks and Mack at once says no, he expects a full game from Robin. Besides, the other relievers are rested, there are three, maybe four guys he could ask to go short. Tonight, in fact, he's recommending two long men share the game, just to spread the work around.

"So should we send him home now?" Carl considers. There's really no need to delay his packing half a day.

"Listen," Mack counsels, "you let the word out he's going all the way up, you're going to have a party on your hands and not a ball game." Carl realizes at once that he's right. Guags is such a favorite that any word of his success will be cataclysmic.

"Yeah," Carl agrees, "I can see waiting until after the game, 'cause these monkeys are going to be ready for a celebration anyway. Might as well give them something better to party on than just the last regular game."

Mack has another piece of sound advice. "Now what about the fans?" he asks wryly. "You want them shut out of it till they read tomorrow night's paper? Now that's just plain unfair!"

Guags is a big crowd pleaser, so Carl doesn't need to be convinced. Rather than explain it all to Mack he just picks up the phone, buzzes Jeff, who's now back in the GM's office, and tells him what's up, all the time keeping Mack's attentive and approving eye.

Freddie Guagliardo's going up to K.C. tomorrow, he tells the GM, but says to keep it quiet. Win or lose, Freddie will pitch the eighth. Let him do his usual one-two-three, and as he comes off the mound Carl will give him the news. That way he walks right out of A-ball and into the bigs. And please have Bill White make the announcement right then to the fans. Mack is smiling again, anticipating the moment's drama. Times like this make all the work of coaching surely worth it.

Banging lockers in the clubhouse signal some early arrivals, and when two or three radios start playing, all blasting out different tunes, the rhythm for tonight's game begins. Its pace includes a half-hour of horseplay around the lockers, suiting up and a few loose throws outside the dugout, then twenty minutes of stretching exercises in left field. Carl and Mack keep sneaking looks at Guags as he goes through these paces with the rest, figuring he'll pull one last prank by which they can all remember him. But their hoped-for drama fails to happen—the late afternoon is going just too damn routinely—and once the game is underway Mack starts playing some scenes himself.

The hapless Eau Claire Kings are their draw for the final series, and their ragtag assortment of utility men gives the Royals little to sharpen on for the league championship tomorrow. So one by one, as the innings roll by and the Mason City lead mounts, Mack calls a pitcher down to his end of the bench to run him through his game. Keith Henley, daydreaming at ease among the other starters, is first.

"Now keep this to yourself," the old coach tells him, "but Guagliardo's going up."

"Next year?" Keith asks.

"Tonight," Mack announces with a smile.

But Keith is all frowns. "Come on, Double A closes tonight with us and they're out of the play-offs. You mean next spring, don't ya?"

"Who said Double A?" Mack prods.

"Tacoma?" Keith gasps. "For their last week? They're in a race, man, they need a stopper? What's wrong with Jeff Copeland?"

Mack is loving every minute, and takes some time to tell him Copeland's fine, getting a save a night, before asking the question, "Who said Tacoma?"

Keith's half-smile keeps him from mouthing a long, protesting "No," and Mack's already cautioning him to keep quiet. But when he tells his young starter to send over Al Elgin, Keith becomes an accomplice and hurries down the bench to call his friend.

By the time Freddie has grabbed his bag and walked down to the bull pen for his customary late-inning duty, most of the squad know he's really headed for K.C. But to keep things straight Carl tells him to start throwing in the bottom of the seventh, that even though the team is sitting on a six-run lead and he's putting in the reserves he wants Freddie sharp "for tomorrow night." It's his own private joke that he hasn't said where.

There's nothing climactic about Guags's eighth inning, as he walks his first runner, erases him in a double play, but then allows two back-to-back singles before working the Kings' weakest hitter to a 2-2 count. The game means nothing, and Carl knows it's hard for Freddie to concentrate, but he shouts some encouragement for a strike-out and thankfully gets it with Guags's big-breaking curve.

"Don't wait so long with the breaking stuff if you pitch tomorrow night," Carl tells him as he meets him outside the dugout.

"If I pitch?" Freddie stammers. "Don't you want me to close for Robin?"

"You're not here tomorrow, Freddie," Carl says with a big grin. "You're going to Kansas City!"

"No lie?" Freddie asks, then turns to notice the crowd, which has just heard Bill White's announcement and is giving him a standing O. His teammates are now out to congratulate, and for a moment he's mobbed like a World Series scene. But Mack is out there to restore order, and with a "Come on, girls" he herds the players back for their bottom of the eighth at-bats and the *pro forma* ninth against Eau Claire.

The game ends quickly and everyone rushes into the clubhouse for a celebration, but it's a strangely serious Freddie Guagliardo who greets them. He's changed to a sweatshirt and jeans, and looks oddly out of place and even immature as he solemnly shakes their hands, much like a high schooler visiting the team might do. Keith and Robin try to make some jokes, but their scrappy little Chicagoan has something on his mind.

Girl-friend trouble? Freddie shakes off Keith's question, but asks him to step aside. And while the boom boxes crank up for the hysterics all the guys feel they deserve, Freddie has settled into the trainer's empty room to implore Keith's aid.

"I thought I was going home this week, man," Freddie says with a worried groan.

"You're going to the big leagues, buddy, cheer up!" Keith says, still bubbling with happiness.

"You gotta help me . . . " Freddie mutters, beside himself with worry, his dark eyes glancing about the unlit room as if Chet's medical gear has ears.

"You bet, buddy, just ask." Keith motions that he's ready for anything.

"You gotta help me," Freddie confides, "get rid of that Benz!"

⊖ Game Time ⊖

For the league-championship game on August 31 tickets jump to four dollars grandstand, five dollars box—damn near major-league prices, one fan angrily notes. But the players are up for it, even better baseball is promised, and attendance is best for any nonpromotional event of the year.

They've had over seven thousand people in the stands for special nights—Credit Union, Eagle Food Stores, Standard Distributing (Schlitz night)—where the lure of free admission and door prizes brings out ten times what the Royals could otherwise hope to draw. Most times it's the faithful four hundred the players prefer. "See y'all next free game" pitcher Keith Henley had shouted at the early-emptying stands on Muscular Dystrophy night when people ignored their come-from-behind play in the ninth. The four hundred came for baseball, and were rewarded with bingo, strike-o, the trivia question (which bizarrely named fans had been winning, most recently "Sue Chief"). On cheap-beer nights it would be a rowdy crowd, but not much bigger, and the emphasis was still on baseball, just a little hotter for the umps. And tonight it's the baseball night of the year.

Robin Haas, 19-6, best in the league, will pitch for Mason City. Ray Majors, for Cedar Rapids, the Southern Division champs. Bill White introduces both teams one-by-one, and World Series-style they stand in ranks along the base paths as the national anthem is played. Robin turns to take his eight warm-up pitches, two straight throws followed by a pair each of fastballs, curves, and sliders. The slider is his favorite pitch, spinning off the side of his fingers then cutting across the plate and away, like a jet fighter peeling out of formation. He's been moving both fingers to the left, gripping it like half a forkball, and it's been popping hard, breaking so late the batter swears it's a fastball and swings two feet above and away. Charting pitches from the dugout, Keith and Matt and the other throwers can guess the pitch just from how the hitter reacts.

For Cedar Rapids Mark Troy, the left fielder, .310 for the season with seven home runs and an astronomical on-base percentage, leads off. He crouches low, Pete Rose-style, and rocks his bat in time with the pitcher's motion. "Boogie, baby!" catcher Jim Smith sings, and the first pitch screams in a called strike. Troy now moves to his other stance, pointing his bat like Rod Carew at the pitcher and drawing it back with his stretch. "Whatta bozo," Jim scoffs and strike two is in there on a curve.

Jim flashes three fingers, the slider, and holds his mitt down off the corner. Robin fires it in, a perfect strike. Three pitches, three called strikes, and all Mark Troy has done is play footsie with his bat. All right!

Ray Tobey, .240 average but a more tactical hitter, bred to hit behind the runner, opposite field, through the box, down the line. All over, where they ain't. A master of bat control.

First pitch he swings and chops the ball over the Royal's dugout, scattering the girls still seeking autographs. He pounds the plate, winces at the pitcher, and is already swinging when the fast-ball leaves Robin's hand. Just a piece of it—rips it back just inches above Jim's mitt and strikes him on the chest, taking his wind. The umpire dusts the plate, calls for more balls, confers with his colleague at first while Jim turns red, then purple, finally a ghastly shade of white as he shakes it off. Chet comes out but Jim is back in his crouch, waving him away. Tobey shakes the bat a few times and mutters back at the catcher, "Next one's got your nuts." The ump, who's caught a few himself from this cowboy, watches the slider break too soon and miss the plate by several inches. "Steerike!" he calls and turns away to duck Tobey's rightful ire.

Two quick strikes on Lou Hill, the Giants' top hitter, bring the crowd to its feet. But he's a dangerous man who hits well in the hole, so Jim calls for some waste pitches to throw off his timing. A curve high, dangerous. Slider low, the ump calls it honest. The crowd groans, falling for the ruse, and to fool the hitter more Jim trots out to "talk his pitcher down." In fact, they say little. Johnny walks in from third and says he's sure the take sign is on, "old

Hamp keeps whispering the signals to himself before he gives them." Jim laughs, says "Listen, I'll show you two and hold out for a wide curve, but just send a straight one down the center hard as you got." Robin is smiling as he delivers, and Johnny hoots as Louis Hill stands looking at the called third strike and the stands erupt.

Eddie is the lead-off hitter, as he's been all month. He has 102 R.B.I.s, unbelievable for such a small guy whose first at-bat is a possible rack-up only if he homers. Bill White reminds the crowd of this feat and they cheer Eddie on. A ball low, another wide. Majors shakes off three signs, it's gotta be a change-up, Eddie figures and tells himself to hold until the pitch is there. It floats in like the Goodyear blimp and Eddie nearly pulls a stomach muscle waiting, but when the time's right he takes an easy swing and strokes it out to left. It was a bad pitch, ball three, and Eddie figures they should keep the take sign on for a few more. He tries to tell Dick Hillier, coaching at first, but Dick can't understand his mixture of Spanish and slang American. "Sure man, good hit," he says, to Eddie's exasperation.

He finally catches Billy's eye as the pitcher talks it over with his catcher. In the old unspoken language, Eddie just shakes his head and Billy gets it. The pitch comes in head-high. Now Dick understands. "Gotcha Eddie, take, take," and Eddie stays close to the bag, since he'll only steal on a swing. Billy takes a called strike, a good pitch he could have easily hit, and Carl flashes the hit and run. Eddie looks down to second, then over to short; both players have from twenty to thirty pounds on him. This he doesn't like, both are Anglos who'd love to plow him down. But he takes a big lead, is surprised when the pitcher fails to throw over, and is off as Billy crouches back to swing. He doesn't see the ball, but from the shortstop's move he senses that it's in the infield between second and short. As he starts his slide the second baseman has the ball, already forcing him out, but to save Billy at first he hooks his arm out to catch the bag and sends legs flailing toward the second baseman's knees. *Mátale*, Eddie sends him flying before he can release the ball, and Billy darts across first.

"Out, yer out" the ump screams at him, for sure, but then runs down toward first jerking his arm up at Billy, too. Interference? Hell no, Eddie thinks to himself, he'd like to argue but can't say a word. Carl is on the field, halfway to second now, asking about the call. "Your man left the base line, we're calling it a double play," the ump explains as if this will let it rest, then turns away. Carl runs around to face him, saying "He had the bag with his left hand!" "He interfered, two outs!" the umpire shoots back, and Carl is livid. "Look here, look here," he argues, and slides into the bag himself to demonstrate. The crowd goes wild, cheering Carl's slide and screaming for him to do it again.

But now Carl is standing off the bag doing a little jump and hop, showing how the Giants' second baseman could easily have cleared Ed's fair slide. "He knew our man had it beat at first, he made the interference happen," Carl is yelling, and the fans have gone bananas. "Listen," the ump cautions him, "stop grandstanding or you're out of the game, I mean it," and Carl stalks off the field, turning every few steps to shout something back. Johnny has been standing just outside the box, taking swings and enjoying Carl's antics, and now looks down to his manager for a sign. "Drill the bastard," Carl yells, and Johnny laughs. His first swing is murderous, but a foot shy of the ball. He takes a strike, then two weak floaters that miss by miles. Two and two, he reaches back to swing but catches only part of it, sending a weak little dribbler to the mound. He's out by five steps.

"N-42, N-42" the bingo girl calls on the PA as Robin takes his warm-ups. "0-67, 0-67" as he tries his new hard slider, "B-8, B-8, we have a bingo" as his curve floats in. He feels good, all his pitches are working, he likes the big crowd and everything's going okay. Cedar Rapids has a lot less strength after its first three hitters so he decides not to waste anything. After a ball and two quick strikes he motions Jim out to the mound. "Hey listen," he says, "I wanna pitch to these guys, let's set 'em down straight," and Jim promises to call good pitches.

Robin's slow curve fools the first two batters, who send soft little pop-ups to the back of the infield grass. But the same pitch to the third hitter hangs in too high, just like that waste pitch in the first, and in a second it's a long hard fly arching out toward right. Donny's been playing shallow for the righty and has to peddle back at full tilt, looking over his shoulder for the ball and trusting Dave Alpert in center to tell him when he nears the wall. "Watch it, watch it," Dave calls, but Donny has the ball in reach and leaps to grab it as the fence blurs into sight. Stay loose, stay loose, Donny tells himself, and with his free hand reaches out to break his fall. The hard fence catches his forearm and he spins around that way, dancing with the Schlitz sign and pulling in his glove with the ball toward his belly. The ump has run out to short center and Donny calls to him "I'm okay, I'm okay," but the ump just yells back "Show me the ball." Donny holds it up, the crowd roars, and the Giants are down six straight.

The next four innings move fast, a few balls slapped to short and a vicious liner that Andy Thompson spears like a swordfish, but otherwise a bunch of pops and some more called third strikes. But with the bingo calls for background as he takes his seventh-inning tosses, Robin begins to think about his perfect game. Eighteen men in order, ahead on all the counts, his slider still working. Now it's the top of their order for the third time, harder work, but he feels confident.

Mark Troy looks at a strike then lunges at a lazy change-up to make it 0-2. Let's get him with another fastball, Robin thinks, and Jim magically flashes one finger. Troy swings, then tries to check it as the ball is high, but it glances off his bat and bounds out toward second. Its high chop eats up time, Troy is fast, and Billy tries a barehand grab. He gets it cleanly but in his haste whips it over to first too fast. It sails nine feet high and gains altitude with each foot, and to shag it Andy must jump forward and up. The throw beats the runner, but Andy's foot has left the bag and Troy is safe. Robin vows not to wait for the call but there it is, Bill White hasn't even asked the writers: "Error on the second baseman, error on the throw. Good play by first baseman Andy Thompson, good play, Andy." '

Robin feels awful, looking over toward Billy, who's risked his gold glove to save Robin's no-hitter. Billy just nods, yells "double play," and Robin feels better. Okay, high fastballs to keep it on the ground. Ray Tobey tomahawks the first to Ed at short, who shovels the ball over to Billy. With a perfect pivot, he rifles it to Andy at first. "Hey, hey!" Bill White is shouting over the PA, and the fans respond. Robin decides to stick with the fastball to get out of this nerve-racking inning, but Lou Hill nails the first one. His line drive is still rising when Johnny times himself for the leap, a trick he learned from Buddy Knox when sitting out those games in June. He's at the top of his jump, stretching toward the stars, when he feels the ball catch in his mitt's webbing and pull him back. He lands in a crowd of Royals—Billy and Ed are slapping his back, and Robin grabs him by the waist and spins him around.

They run to the dugout together, where Jim chides Robin for that last pitch. "They're reading your fastballs, man," he cautions, "they're meatballs, you gotta mix, lay off the straight stuff for an inning," and Billy slides over on the bench to talk about the scoring. "That shouldn't have been an error," Robin tells him, but Billy laughs back, "If Johnny didn't snag that last one we'd have called an error on the pitcher. Bad pitch, man, bad pitch!"

The eighth inning is a breeze. The homestretch rally has given him four runs and a healthy rest, and he sets them down with two infield grounders and an easy fly to center. The trivia quiz has been to guess Robin's ERA, and out of respect the bull pen stays out of it, because they all know the magic numbers, 1.70. If he wins this game he'll be the first twenty-game ace in the league since the sixties, and if he shuts them out his ERA will dive another point, and if he doesn't allow a hit—that's the question as he sits watching Johnny, Jim, and Donny take their final swings in Class A baseball. Bill has been reminding the crowd of all the records waiting to be shattered, but Robin's not nervous yet. He'll face the bottom of the order and Cedar Rapids hasn't any pitch hitters worth the effort.

Keith Henley has walked in from the bull pen, all the guys are in, this must be Mack's show of confidence, as the bench is empty. Keith assumes he's edgy, starts telling his endless hunting stories to keep Robin's mind off the game. The three-quarter beagle, one-quarter black-and-tan, who was so good he'd walk up beside his deer. The south Georgia white tails that grew like giants because the peanut farmers let them eat the gleanings. But Keith is talking with his eye on the field, hoping that the power hitters get a few more runs and give Robin more time. "I'm feeling good man, okay," Robin tells his buddy. Donny fans and they're off the bench. "Go get 'em," Keith yells out as Robin takes the mound.

No announcements, no games for the fans, Robin takes just four warm-ups because the silence scares him. Swede Morgan, clumsy first baseman, low average, a sucker for curves. Strike one, strike two. Try the hard slider on the corner, it misses, ball one. Fastball, high, ball two. "Easy, easy," Jim calls out, but Robin is turned around and staring out toward left center field. The scoreboard. For the first time he's noticed all those zeroes, eight of them across the board, advertising what he'd thought was his own personal drama. Now he really feels spooked. Best he's done before was a two-hitter, a game lost on his own fielding error. He stands there so long the ump motions over, play ball. Slider again, strike three.

Jim trots out. "You're shaking," he says, and Robin looks down at his hand, fluttering so hard he fears he'll drop the ball Jim's handing him. "A no-hitter's shit, man, it's carnival," his catcher tells him, and Robin knows he's right. Win the game, it's won already, just throw some pitches and tuck away the flag. "Listen," Jim is saying, "take something off your fastball, you've been missing with it high and I think you're pissing off the ump, you're making him stretch his calls."

One finger, mitt dead-center in the zone, and Robin fills it with a fastball harder than he'd wanted. Jim shakes his head, the batter dumps his bat and stumbles back toward the on-deck circle for a different helmet. Robin is anxious. Now the batter—shortstop Brandt King, as Robin notices for the first time—steps back in. Where's my concentration? Robin asks himself. Another strike. A ball, with his curve. Now some easy fastballs, if they hit they hit, first walk of the game would hurt more. Ball two, too hard again and too high. "Bring it down, dammit, bring it down," Jim is hollering, and Mack is yelling something about his release. That's right, the nerves have sprung his grip, he's releasing too soon. He's determined to take a lot off the fastball, keep it in the slot, not hitting all day these guys' timing is shot to shit, they couldn't hit a pregnant cow. In the dirt, he's held it too long, stop listening to Mack, he knows how to throw a fastball. Stretch, set, delivery: the pitch is low but somehow it tails up at the end, catches the knees honestly, and the ump yells "Strike!" The crowd roars.

Fifteen strike-outs, a new league record Bill tells the crowd, and as the weak-hitting center fielder walks toward the box everyone's on their feet. A pinch hitter? There really aren't any better swingers on the bench, and down 5-0 the Giants don't want to play poor sports and schneider a finely pitched game. Jim Blankenheim steps up.

Robin takes his time, but Blankenheim stays in the box looking down at him as if to say "I'm no chump, you gotta pitch to me, too." Robin is still just standing, so Jim Smith walks out to the mound, giving him even more time. "Shakey again?" he asks, but Robin says no. "I'm thinking," he says, "I want to make it clean. No more errors, no gift calls. I want a strike-out." Jim scratches his head. "I hear you man." "Fastballs?" Robin asks, "No, you're up and down, it's not your pitch anymore. Listen, your good thing is your slider, the popper, and you haven't overdone it. Three hard sliders, pop them in there, and you're home."

All right. Jim runs back, takes his crouch, and Blankenheim stares without a smile. Waves the bat twice. Robin leans back and comes down a bit on his right side to give the slider its whip. Tips off a sharp-eyed hitter, but the pitch needs it to work. Low but not too low. Jim's mitt pops and everyone in the ball park hears it sing. "Strike," the umpire motions, a quiet call to keep the drama on the mound.

Robin wipes his forehead, tugs his cap, his belt, steps back on the rubber. Looks back at Ed and Billy playing deep, a prevent defense, trusting their arms to throw out any infield grounders. Robin doesn't like it and motions them in. Johnny walks over from third, asks what he's throwing. "Sliders," Robin mutters back. Jim shows three fingers, jiggles his glove, and Robin throws it in and Blankenheim waves, miles away. The crowd hoots, still standing.

Now Robin walks behind the mound. He's realized it's more than a no-hit championship contest. It's certainly his last A-ball game. Mack's been talking Triple A. Four umps. Bigger salary, more meal money, no more Panama Pizzas. Dead-serious players, their eyes on the bigs. No buses, a charter plane. Half these guys he'll never see again, and even if some—like Eddie—come up to Triple A with him it won't be the same. They've been kids together, earning their first money playing pro ball, less than working a car wash or Mac's for the summer but still hard cash for playing the game they love. Take Keith: he could put in winters with his dad's insurance agency, could even play in the instructional leagues, but he just hunts and loafs to keep himself pure for A-ball. As tenuous as it is, the Class A Mason City Royals are still a link in the great chain that runs up through the majors to the World Series, the great dynasties like the Yankees and Milwaukee in the fifties, Hank Aaron, Willie Mays, Ruth, Gehrig, and the Hall of Fame.

Robin turns around, faces the three fingers from Jim, takes his grip on the ball and sets himself toward the plate. He rocks a bit, swinging everything into his back muscles to whip the slider from the side. He twists his wrist to make the ball slip off his fingers, and as it sails toward the plate he swears he can see it rotate each sideways turn.

It looks like slow motion, and Robin stares after the ball as it slides toward the plate—Blankenheim, Smith, the ump no longer existing—just the white ball, red seams sailing from his hand toward the darkness that now clouds his target. A thousand things run through his mind. Eddie and his *niña* sweetheart. Buddy. Billy and Ed behind him. Spring camp next March, a Triple A slot, maybe a shot at the parent club.

He's lost the ball. His eyes tear, he panics. Has he thrown it into the screen? He wants to look around but can't move.

He hears a sudden roar, like surf in Oregon, the subway in New York, the sound he'd heard in high school when he raced his parents' Buick on the freeway. He's more afraid than he's ever been in twenty years of living but he's still looking straight ahead, he'll face it square.

And this is what he sees: a blur of the hitter's bat, Jim's mitt puffing dust, and the ump's right arm shooting straight up, showing "Strike." Smitty has hit him with a flying tackle, Billy is jumping and laughing around him in a crazy dance, Eddie is smiling his shy smile, and Andy has an armlock around his neck. His infield takes him off his feet and carries him toward the dugout, the crowd roaring like a white-water rapids and everyone around him looking up and shouting.

Robin is swept away into the clubhouse by the other pitchers. They'll toss him in the shower clothes and all, cleats squeaking on the wet tiles, their hoots and hollers echoing out to the field. Few fans have left, the stands are still crowded with milling people anxious to love their Class A players while they're here. Next year, they know, a few of the weaker youngsters will be back. But the weakest will be out of baseball and the best sent up closer to the major leagues.

Robin, Donny, Johnny, and probably Billy are sure about a better league next year. So is Eddie—he hasn't done much this game, one for five, but he's the season's star and a baseball oddity, a shortstop who can hit with power, and the future is his.

But right now there's the present. Elias Cedeño, the Giants' reserve second baseman and to Eddie's knowledge the only other Panamanian in the league, has pulled the Royals' shortstop away from his teammates and brought him over to the boxes behind the Cedar Rapids bench. "Eduardo, mi compadre, aquí esta mi niña." Eddie glances about, worried that he has Jolene hidden in the dugout, but Elias is pointing to a smiling dark-skinned girl of twenty holding a little baby just a few months old. Eddie smiles, is introduced to Elias's wife and infant daughter, and happily takes the child in his arms.

The *Courier* photographer, who still can't get into the locker room, is passing by and motions Eddie for a shot. Next morning, as the world turns to the final month of major-league baseball, the World Series, and the NFL, Eddie, Elias, and the *niña* smile out from the sports page. Eddie winks as the short season ends.

Jerry Klinkowitz
is executive director of the Waterloo Indians, a farm team of the Cleveland
Indians and 1986 Midwest League champions. In the off-season, he teaches at
the University of Northern Iowa and has published twenty books of literary and
cultural criticism, including *Literary Disruptions*, *The Self-Apparent Word*,
and *The New American Novel of Manners*. His award-winning short stories
have appeared in a number of magazines.